# The Dying of the Year

A Yorkshire Murder Mystery

Tom Raven Book 3

## M S MORRIS

# PROLOGUE

It was dark. Proper winter dark. Late November, and rain drummed loudly on the nylon fabric of the golfing umbrella. A storm had been promised and had arrived at last. Sam Earnshaw kept a firm hold of the umbrella as a gust of wind seized it, making it duck and dive in his hands. Sam had never liked storms, and winter was his least favourite time of year. But tonight, bad weather was the least of his problems.

His mind was in turmoil.

What had he just seen? He wished he could unsee it, but there was no chance of that happening in a hurry. The image was etched firmly on his mind's eye. He didn't think he would ever forget it.

Now he just needed to get away, to find some space and time to think things through.

He stood at the roadside, his shoes and trousers getting steadily soaked. The sensible thing would be to go back indoors and wait, but that wasn't going to happen, not after what he'd just witnessed. Above the roar of the wind he could still hear the sound of music from within the building, the rhythmic beat drumming along with the rain.

Everyone else was still inside and as far as he knew he was the first to leave.

He had to get away before he was followed.

The street was empty, painted a dirty orange by the streetlights. Sam peered at his watch under the dim glow. Just after ten o'clock. The taxi would be here any minute and he could make his exit, put all this behind him and work out his next move.

He already knew what he would do first.

He'd go straight to Becca and tell her what had happened. Not only was his girlfriend a police detective, but she had good instincts about people. She would know exactly what to do. In any case, it would be pointless trying to keep this from her. She would know immediately there was something troubling him. That detective brain of hers always ferreted out the truth.

White headlights glowed in the distance, turning into the road. The throb of an engine over the howl of the wind. The taxi, at last! Sam stepped forwards so the driver would have a clear view of him beneath the streetlight.

But something wasn't right.

The vehicle was approaching fast. Too fast. As it drew near, Sam saw that it wasn't a taxi, but a van. It hurtled along the road like a mad thing, wipers whipping left and right across the windscreen at top speed, tyres cleaving through pools of surface water like a surfer riding a wave.

He stepped back to avoid being splashed, but as he did so he felt a pair of hands in the centre of his back.

He tried to turn around to see who was there but the wind chose that moment to grab the umbrella, forcing him to switch his effort into regaining control before it took off.

And then everything happened at once.

The van sped closer. The hands against his back gave him a forceful shove. The wind snatched the umbrella from his grasp as the unseen assailant propelled him into the road. He opened his mouth to cry out, but the wind stole his words away, just as it had taken the umbrella.

The van smashed into him like a juggernaut, packing

enough mass and violence to bring time to a juddering halt. Like being caught in a bomb blast. One massive whump, and a crack opening up in reality.

Then he was flying through the air, headlong into the night. As he tumbled over the windshield of the van, he thought he caught a glimpse of the umbrella, white and green, sailing gracefully into the sky. But there was no sign of his attacker.

His head bounced off metal, hard as rock, and he plunged into a bottomless pit. His final thought before the darkness swallowed him was, 'I must tell Becca.'

# CHAPTER 1

*Twelve months later*

B ecca Shawcross rubbed her eyes and yawned. It was
nearly six o'clock in the evening. Her colleagues,
DC Jess Barraclough and DC Tony Bairstow, were
shutting down their computers and preparing to leave for
the night. Sensible folk. But Becca wasn't ready to go. She
returned her gaze to her computer screen, trying to make
sense of the words that swam before her.

Names. Dates. Times. Locations. The nuts and bolts
of police work. She tried to focus her attention on what
they meant.

Jess came over and leaned against the desk, loosening
her long blonde hair and retying it into a ponytail. 'Hi,
how's it going?'

'Okay. Good.'

Jess gestured at the information on Becca's screen.
'You look tired. Can't that wait until morning?'

'I guess so.' Becca glanced over at the door. 'I'm
waiting for Raven. But he still hasn't come back from the
hospital.'

DCI Tom Raven was the real reason Becca was still at her desk so late in the day. She was desperate to hear what he had to say.

She'd spent the whole day stuck behind her desk, staring blankly at her screen, her mind roaming anywhere but on the job in hand. Normally she was a diligent, hardworking investigator, keen to get up and running with a new case. But today the job she'd been assigned had left her bored and listless. It was hard for her to drum up much enthusiasm over the theft of electronic goods from a warehouse in Pickering, even though as a detective sergeant with Scarborough CID it was her professional duty to investigate all crimes with the same high level of attention to detail. No doubt for the owner of the warehouse the disappearance of a substantial number of laptops was a devastating blow to his business. But Becca was struggling to care when she had so much else weighing on her mind.

She couldn't stop replaying the day, almost two weeks earlier, when her boyfriend had woken from his year-long coma.

Becca had been at Sam's bedside, expecting him to die. Sam's parents, Greg and Denise, had made the decision to switch off his life support, in agreement with the hospital consultant, Dr Kirtlington. After a whole year in a comatose state with no sign of improvement, it had been the doctor's opinion that Sam would never recover and that it was in the best interests of everyone involved to bring his life to an end.

Becca hadn't been consulted, merely informed of the decision. She had argued for Sam to be given another chance, for the day to be pushed back. For just a little more time. But she had been overruled.

Then, when the moment came, Sam had confounded expert opinion by regaining consciousness. Perhaps, Becca liked to think, it was her own last-ditch efforts to rouse him by playing music to him that had finally reached him and brought him back from the dead. Maybe sitting at his bedside for an entire year had made a difference too.

Whatever the reason, she had been sitting with Sam at the moment he came round. When he blinked open his eyes and looked up at her, her heart flooded with so much joy she thought it would explode. It was a miracle – the answer to all her prayers. She wept tears of happiness. But then her joy turned to shock when Sam told her that he had been pushed in front of the vehicle that had left him for dead. Who would have done such a thing? Sam was such a kind, gentle person.

Becca hadn't known what to do for the best. By rights she ought to have told Sam's parents straightaway. But she had held back from confiding in Greg and Denise. As far as Becca was concerned, they had given up on their son, whereas she had never stopped believing. So instead of speaking to them, she had turned to Raven, her boss of barely two months.

Although she hadn't known him for long, in that short time they had worked together on two murder cases. Raven was still something of a mystery to her – she knew next to nothing about his personal life – but he had earned her respect.

She trusted he would take Sam's story seriously.

Raven had gone to interview Sam at the hospital earlier that afternoon. Becca had wanted to go with him but he'd said it was better if he went alone. He'd argued that it was unethical for her to have any involvement in a criminal investigation involving her boyfriend. She had reluctantly conceded that he was right. But at the same time a misgiving had entered her head. Did Raven want to conduct the interview without her present because he doubted that Sam's story was reliable? She had put her trust in Raven by confiding in him. She hoped he wasn't going to let her down.

She checked the time again. Raven definitely ought to be back by now. The staff nurses were strict about visiting times, under doctor's orders, and would have thrown him out long ago. So where the hell was he?

Jess was the only other person at work who Becca had confided in about Sam. 'You know how Raven is.'

Becca knew all right. Raven had plenty of good qualities – drive, loyalty, dogged determination – but communication wasn't one of them. The fact that he hadn't returned to tell her what Sam had said should have come as no surprise.

She took another quick look at the door, but there was no sign of him. 'It doesn't look like he's coming back to the station tonight.'

'No,' said Jess kindly, 'so go home.'

Becca felt her spirits sink even further. It looked like Raven was going to let her down after all. Perhaps her worst fears had been realised and he had concluded that Sam was an unreliable witness and his story untrue. Now he was too ashamed to face her with the news.

Becca was too tired to put up any resistance to Jess's friendly cajoling. She switched off her computer and packed up her things. She would waylay Raven as soon as she saw him in the morning and demand an update.

He owed her that, at least.

★

The man lying in the bed looked like death. But he was, by no small miracle, alive.

Detective Chief Inspector Tom Raven dragged his chair nearer to the bed and leaned in close to catch the faint sounds that emerged from the mouth of Sam Earnshaw. A voice that hadn't uttered a single word for a whole year and was now striving to make itself heard above the background hubbub of a busy, modern hospital. In the corridor outside the private room a trolley with squeaking wheels trundled past, and on the next ward nurses called to each other as machines hummed and beeped. Rain pattered against the darkened glass of the window, and beyond it the evening rush-hour traffic rumbled on. But it was important that Raven didn't miss a single word, because what Sam had to tell him was a matter of life and death.

The patient's wasted arms lay motionless on the crisp white hospital bedsheets. Fine blond hair framed his regular features, but his skin held an unhealthy grey pallor. His sunken eyes were turned towards Raven. 'I want to tell you as much as I can remember.'

'Go on, then,' said Raven encouragingly.

When DS Becca Shawcross had come to Raven the previous week in a state of extreme agitation quite unlike her normal calm, professional self, it had taken him some time to disentangle the threads of her jumbled narrative.

'It's my boyfriend,' she'd told him. 'He's woken up at last.'

Raven's first response to her news had been, to his shame, 'What boyfriend is that, then?' The look of disappointment, even dismay, on her face had alerted him immediately to his mistake. Becca had mentioned a boyfriend once in passing, but had never given his name. And with no further mention of a boyfriend and no evidence of any such person materialising, Raven had given his existence no further thought. He had pictured Becca as a single woman who went home every night to her parents' Bed and Breakfast on North Marine Road.

How little he knew his own team.

The astonishing fact that Becca had spent most of her evenings and weekends for the past twelve months sitting by the hospital bedside of an unconscious and unresponsive hit and run victim had cast her in a whole new light. Raven had already held her in high regard. Now his admiration for her increased further.

That kind of commitment, he reflected ruefully, was something he had been rather deprived of in his own life. There was no one who would sit by *his* bedside and talk to him for hours. There was hardly anyone who wanted to talk to him at all. His estranged wife, Lisa, would probably have instructed the doctors to switch off the machines long ago.

But Becca had never given up hope, and her steadfastness had been rewarded. Sam had, against all medical expectations, come round from his coma. And Becca had been there to witness his return to consciousness. Her joy was plain for Raven to see. But upon waking up, he had made a startling revelation.

According to Sam Earnshaw, it was no accident that had left him fighting for his life. It was attempted murder.

In response to Becca's plea, Raven had agreed to speak to Sam and find out for himself if there was a strong enough case to open an investigation. If there was, he had promised to do whatever he could to bring Sam's would-be killer to justice. A bold statement, made on the spur of the moment. He hoped he wouldn't live to regret it.

'Take your time, Sam,' he murmured to the young man in the hospital bed. 'I can come back later if you'd prefer.'

Raven was aware of the strict time limit that had been set for him by the staff nurse on duty. 'Twenty minutes,' she had said in that officious way that seemed to come so naturally to certain people. 'And not a minute more.'

Raven checked his watch. He was already close to exceeding his allotted timeslot, and they had barely got started.

The young man murmured something too faint to catch and Raven leaned closer still. 'Sorry, could you repeat that please?'

'It was the eighteenth of November,' said Sam, forcing the words out with obvious effort. 'There was a party that night, at work. A private event for employees and their families.' His voice was barely above a whisper, but there was a steely determination in his eyes; a desire for his story to be heard. Raven listened attentively.

'It was at Salt Castle Brewery. That's the family firm, the one my father founded. I work there, alongside my two brothers.' Sam's face fell. 'Or rather, I used to work there. Before this happened.'

Raven refrained from saying anything. It would have been nice to be able to reassure Sam that soon he would be fit and well enough to return to work, but Raven was no doctor and knew nothing about how long Sam's road to recovery might take, if such a path was even possible. Raven had been forced to quit his own short-lived career as a soldier after a battlefield injury, which was how he had ended up in the somewhat unlikely role of police detective. He was hardly the best person to dispense career advice.

'Why wasn't Becca with you at the party?' he asked Sam. 'You said that families were invited. I assume that applied to girlfriends too.'

'She was on duty that evening. But I arranged to meet her after work.'

'At the party?'

'No, in town. That's why I left the party early.'

Raven nodded. Sam's account matched what Becca had told him – that she would have gone to the party too if she hadn't been called away at the last minute for a surveillance op. Sam had arranged to meet her in town later, but had never shown up. At first she had been cross, thinking he was having too much of a good time and had forgotten about her. But then she'd received a call from Sam's distraught father. Sam had been the victim of an accident and had been found unconscious in the middle of the road. He had been rushed to hospital. 'We'd been planning to move into a flat together in the new year,' Becca had told Raven. 'But then everything fell apart.'

Raven wondered how differently things might have turned out if Becca had been able to go to the party with Sam. Would that have altered the course of events, saving him from his fate? Might they have moved into their flat after all, and now be living happily together? He knew it was fruitless to speculate that way. Any number of conscious choices or random events might have conspired to alter the outcome of that evening. Until Raven knew more, it was impossible to say.

Besides, the unexpected overtime that had prevented Becca from attending the party was inevitable in police work. It was hard to juggle the job with a social life, or family life for that matter. That had been the root cause of Raven's marriage breakdown. He wasn't personally to blame for Lisa walking out on him. At least, that's what he liked to tell himself. If he repeated it often enough he might even come to believe it.

'I was waiting on the roadside for a taxi,' continued Sam. 'It was dark, and raining, and the visibility wasn't very good.'

'Focus on what you can remember about the hit and run itself,' said Raven, conscious of his allocated time running out and anxious to steer Sam towards the nitty-gritty of his account. 'Did you see the vehicle that hit you?'

'Yes. It wasn't the taxi. It was a van.'

According to Becca, no van had been mentioned in the original police report into the incident. There had been no eyewitnesses and no vehicle had stopped at the scene. Nor had any driver come forward to admit responsibility. 'Can you describe the van?'

'Not really. I didn't see it clearly.'

'What about the colour?'

Sam grimaced with the effort of recalling the scene. 'All I can remember is that everything looked orange.'

That would have been because of the cast from the streetlights. Most of the old sodium vapour lamps in the town had been phased out, replaced by white LED lights. But a few of the old streetlamps remained. They were notorious for making it hard to discern true colours.

'What about the type of van? How large was it?'

'It felt pretty hefty when it smashed into me.' Sam gave Raven a wry smile.

The lad had clearly managed to retain a sense of humour despite his terrible ordeal. That pointed to a lot of mental resilience. Raven tried to picture Sam and Becca as a couple. He reckoned the two of them would make a good pair.

'And you say that somebody pushed you into the path of the van?'

'Yes. I didn't see them, but they crept up behind me

and shoved me into the road.'

'Could it have been the wind?'

'No, I felt their hands against my back.' Sam closed his eyes and after a moment or two Raven wondered if he had reached his limit for the day. It was probably time for him to leave, but he would happily return for as many sessions as it took for Sam to tell him everything he remembered.

He rose from his seat and touched Sam's hand, saying, 'I'll come back tomorrow.'

Sam's fingers suddenly curled around his. The movement was unexpected. His eyes flicked opened and he frowned. 'I was trying to remember what else happened.'

'Something about your attacker?'

'No. There was... something else. Something that happened before I was pushed.'

Raven sat down again. 'What was it?'

Sam groaned in frustration. 'I don't know. It's just a blank.'

'Don't worry about it now,' said Raven.

A gap in Sam's memory was entirely to be expected. He had done well to recall as much detail as he had, although Dr Kirtlington, the consultant in charge of Sam's care, had warned Raven about giving too much credence to anything that his patient recounted. 'Sam has suffered a traumatic head injury, and his memories are not to be relied upon. All things considered, he's lucky to have survived at all.'

*Lucky*. That would be the same kind of luck that Raven had been told he had when he woke up in a military hospital to learn that he wouldn't lose his leg after all, but would merely suffer from a limp for the rest of his life. It wasn't the sort of luck that lottery winners enjoyed, but a special second-rate kind, reserved exclusively for the unfortunate.

'I need to remember what else I saw.' Sam was becoming agitated. 'I know it's important.'

'I'm sure it will come back to you.'

The door opened and the staff nurse bustled in. 'Still

here, Chief Inspector?'

'I was just leaving.'

The nurse arched a stern eyebrow. 'I did tell you not to tire Sam out. He needs to rest if he's going to make a full recovery.' She stood there, clearly waiting for Raven to move.

Raven rose again, patting Sam on the shoulder. 'Don't worry about anything for now. Whatever it is you're trying to remember, it'll come to you, I know it will.'

# CHAPTER 2

Raven headed out into the dark, turning his collar up against the wind and the rain. It was the last day of November, just over a year since the hit and run. According to Becca there had been a storm that night too. Raven liked storms. He enjoyed the wind in his hair, the feeling that the elements were at large, demonstrating what they could do when they really put their mind to it. Lisa had called him mad to enjoy winter weather so much.

'What's wrong with summer, Tom?' she'd demanded. 'Spring's not so bad either.'

But Raven felt most at home during the darkest part of the year. Perhaps it was something to do with setting expectations. When the days grew short, no one expected much from them, so the occasional burst of sunshine or unseasonal warmth meant far more. During summer, when long hot days were taken for granted, it was so much easier to be disappointed. And Raven had endured enough disappointment in his life already.

He shoved his hands deep into his coat pockets and made his way across the windswept tarmac of the hospital car park. Pressing his key fob, he was greeted with a welcoming blink of lights by his silver BMW M6 coupé. A lonely beacon shining in the darkness. His one true companion. He slid inside and started the engine.

He knew that Becca would no doubt be waiting for him back at the station. She would want to hear every last detail of his conversation with Sam. She would expect him to say that he was now ready to begin an attempted murder inquiry and explain precisely how he intended to pursue the investigation. She'd probably want to get involved herself, even though he had already ruled out that possibility, hence her assignment to an unrelated burglary case. Still, she would no doubt expect Raven to keep her in the loop.

In her position, he'd have been exactly the same.

The problem was, he didn't have anything to tell her, at least nothing that she didn't already know herself. And as for theories about what exactly had happened, he needed to gather more information before he could begin to formulate a hypothesis. So instead of returning to the station after leaving the hospital, he drove straight home, hoping he might be able to find some clues to another conundrum that was perplexing him – what exactly his builder was doing with his house, and whether there was any possibility that it might be made habitable in time for Christmas.

To describe Raven's house in Quay Street as a three-storey Georgian terrace would have made it sound rather grander than it was. In reality, the old brick house was narrow and rickety, hemmed in on either side by its neighbours, and worn down from decades of neglect. Its history was murky, much like the personal stories of its current and past occupants, but it was at least two hundred years old. Not as ancient as some of its neighbours, which had stood in the shadow of the castle headland since the fifteenth century, but old enough to have seen a bit of life and death. It had belonged to Raven's father, Alan, and before that to his grandfather, Jack. It was the house in which Raven had grown up, the house he'd fled when he left Scarborough at the age of sixteen, and the house he'd inherited when Alan Raven dropped dead of a heart attack on his way back from the pub.

Raven had returned to his hometown from London to make arrangements for his father's funeral. But instead of doing the sensible thing and putting the house on the market for some enterprising property developer to turn into a holiday let – Becca's brother, Liam, did that kind of thing for a living – Raven had decided to live there, and had contracted the services of a local builder, Barry Hardcastle, to do the place up. He must be getting sentimental in his old age.

With any luck he would catch the builder before he clocked off for the day. Raven had given Barry a key so he could come and go as he pleased, but his working hours were a mystery. Sometimes he started work at the crack of dawn, before it was properly light. On other days he didn't show up until late, if at all. As for finishing each day, that could happen at any time. But at least work on the house had begun, after a shaky start.

Raven left the BMW in the car park at the end of the street and walked down the central line of cobbles – no more than two feet wide – that denoted the original width of the road before the houses on one side had been knocked down in the nineteen-sixties and the road widened. But it was still a narrow street, and Barry's van and the skip he'd deposited in front of the house were fast becoming a source of tension with the neighbours.

But what could Raven do about that? He wanted the builder gone as much as anyone.

This evening the van was still there, so Barry hadn't disappeared early for once. Raven pushed open the front door of the house and nearly put his foot through a hole in the floor. 'Christ's sake,' he muttered.

Half the floorboards in the hallway were missing, leaving a gaping void and just a few precarious joists like hollow ribs to walk on. Beneath the sparse timber frame, a gap of about a foot led directly to bare soil. Raven peered at the shallow space in alarm. So much for foundations. It seemed there was hardly anything holding the house up. At least being part of a terrace, it had its neighbours to lean against, like a line of drunks propping each other up.

A smell of damp rose from beneath the floor, pervading the hallway like a fog. Quay Street was just yards from the harbour and, as its name suggested, had been the original quayside in medieval times. Raven wondered whether during high tides, seawater might percolate up through the ground, seeping into the fabric of the house. No wonder the walls of the old building were riddled with damp. The thought struck him that the whole edifice might topple over in a storm the way his father had collapsed and met his end that night as he staggered home from the Golden Ball. What would be the point in all this construction work then? Not for the first time, Raven questioned the wisdom of continuing to sink so much of his money into this wreck of a house. But no one would want to buy it from him in its current state. Now that he'd begun the renovations he had no choice except to see them through.

'Watch where you put your feet!' Barry's ugly but relentlessly cheerful face appeared at the top of the landing. From somewhere in the depths of the house, his youthful apprentice, Reggie, was making a hell of a noise with a hammer. He appeared to be in direct competition with Barry's portable radio which was blaring out pop songs from the eighties. 'Just finishing off,' said Barry, clumping down the rickety staircase. 'We've started ripping out all the rotten bits of wood. Half of it's gone in the skip already.'

Raven knew that this would only further inflate his already eye-watering bill for the work. It seemed that every time he spoke to his builder, Barry had identified some new problem that needed fixing. The estimate for the work was spiralling and the finishing line was rapidly receding into the distance.

Raven eyed the pit of doom that he had almost fallen into. 'I hope you're not going to leave the hallway like this with all the floorboards up.'

'Nah,' said Barry. 'Course not. I'll get Reg to lay a few planks over the gaps. Then we'll get out of your way for the night.'

'Stay as long as you like.' Raven would gladly have put up with Barry and Reggie until bedtime if they would only get on and finish the job. It was proving far more challenging than he'd anticipated to restore some kind of structural integrity to the house, let alone to drag it into the twenty-first century. But what did he know about building work? He was just a detective.

He'd originally hoped that Barry would have the place finished within a month, enabling him to invite his daughter to come and stay with him over the Christmas period. Hannah was a student of Law at Exeter University and he hadn't seen her since the summer. Their communications had dwindled to occasional emails and text messages, and he'd hoped to use the house as a means of rekindling their relationship. But even without asking Barry for a progress report, Raven could see that the chances of having the house ready in time were fast shrinking to the size of a pinhead. At the moment, the place was a death-trap.

He stepped carefully across the hole in the hallway and ventured into the kitchen. Fresh horrors greeted him. The ancient gas cooker, which had stood against the nearest wall for as long as Raven could remember, had been consigned to the great appliance graveyard in the sky. Only a stub of capped-off pipework and some hideous sixties-era mosaic tiles remained in the space it had occupied these past fifty years.

'I bet you're glad to see the back of that old thing,' said Barry.

Raven stared at the gap in the kitchen, dumbstruck. The old cooker had been a bugger to use and would never have passed even the most basic of safety tests, but seeing it gone he felt its loss like a body blow. A piece of his childhood had been ripped out and tossed aside. More to the point, how was he going to cook his meals?

'Reckon you'll be heading down the chippy tonight,' said Barry. 'What do you say, Reggie?'

The lad, who was busy hammering away at the cupboards on the kitchen wall, paused in his demolition work. He turned his eyes to Raven, but kept his opinion on the matter to himself. To date, Raven had never heard him utter a single word.

'Yeah,' continued Barry, 'we'll have this kitchen ripped out completely by the end of tomorrow.'

'Then how long until you put the new one in?'

'Well, it'll be a bit,' said Barry, spreading his palms in a vague kind of way. 'We'll have to knock out the bathroom wall and make everything good before we can start installing anything new.'

'How long will that take?'

'Hard to say, squire. There'll be rewiring, replastering, new plumbing, and a new floor to put in before we can even think about getting the kitchen guys started.' Barry stroked the thick stubble on his chin, contemplating Time's deep mystery. 'How long, you ask? It all depends, doesn't it, Reg?'

Reggie said nothing, but returned to his hammering.

Raven nodded in glum resignation. Each time he came home in the evening, another piece of the interior of his house had been demolished. Soon there would be nothing left. So far Barry had wreaked nothing but destruction, and never seemed to know how long anything would take. Raven knew that he had inflicted this nightmare on himself, but that didn't make it any easier to stomach. He could only pray that eventually a phoenix would rise from the ashes.

'Let's call it a day,' said Barry. 'Come on Reggie, put that hammer down and drag a few planks across the floor to stop Raven doing himself an injury.'

Raven waited until they had gone, the wooden planks forming a narrow runway down the centre of the hall as promised, leaving a drop to bare earth either side. He returned to the kitchen and flicked on the kettle to make a cup of coffee. The wiring crackled gently as the water boiled, bolstering Raven's confidence that he had made the right decision in unleashing Barry's destructive force to carry out the renovations. He hunted in what was left of his cupboards for a clean mug, and unable to find one, selected the least dirty specimen from the pile that Barry and Reggie had left in the sink. No wonder work on the house was progressing so slowly if the builder and his apprentice spent all day drinking tea. Raven rinsed the mug under the tap before heaping a spoonful of coffee granules into it and splashing boiling water on top. He detested instant coffee, and could only hope that one day soon his dream of a gleaming new kitchen with a proper espresso machine taking pride of place would be realised.

He took a sip of the stale-tasting drink and reflected that the next day would be the first of December. It was getting on for two months since he'd left London and returned to his hometown, quitting the Met and transferring to North Yorkshire Police. Christmas was just around the corner and already the lights were up and the shops crammed full of the kind of sparkly tat Raven despised. Posters for the annual pantomime at the Spa Theatre – *Aladdin* – adorned every billboard in town. There was talk at the station of a Christmas party, which Raven planned to use his best endeavours to avoid. And the duty sergeant was already badgering him to buy raffle tickets. Since the top prizes consisted of a golfing day, a wine hamper and a bottle of whisky – none of which held even the slightest appeal to Raven – he had politely declined. Despite his fondness for winter, he had never got on with Christmas. During his childhood, festive family celebrations around the tree had always ended with his father passing out drunk. And as an adult, Raven had tended to seek out opportunities to work unsociable hours rather than spend time cooped up at home. Terrified of repeating the mistakes of his father, he had wreaked his own kind of havoc on his wife and daughter.

He sighed. There was no way Barry was going to have the house in a fit state for Hannah to come and stay by the twenty-fifth. He was facing the prospect of Christmas alone.

No family. No friends. And at this rate, quite possibly no roof over his head.

# CHAPTER 3

Becca was already wide awake when her alarm went off at seven. She'd lain in bed tossing and turning since the early hours, sleep an impossibility with the questions that kept spinning through her mind. Why hadn't Raven returned to the station the previous evening? Why hadn't he at least phoned her? Had he even spoken to Sam, or had the nurses chased him away? They could be formidable – one in particular – although Becca had won them over during her year of vigilance at Sam's bedside. Then again, what if Dr Kirtlington had convinced Raven that Sam's memory was not to be trusted?

Becca needed Raven on her side if there was to be any chance of finding out who had tried to kill Sam. Her worst fear was that the killer might try again.

The problem was that she had no evidence, apart from Sam's own claim. That was enough for her, but would it be sufficient to convince an outsider like Raven? If not, then her only hope would be to plead with him for his support. That would test his loyalty towards her. She and Raven had forged a bond working together on two murder investigations. But she had no idea how strong that bond would prove to be.

She showered and dressed, parting the curtains for a quick peek at the world outside. Her window at the top of the guest house had a grand view over the entire sweep of the North Bay, and on a clear day she could see for miles, from the sands of Scalby Ness to the tip of the castle headland, and out across the flat expanse of the North Sea. This morning it was still dark, although a grey-pink glimmer at the line where the sky met the sea indicated that the day would soon begin.

When it came, Becca would be ready for it.

She went downstairs to the kitchen where the family ate. As she'd expected, her mother, Sue, was already hard at work, preparing breakfast for the guests. She looked up from the cooker to greet Becca. 'Morning, love. Ready for a full English?'

Becca had half a mind to decline. She wanted to get into work early so as not to miss Raven, and she wasn't sure she had much appetite. But today was going to be a tough one, and she needed all the fortification she could get. 'Thanks,' she told her mum. 'I'll put the kettle on.'

By the time she'd brewed a mug of strong tea for herself, Sue had heaped a plate with bacon, sausages, eggs, beans and fried bread. 'Hang on,' she said, 'I've got some mushrooms too.' She placed the steaming black cups beside the scrambled egg, filling the last empty corner of the plate.

Becca eyed the mound of food, knowing that her waistline wouldn't thank her for consuming it, but suddenly feeling ravenously hungry. She plunged in, enjoying the comfort of hot, home cooking. The salty tang of the bacon, the reassuring hot fluffiness of the egg, the delectable inky juice of the mushrooms. There was nothing like it to set you up for the day.

'Liam's on his way,' said Sue. 'He should be here any minute.'

'Mm,' said Becca, her mouth too full to speak. Her brother hadn't been her favourite person recently. When

Sam had been in a coma, Liam had tried to persuade her that it was time to move on and find someone new. They'd had a falling out, and Becca had spoken angry words to him. He had since apologised, conceding that he'd been wrong about Sam. He'd begged her forgiveness and she had grudgingly given it. But still the memory of his disloyalty lingered. She couldn't regret what she'd said to him. Her brother ought to have supported her at a time when she'd needed him most.

The back door opened. Not the usual crash that announced Liam had entered the building, but a muted, circumspect opening and closing of the door, as if he was afraid of the reception he might receive.

'Hi, Sis. Hi, Mum.'

He stood on the threshold, waiting for permission to enter.

Becca hid a smile. She doubted that this new, deferential version of her brother would last long, but for the moment she was enjoying it. 'In search of free grub?' she teased him.

'Um, if there's any spare?'

Sue bustled over to the table and deposited another heavy plate of food. 'Of course there is, Liam. Stop being silly. Becca isn't going to bite your head off. Come and have some breakfast.'

Yet still he hesitated until Becca took pity on him. 'Come on, Bro. Get some food down your greedy gullet whilst it's hot.'

Finally given leave to join her, Liam left the threshold and came over to the kitchen table, shrugging his leather jacket onto the back of the chair. Whatever the weather, he never wore a proper coat. He tucked into the cooked breakfast like he hadn't eaten for a week. 'So, any news about Sam?' he managed between mouthfuls of food.

'Raven went to see him yesterday.'

'And?'

'And I'm going to speak to Raven this morning.'

'Good. So is he going to start a proper investigation? Is

he going to find out who tried to kill Sam?'

Becca's heart leapt at the conviction in Liam's voice. Whatever doubts he may have harboured before, her brother was totally behind her now. She speared a piece of sausage with her fork. 'He damn well better.'

★

The look on Detective Superintendent Gillian Ellis's face was not encouraging. Never an easy person to win over, this morning she seemed to have come into work bringing even more than her usual quota of grumpiness. She scowled as Raven knocked and entered her office, her heavy jowls quivering with displeasure.

'This is a very early call, Tom. I hope there's a good reason for it.'

'There is, ma'am.'

Raven had fled his house earlier than normal in order to get out of Barry's way. The builder seemed to be on a roll, arriving first thing and promising to "crack on and rip out the rest of the kitchen today". It hadn't even been fully light when Raven had closed his front door behind him and stopped off at a harbourside café for eggs, sausage and a mug of coffee.

The storm of the previous night had eased, and a few hardy fishermen had gathered on Sandside debating whether it was worth setting out that day. After staring at the sky and watching foamy waves batter the shore, they appeared to be having serious doubts, and by the time Raven had drained the last of his coffee, they were already heading for home, another day's work lost.

Gillian's face appeared equally stormy. 'So, what is it?'

'It's Sam Earnshaw, ma'am.' Raven had briefly raised the issue with Gillian before his visit to the hospital. Normally there would have been no need to report such a routine matter as an informal interview with a victim, but in the case of a serving officer's partner there was a certain sensitivity involved. Raven wanted to make sure that

Gillian was fully onboard with what he was doing.

'What did you make of him?'

'I thought Sam made a very credible witness. He reported the events he recalled in some detail and even acknowledged the areas that were hazy, or where there were gaps in his memory. I believed what he told me.'

Gillian shuffled some papers on her desk. 'I know you want to look into it, Tom, but a thorough investigation into the accident has already been conducted. Why do you think this fresh account changes anything?'

Raven noted with disappointment her use of the word "accident". She was clearly clinging to the official line and was going to need some convincing that the "accident" was no such thing. 'The victim alleges that he was pushed into the path of an oncoming vehicle. That makes it attempted murder.'

The original police investigation had reached its conclusion months earlier, but Raven was determined to see it reopened. He had taken the matter very much to heart, and not only for Becca's sake. There was something more personal at stake here.

His own mother had been killed in a hit and run incident when he was sixteen years old. She'd been out searching for him when he ought to have been at home revising for his exams. His feelings of guilt over her death, coupled with his father's drink-fuelled violence, had forced him to flee Scarborough into the embrace of the British Army. The army had enabled him to win back his self-respect, but it had also sent him into a conflict zone – Bosnia – where he had taken a bullet to his right leg, bringing his short military career to an abrupt and painful end. It was thirty-one years before he again set foot in his native town.

'I see.' Gillian removed the reading glasses from the end of her nose, a sure sign that she was giving the matter her deepest consideration. She leaned forwards heavily over her desk. 'Tell me exactly what the consultant at the hospital said about the reliability of Sam's account.'

Raven knew that to quote Dr Kirtlington verbatim would be fatal to his hope of reopening the inquiry. The consultant had made it perfectly clear that in his opinion, Sam's memory could not be relied upon. Yet everything that Sam had told Raven was consistent with Becca's account of that night, and he'd appeared to be perfectly lucid, so Raven was prepared to give him the benefit of the doubt.

He needed Gillian to trust him on this, and the best way of achieving that was by telling her a lie. 'Dr Kirtlington said there may be gaps in Sam's memory. We shouldn't expect him to remember everything immediately.' Not so much a lie, more a selective truth. Raven hurried on. 'But Sam's already given me enough information to move things forward. What I'd like to do now is re-interview the witnesses who were at the party on the night of the incident.'

He waited to see if Gillian would see through his subterfuge or quibble with his use of the word "incident". She had an uncanny ability to sniff out a single falsehood in a field of truths.

She regarded him with suspicious eyes, clearly drawing her own conclusions about Sam's ability to supply reliable evidence. 'I'm prepared to cut you a little slack, Tom. But proceed with caution. All we have is a vague claim by a witness who's only just woken up after a year unconscious. Who knows how much confidence we can place in what he says?'

'We won't know unless we investigate thoroughly, ma'am.'

'Don't patronise me, Tom. It's too early in the morning for that. Go and ask your questions, then come back and tell me if you still think you have a case. But I'll want real evidence to convince me that this is worth pursuing.' She softened her voice. 'Even though DS Shawcross has a personal interest in the matter.'

Raven nodded. There was no suggestion of bias in Gillian's words. But Becca was one of their own. And that had to mean something.

Gillian hadn't quite finished. 'And because of that personal interest, I take it you understand that she can have no involvement in the inquiry?'

'Totally. I've already assigned her to other duties.'

'Very good, Tom.' Gillian slipped her reading glasses back over her nose and returned to whatever report she'd been reading when he came in.

The meeting was over. Raven slipped out of her office before she could have second thoughts.

*

Becca was waiting for Raven when he left Superintendent Ellis's office, his approach heralded by his slightly uneven gait as he negotiated the stairs.

She was miffed that despite getting up early to intercept him as he arrived at the station, he had beaten her to it and gone straight to speak with Gillian before she'd even had time to get her coat off. No doubt their meeting had been to discuss Sam. She felt aggrieved that he hadn't come to see her first. If Raven sent Gillian the wrong signal at this stage, the investigation would be sunk before it left harbour.

She wasn't going to wait for him to disappear again, but stepped out to meet him in the stairwell. He stopped on the landing as soon as he saw her.

'Becca.'

'Raven.'

Although Becca's colleagues called the DCI "sir", Raven had specifically invited her to call him by his surname. An intimacy, of a kind. She was also, as far as she knew, the only one who knew about his military service. She figured that must count for something. Well, the closeness of their relationship was about to be put to the test.

'You're in early today. How are you getting on with that burglary in Pickering?'

Raven could be infuriating when he wanted. Becca's reason for waylaying him in the corridor must be as transparent to him as polished glass. She had no patience for small talk. 'Were you in a meeting with Detective Superintendent Ellis just now?'

'You know I was.'

'Well?'

'Shall we go into my office?'

'No. Just tell me what happened. Did you speak to Sam yesterday? Did you believe him?' The words tumbled out before she could stop herself. If Raven cast doubt on Sam's story, or worse, if he sided with Dr Kirtlington and his "expert" opinion, she would never forgive him. The hospital consultant had been wrong about Sam recovering, and he was wrong about this too.

'Hey, calm down. Of course I believed Sam.'

Becca's face flushed with relief. 'You did?'

'I don't know why you doubted me.'

'So you'll reopen the investigation?'

'The boss just gave me the okay.'

Becca was lost for words. Her night of broken sleep had been for nothing. Her battle-readiness, her determination to fight Sam's corner... all of it unnecessary. She felt like throwing her arms around Raven and giving him a huge hug.

But that would have been well out of order. There was no sense in testing their relationship that far.

'But,' said Raven, 'Gillian asked me to make one thing perfectly clear to you.'

Becca knew what was coming. 'Yes?'

'You can't be involved with the inquiry in any way. Leave it to me and the rest of the team. I promise you that we'll do our best.'

Becca couldn't help feeling deflated by the news, even though it had been expected. How frustrating was it going to be, standing back helplessly and watching others try to find the person who had pushed Sam into the road? But she didn't try to argue with Raven. She knew that if she were found to be interfering it could undermine the entire case. 'So it's back to burglaries in Pickering for me, then.'

'I'm afraid so.'

She stood aside to let him past. She might be forbidden from getting directly involved, but she had ways of finding out what was happening in the investigation. If she thought it was getting bogged down or heading in the wrong direction, she wouldn't hesitate to put things right.

Raven started to leave, then stopped and turned back. 'One more thing... do let me know if Sam remembers that thing he's forgotten.'

# CHAPTER 4

Having got the go-ahead from Gillian, Raven set about organising his team. With Becca side-lined he had lost his most capable detective, but he knew he could rely on his two detective constables, Jess Barraclough and Tony Bairstow. They would be determined to give their best, for Becca's sake.

When he'd bumped into Becca just now – or rather, been ambushed by her – he'd been tempted to dampen down her expectations. As Gillian had pointed out, all they had to go on was the testimony of a recovering coma patient. The incident had taken place over a year ago, and while they had access to the original witness statements taken at the time, the investigation had proceeded on the assumption that it had been a straightforward accident. Sam's evidence changed all that. They would have to reinterview everyone from scratch, one year on. Memories faded after such a long time, and not only for coma patients.

But in the end he had said nothing that might suggest to Becca he wasn't taking the case seriously. Partly because he was, and partly because she would have flown off the

31

handle if she'd detected any hint of reticence on his part. And Becca off the handle wasn't a prospect he fancied facing.

'Right,' he said, 'let's start by reviewing what we already know. Tony, can you fill us in?'

Raven had already assigned Tony the task of reading through the report from the original investigation and making himself familiar with its conclusions. Until he was completely up to speed on the case he would be relying on Tony's knowledge to fill in any gaps.

As usual, Tony had all the facts at his fingertips. 'Last year, on the evening of the eighteenth of November, a social event was held at Salt Castle Brewery in Scarborough for employees and their partners.'

Raven couldn't resist the obvious quip. 'A piss-up in a brewery, you mean?'

'You could call it that, sir.'

'Carry on.'

'It's a family-run firm located on a business park just off the A64. The owner is Greg Earnshaw, Sam's father. Two older brothers are also involved. They were both present, along with their wives.'

'How many employees work at the brewery in total?'

'Around twenty-five if I remember rightly, sir. Most of them attended that evening, along with a similar number of guests.'

'We'll need to speak to all of them if possible.' Any one of the people present might have noticed something that had been missed in the original investigation. And any one of them might have been Sam's assailant. It would be a big task, but Raven knew that Jess and Tony would put in the hours needed to make it happen.

Tony continued with his briefing. 'Sam was found unconscious on the road outside the brewery by a taxi driver who'd come to pick him up. He'd been hit by a vehicle. Not the taxi, I hasten to add. That was checked thoroughly at the time.'

'Wasn't there CCTV?' asked Jess. 'Businesses like that

usually have some kind of security.'

'There was a camera near the entrance,' said Tony, 'but its coverage didn't extend to the road.'

'And no one at the party saw what happened?'

'No. Sam was the first to leave, so all the other guests were inside the building when the incident took place. Everyone attending the event was interviewed, and a door-to-door was carried out at nearby businesses, but no one witnessed the hit and run or even realised what had happened to Sam until the taxi driver arrived and raised the alarm.'

'And there were no clues to the identity of the driver or the vehicle involved?'

'None.'

'All right,' said Raven, picking up his coat. 'I think it's about time we paid a visit to the brewery, don't you?'

★

Greg Earnshaw was a man on a rollercoaster ride. Twelve months ago he'd thought he'd lost his youngest son in a hit and run accident. Then Sam had regained consciousness, only to reveal that it had been no accident. Someone had wanted him dead.

The strain showed on Greg's face.

But there was no doubting the resolve and determination he displayed as Raven sat in his office, outlining his plans for the investigation.

'I guarantee you my full cooperation, Chief Inspector. I'll ask my staff to give you as much time as you need to complete your enquiries. No one wants to get to the bottom of this more than me, I assure you.'

Greg's voice was deep and earnest. He exuded a natural authority and fitted his role of enterprising local businessman to a tee. According to Tony's briefing, he was a self-made millionaire, the son of a bus driver, who had hauled himself up by his bootlaces to forge a business that was carving out a growing niche in the independent brewery sector and had built a reputation to match.

But Greg's face wore unmistakable signs of the torment he'd had to endure this past year. His eyes were sunk in shadow, his forehead furrowed with worry lines, his iron-grey hair as dark as the sky that filled the broad window behind his desk.

Salt Castle Brewery was situated on a small business park off the main road running south out of Scarborough. Its nearest neighbours were warehouses, wholesalers and a car body repair workshop. The area was busy enough during the day, with vehicles coming and going all the time. But in the evening it would be quiet and deserted. Just as it had been the night Sam had stood on the access road in front of the brewery waiting for his taxi.

The main part of the building was given over to production facilities, with a large open-plan office for management and admin staff located upstairs. Greg enjoyed a private office to himself, with a view over fields towards the flat top of Oliver's Mount. Raven sat across the desk from him, facing the window.

Despite the best efforts of the air conditioning, a yeasty smell pervaded the atmosphere, making Raven's nose wrinkle. He had known officers in the Met who would have jumped at the chance to visit a brewery in the hope of being offered a taster or two. But as a confirmed teetotaller, Raven was immune to such temptations.

'As you can see, it's just me in the office today,' said Greg. 'If I'd known you were coming, I'd have arranged for the rest of the management team to be here too.'

Raven had noticed a couple of unoccupied desks in the main office space. 'It's no problem. I can catch up with everyone else later. In fact, I prefer to chat to people one-to-one. I find it easier to get to know them like that.'

Greg nodded his agreement. 'That's always the best way. I'll give you everyone's home address in case you want to visit them at any time.'

'That would be helpful, thank you.' Raven would have put Greg somewhere in his early sixties. He was a solidly-built man who looked like he might rise to the occasional game of golf but didn't particularly take care of himself. He wore a V-neck pullover over a checked shirt with a pair of beige chinos. Smart casual, rather than CEO material. He was clearly at ease in his own skin.

'Tell me about Salt Castle Brewery. I understand that you founded the business yourself.'

There was more than a hint of pride in Greg's voice when he answered. 'Aye, me and a couple of pals back in the mid-eighties. It was a good time to set up a business. Lots of money sloshing around and a government that encouraged enterprise. Things were looking up after the dark days of the seventies and early eighties. We thought we could do anything. And if we worked hard, we could.'

'The name, Salt Castle Brewery, where did that come from?'

'Salt for the sea, Castle for the town's most famous landmark. For a small independent brewery, provenance is vital. Customers want to know where your beer comes from and what makes you special. It's all about creating a strong regional identity, and I wanted the name to reflect that.'

'You brew all your beer here?'

'Yes, from locally-sourced malt. It's all Yorkshire-grown barley.'

Raven knew little about beer but could tell that Greg was a down-to-earth Yorkshireman, justifiably proud of the business he'd built from scratch.

'Who else works in the management team?'

'It's very much a family firm.' Greg handed Raven a framed photograph that stood on the desk in front of him. The photo showed himself with three young men. It had clearly been taken in the brewery tap room and all four were holding up bottles in a celebratory gesture. Raven recognised Sam in better days. The other two must be his older brothers.

'Marcus is the eldest,' explained Greg. 'He's finance director. At the moment he works from home whenever he can because he and his wife have a nine-month-old baby.'

'And your middle son?'

'Anthony. He's head of sales, currently away on a business trip to Edinburgh, trying to persuade the Scots of the superiority of Yorkshire beer. I've no doubt he'll be successful. I used to do that job myself back in the day.'

'And what was Sam's role? Before the incident, I mean?'

At mention of the hit and run, Greg's demeanour grew more gloomy. 'As the youngest, Sam hadn't been in the business for long. To tell you the truth, he'd taken a bit of persuading. He had grand ideas about travelling the world – you know what youngsters can be like. But he came round in the end. I offered him an attractive package – not money for nothing, mind you, I expect my sons to earn their keep – and he took on the role of account director, looking after our existing customers. He made a good job of it. Everyone likes Sam. He has a warm personality.'

'So who's been doing Sam's job for the past year?'

Greg brightened at the question. 'That would be Ellie, my niece. She's been a real trouper, stepping into the breach, so to speak. She's out visiting clients today.'

'It really is a family business, isn't it?' said Raven. He could never have contemplated working alongside his own father, not that Alan Raven had done much work if he could help it. Stepping into his father's shoes and becoming a fisherman would have been Raven's last choice of career. But with a different kind of father, perhaps things might have been different. If Raven had stayed on in Scarborough instead of leaving to join the army, what kind of life might he be living now? It was an unanswerable question. 'How do you all get on, working so closely together?'

'There's nowt more important than family,' said Greg.

Raven detected a slightly defensive tone in the answer. Was this a hint of murky undercurrents beneath the rosy picture that Greg had sought to paint of his family and firm? 'Even brothers can have disagreements from time to time,' he suggested.

Greg folded his arms and planted his elbows firmly on the desk. 'I know what you're getting at, Raven. You don't mind if I call you that, do you?' Greg didn't wait for a response before pressing ahead. 'I'm not going to pretend there have never been any differences of opinion between the three boys. There's bound to be sibling rivalry in any family. But Sam, Anthony and Marcus are good boys. Always have been.'

'All right,' said Raven, deciding not to push the matter. 'Can I ask if you have any views yourself about who might have wanted to kill Sam?'

There was never any harm in asking, was there? Not that Raven expected to be handed the solution to his problem on a plate.

Greg leaned back in his chair. 'None at all, I'm afraid. As I said before, everyone likes Sam. Of the three boys he's always been the one with the most talent to make friends. Perhaps that's what comes from being the youngest of three. My wife is distraught at the idea that anyone would want to kill him. But can I ask you a question in return?'

Raven nodded his assent. 'By all means.'

'The doctor at the hospital, Dr Kirtlington, says that we can't rely on Sam's memories. He thinks this would-be killer might all be in Sam's head. What do you think?'

Raven didn't like being put on the spot like that. He had formed his own opinion of Dr Kirtlington, but he wasn't about to share it here. 'We have to keep an open mind.' Turning the question back on Greg, he asked. 'What do you make of Sam's allegation?'

Greg hesitated for a moment. Then he seemed to make up his mind. 'If Sam said it happened, then it happened. He's my son and I trust him completely.'

'I wouldn't have expected anything less.'

Greg rose to his feet and reached across the desk, seizing Raven's hand and holding it firmly in his grip. 'Thank you for agreeing to investigate this, Raven. You will find out who tried to kill my son, won't you?'

Raven knew the size of the challenge that lay ahead. He wasn't about to make a promise he couldn't be sure of keeping. But he also knew that with Greg's backing he had the green light to start digging. And dig he would. 'You have my word that I'll do whatever it takes to uncover the truth.'

# CHAPTER 5

While Raven had disappeared into Greg Earnshaw's private office to introduce himself to the managing director of the brewery, Jess and Tony had been left to start tackling the rest of the staff. Tony, expressing a keen enthusiasm for the brewing process, had taken off in the direction of the fermentation hall, eager to see where all the action took place, leaving Jess in the company of the office secretary who introduced herself as Sandra.

'Would you like a nice, hot cup of tea and a biscuit, love?' Sandra was a plump woman in her fifties with bottle-blonde hair and a relentlessly cheerful disposition. Her corner of the office was stuffed with filing cabinets covered by a small jungle of pot plants, some of them trailing tentacle-like foliage almost to the floor. It was homely in a chaotic kind of way. Without waiting for Jess's response she proceeded into the tiny kitchen next to the office, returning a minute later with a tray of mugs and a seasonal biscuit tin bearing an image of snow and holly.

'It's right parky out there this morning,' she said, depositing a mug of milky tea in front of Jess and sliding the biscuits in her direction. 'Go on, help yourself. You're here just in time for elevenses.' She settled her ample frame into her swivel chair and bit into a ginger snap.

'Thanks.' Jess selected a chocolate Viennese. She hadn't realised that elevenses were still a thing, and she wasn't really a biscuit person, but if it helped break the ice with Sandra she was happy to go along with it. Not that the office secretary needed much encouragement to start talking.

'Greg told me you're here to talk about Sam. What a terrible business, that hit and run. And Sam such a lovely lad. I've really missed having him around the place. Greg was bowled over when he came round, and I can tell you that I was too.' She leaned confidentially across the desk, pushing her bosom before her like a snowplough and lowering her voice to a loud whisper. 'Sam's always been my favourite of the three brothers. Don't write that down though, it's just between you and me.'

'How long have you known him?' asked Jess, taking a sip of the sweet, hot tea. From the way Sandra spoke, Jess figured she must have been with the firm for a good while.

Sandra gave a throaty laugh. 'Since the day he was born, love. I've worked for Greg right from the very beginning. I'm practically part of the furniture.'

'So you'll know everyone who works here.'

'I should say so. It's a real family firm, that's what I like about it. Close. Friendly.'

'Were you here the evening Sam was run over?'

Sandra sighed. 'We all were. Greg wanted everyone to come – staff and their partners. We made quite a crowd.'

'How many, altogether?'

'Thirty-nine, to be exact. That's twenty-four employees including the directors, plus fifteen guests – wives and girlfriends.'

'And husbands and boyfriends?'

'Aye, them too.' Jess noticed that Sandra wasn't wearing a wedding ring. 'You'll want to know how I can be so certain about the numbers, I expect. It's because I organised the guest list and had to give all the names to the police during the original investigation. I can print a copy of the list for you to take away, if you like.'

'That would be really helpful, Sandra.'

'No problem.' Her fingers moved nimbly across her computer keyboard as she searched for the relevant file and sent it off to the printer.

'Can you tell me everything you remember about that night?' asked Jess as the printer whirred into action.

'Everything?' Sandra raised an eyebrow. 'Everything is a lot, love. I have a good memory for people and conversations. But the gist of it is that we were all having a lovely time. Well, folk do when there's free beer on the house, don't they? Sam needed to leave early because he was going to meet his girlfriend, Becca – who you probably know, since she's one of your lot – so he asked me to call a taxi for him, which I was happy to do. I didn't see him again after that.' She paused to dab at her eyes with a handkerchief. 'Then at about half past ten the taxi driver – Ricky, his name was – came rushing inside, all in a tizz, yelling that there's a body lying in the road. Well, you can imagine! Everyone rushed out to see – even though it was tipping down with rain – and someone – I think it was Greg – phoned for an ambulance. Poor Denise – that's Sam's mum – was beside herself, as any mother would be. I looked after her and made her a cup of sweet tea. That's what they say you should give someone who's had a bad shock. Hot sweet tea. Anyway, the ambulance turned up after about ten minutes and took Sam away, with Greg and Denise following in the taxi. And that was the end of the party. Dreadful, it was.'

Sandra was right about having a good memory. Not only had she remembered the exact number of guests at the event, but her recollection of the evening seemed sharp even a year on, even though it was peppered with extraneous detail. Jess noted it all down just in case. 'What exactly was the party for?'

'We were celebrating the signing of a new contract.

Greg always insists on marking achievements in some way. He says that if we don't take a moment to give ourselves a pat on the back, what's the point in working so hard?'

Jess could tell from the admiration when Sandra spoke about Greg that she was likely to prove unswervingly loyal to her boss. But that didn't mean she would be unwilling to share any juicy items of gossip given half a chance.

Jess framed her next question carefully. She didn't want to get on the wrong side of Sandra after such a good start. Nor did she want to reveal that this was now an attempted murder investigation. 'How well did Sam get on with everyone who was at the party that night?'

'What do you mean? Sam's always been well-liked by folk.'

'But is it possible he might have fallen out with someone?'

Sandra reached for another biscuit and bit into it before replying. 'Well, I'm not one for tittle-tattle, you understand…'

'Of course not.'

'But between you, me and the gatepost, there was a bit of a bust up that day between the three brothers.'

'At the party?'

'No, earlier in the day, at work.'

'What was it about?'

Sandra shook her head. 'I didn't overhear the details' – Jess surmised that this wasn't from lack of trying on Sandra's part – 'but I can tell you that it wasn't the first time those three had a go at each other. They were always squabbling. Brothers can be like that.'

'I thought you said everyone liked Sam.'

'Well, yes. Most folk did. But family – that's another matter. Those two older brothers, I sometimes thought they had it in for Sam. But like I said before, I hate to gossip.' Sandra pushed the open biscuit tin in Jess's direction. 'Go on, have another one, love. You look like you could do with feeding up.'

★

Tony Bairstow fancied he knew a thing or two about beer. He was a modest drinker – nothing too much, no heavy sessions down the pub or anything like that – but he did enjoy a quiet pint or two in the evenings in front of the telly. He liked to sample craft beers from the many microbreweries that had sprung up in recent years, and even ran a home brew kit in his kitchen, producing just enough drinkable beer to keep himself going. But Salt Castle Brewery was on an altogether different scale from his own setup. Tony whistled through his teeth as he gazed up at the gleaming stainless-steel tanks and fermentation vessels that rose to the ceiling, connected by a complex network of pipes and valves. Metal steps led up to a high-level walkway that ran around the top of the building.

'I can give you a quick tour if you like,' said the head brewer, who had introduced himself as Gavin Thompson. He was a big man, the large dome of his head perfectly bald, his handshake firm and strong. He regarded Tony as if appraising a fellow enthusiast.

'I'd love that,' said Tony. He pulled out his notebook and pencil, ready to record any pertinent points.

'No problem.' Gavin gave some instructions to a couple of employees he'd been supervising and broke off to show Tony around. 'Let's start with the ground floor.' He set off across the polished concrete floor, Tony scurrying in his wake to keep up. He pushed open a door and pressed some switches. A large number of lights flickered on, illuminating the room beyond.

'So down here we have the tap room,' said Gavin. 'Sometimes we open this up to the public, other times we invite industry reps to come and sample our wares.'

Tony stuck his head inside to have a good look around. It was like a normal bar, with tables, chairs, table football, and a vintage jukebox in one corner. But the back wall was made entirely from glass, showing the working brewery behind, and at the bar itself the only drinks on offer were beers – ales and lagers; draft and bottled.

'Is this where you held the party the night Sam Earnshaw was injured?'

Gavin looked Tony up and down again, reassessing him carefully. 'Is that why you're here? To investigate what happened to Sam?'

'That's right.'

'The police did all that a year ago.'

'We're following a new line of enquiry.'

Gavin nodded slowly. 'Well, all right. If it helps catch the bastard who ran into Sam, I'll tell you whatever you want to know. And to answer your question, yes, this is where everyone was that night.'

The room was empty and silent now, but Tony tried to picture it as it might have been during the party. Late November, the night as dark as pitch, rain hammering down and music turned up loud. Nobody inside the bar would have seen or heard anything happening outside.

'Seen enough here?' Gavin switched the lights off, returning the tap room to darkness and set off again, heading back into the main part of the brewery. There was a restless energy to the man, as if he was eager to show Tony the best bit of the brewery. He gestured at a staircase leading up an inside wall of the building. 'That takes you up to the offices. But my domain is here. We call this the brew deck. It's where the magic happens.'

Tony allowed his gaze to wander once more around the vast open space of the brewery. It was an awesome sight, like a cathedral to beer.

Gavin led the way over to a cluster of steel vats, each about ten feet tall. A modern control panel set into the wall bristled with dials, buttons and electronic readouts. 'These are the mash tuns where we mix the malt with water to make a mash. By heating it we convert the starch in the grains into sugars ready for fermentation.'

'Sure,' said Tony. He was familiar with the process. At home he did the same job using a small mashing bin that sat on his kitchen worktop.

Gavin pointed to a series of steel pipes leading from the tuns to a set of large kettles. 'You'll know what these are for, I expect?'

'For boiling the wort?' Wort was the name given to the end product of mashing. It was the sugary liquid that would then be brewed into beer.

Barley, malt, wort, beer. Alchemy.

'Right. After we've extracted the wort from the malt, we sterilise it by boiling it with hops in these kettles. Then we cool it quickly to prevent contamination.'

Gavin was moving again, heading this time up the stairs that led to the upper level of the brew deck. He hauled himself quickly up the metal steps, his long legs taking them two at a time. Tony huffed and puffed to catch him up.

The brewer stopped once he reached the walkway that spanned the top level of the brewery. From here, Tony could see that the steel platform was designed to give access to the upper sections of the huge fermentation vessels that reached almost to the ceiling like the pipes of a vast organ. Dials and controls were set into the sides of the cylindrical fermenters.

'This is really the most important part of the whole process,' said Gavin. 'After filtering, the wort and hops are pumped into these vessels and we add the yeast. Fermentation turns the sugar into $CO_2$ and of course, ethanol. After fermentation we move the beer into conditioning tanks to mature, then filter again. Finally it goes to be packaged in kegs or bottles.'

'It's an impressive set-up.'

Gavin shrugged modestly. 'We moved to the present location about ten years ago to scale up production. The company's grown over the years but it's still a small operation compared to the big breweries. When we started out we were in a much smaller building in town. We really were Salt Castle back then. You could see the foreshore, smell the spray from the sea. We used copper vats in those days too.'

'Is copper better?' At home, Tony used a plastic bucket for heating his mash, but he didn't think Gavin would want to hear about that.

The brewer's strong hands gripped the metal railing that ran along the edge of the walkway. 'Stainless steel provides a sterile environment and produces a more predictable result. But copper's the old way of brewing.'

There was nostalgia in Gavin's eyes and a longing for past traditions, yet it was obvious from the way he talked about the brewing process and how his gaze returned constantly to the equipment he described that he still felt a deep passion for his work.

'You enjoy working here?' Tony asked.

'Love it. I look forward to coming in each day, and there aren't many people who can say that about their job.'

'No, there aren't,' agreed Tony. 'So tell me, what's the family like to work for? It's quite unusual having a father and his three sons running the place.'

'I suppose so, but Greg and I go all the way back. We were at school together.'

'Really?' Tony made a note. 'And what about his sons?'

Gavin seemed in no hurry to express an opinion. He turned away to inspect the dials on the nearest fermenter, giving them a gentle tap. 'Sam's a nice lad and he was good at striking a rapport with the customers. I was very sorry about what happened to him.'

'And the other two?'

'Marcus and Anthony have big plans for this place. They're not short on ambition.'

'That's a good thing, isn't it?' said Tony. 'When you're running a business?'

'As long as you don't lose sight of what it's really about.'

'And what is it about?'

Gavin turned his large head to take in the expanse of the brewery building, the vats and tanks, the pipes and gantries. He breathed in the heady smell of hops, malt and yeast. 'Like I said, it's a family firm. We're independent.

We produce a high-quality product from local ingredients. Sam understands that, and Greg does too, or at least he always did.'

'You think Greg shares the same ambition as Marcus and Anthony?'

'He's always been hungry for success. You have to be, to conjure an operation like this out of thin air.' Gavin gazed out from the gantry at his realm, like a farmer surveying ripe fields before harvest. 'But I guess Greg's getting ready to hand over to the next generation. You can't fight progress. You have to face the future.'

Tony nodded. He was keen to move the interview on to the night Sam had been hit and left for dead, but he held back, sensing that the brewer wasn't quite done with his reflections.

Sure enough, after a moment Gavin leaned towards him and lowered his voice. 'Mind you, the company's had a run of bad luck, if you ask me.'

'What do you mean?'

'I don't know what else you'd call it, this accident happening to Sam so soon after the old finance director passed away.'

'The old finance director?'

'Jeremy. He founded the company alongside me and Greg. But he died in an accident just a year or so before Sam was run over.'

Tony licked his pencil and turned to a fresh page in his notebook. 'Tell me more about Jeremy,' he said to Gavin.

# CHAPTER 6

There were many attractive sights to see in the town of Pickering, such as the medieval castle, the heritage railway station with its brightly-painted steam engines that took visitors across the North York Moors to Whitby, and the old stone houses, shops and churches of the town centre.

But the place where Becca found herself now wasn't one of them.

The industrial park on the outskirts of the town was grey, windswept and devoid of charm, but at least the half-hour drive from Scarborough had given her an excuse to get out of the police station. Anything had to be better than sitting at her desk waiting for Raven, Jess and Tony to return from the brewery so she could quiz them and find out what progress they'd made. None of the team had told her where they were going when they left the station together that morning, but Becca hadn't reached the rank of DS without the ability to make her own deduction about something so blindingly obvious.

The electronics wholesaler that she was visiting was situated between a commercial printer and a company that manufactured custom motorcycle parts. She found the owner of the business in front of the warehouse, signing off a fresh delivery of laptops and barking orders at the unfortunate delivery driver who had brought them.

'Mr Owens? Becca Shawcross from Scarborough CID. I'm here about the theft you reported.'

'Ah, good, about bloody time one of you lot showed up.' The man was heavily bearded and dressed in a white shirt straining to contain the bulge of a paunch. He wore a hard hat on his head and had his sleeves rolled up, despite the nip in the air. 'Come inside to the office.' He turned his back on her and stomped away into the building.

Becca followed him in. The office attached to the side of the warehouse was cramped, the desk a sea of delivery notes and invoices. A single dirty window gazed onto the corrugated metal wall of the neighbouring unit. It looked a thoroughly depressing place to work. No wonder Owens was so ill-tempered. He took a seat on a squeaky swivel chair and looked at her expectantly. No tea or coffee was on offer, not that Becca would have fancied one anyway. The place looked decidedly unhygienic.

'Have a seat if you want,' the manager suggested.

Becca cleared a pile of random invoices off a spare chair and dumped them onto the floor. The seat shifted alarmingly as it took her weight, and she hoped it would hold up for the duration of her visit. 'Mr Owens, perhaps you could start by explaining the nature of your business exactly?'

Owens gave his armpit an impatient scratch. 'Wholesale and distribution. It's not rocket science. We import goods and distribute them to retailers in the Scarborough and York area.'

'You reported the theft of a consignment of fifty laptops at the weekend.'

'Aye, that's right.' He manoeuvred his paunch closer to his desk and began tapping away at a battered-looking keyboard. He swivelled the computer screen towards Becca. 'This lot. High-spec laptops straight from the manufacturer. They were top end, no cheap rip-offs. I only do quality.'

Becca peered at an electronic delivery note. 'Maybe you could print that off for me?'

'Hey presto.' Owens clicked a mouse, and a printer in the corner of the room spun into action.

The man made no move to get up, so Becca retrieved the printout for herself. She studied the delivery note, checking that it matched his description. 'Where were the items stored?'

'In the warehouse, close to the main entrance. They'd only been brought in the previous day.'

'I see. And do you have any CCTV footage from the night of the burglary?'

'Of course. I'm not some idiot.'

Owens inserted a flash drive into his computer, bashed more keys, and a somewhat grainy image of the warehouse appeared. It was dark, and a steady rain was falling. The date and timestamp on the video showed that it was Saturday night, just after eleven-thirty, a time when the industrial park would presumably have been deserted.

'Would anyone have been around at that time?' Becca asked.

'No.'

'What about a security guard?'

'Don't have one,' grumbled Owens. 'Look, here he comes now.'

He pointed at the screen just as a male figure in a dark hoodie came into view, a baseball cap pulled low over his eyes, his back to the camera. He levered open the side door of the warehouse with a crowbar and disappeared inside. A few minutes later the man reappeared through the main entrance, wheeling a pile of boxes on a trolley. The cap and hood hid his face from the camera. He quickly disappeared from view. For another minute or so, the figure was lost to sight. Then the camera caught the tail-end of a white vehicle as it left the scene.

Owens hit the stop button. 'That's all there is.'

'Do you have an alarm system installed?' asked Becca.

'Of course I do! But it was late on Saturday night and you lot were too busy dragging drunks off the streets to do anything about it. By the time someone arrived, the thief was long gone. In any case, the plods who showed up weren't much cop. They didn't even dust for prints, like they do on TV. Just told me I needed to fit a better lock. Well, I'd already worked that out for myself, hadn't I?'

The warehouse manager's relentless belligerence was beginning to grate on Becca, and she was tempted to agree with the "plods" that the case was a lost cause. But it wasn't as if she had anything else to fill her time right now. She needed a challenge to take her mind off Sam. 'Well, I'm on the case now, Mr Owens. And I assure you that I will do my very best to get to the bottom of this.'

For the first time since she'd arrived, the man's face broke out into a smile, suggesting there might be an ounce of sensitivity beneath his hard hat and grumpy demeanour. He gave her a thumbs-up with two chubby digits. 'Well, that's more like it. Let's nail this bastard!'

Becca returned his smile weakly, figuring she must have done something to impress him. Though how she was going to track down the burglar with so little to go on, she had no idea.

\*

After their morning session at the brewery, Raven gathered Jess and Tony together in his car for a quick debrief. It was quicker than driving back to the station, and Raven was keen to avoid Becca who, no doubt, would be pestering him for an update as soon as he returned.

The interior of a sports coupé didn't make for an ideal incident room – even a temporary one – but Raven swivelled round in his leather seat to address Jess, who was sitting beside him, and Tony, who had taken up residence on the cramped back seat of the car. The M6 wasn't really a four-seater. More like a two plus two, or perhaps a two plus one. Fortunately Tony's legs weren't that long. And besides, the DC never complained about anything.

'So, what do we have so far?' Raven had to admit that apart from Greg's reassurance of full cooperation he had little to show for his work, just a potted history of the business and a summary of the roles of the various family members: Greg's eldest son, Marcus, as finance director; Anthony, the middle son, as sales director; and Ellie, Sam's cousin, now filling his position as account director. He hoped the others had managed to gather more interesting intelligence.

'I spent some time with Greg's secretary,' said Jess. 'She was quite chatty over tea and biscuits. She told me there was a big argument between the three brothers on the day of the party, and this wasn't the first time she'd seen them quarrelling.'

'Interesting.' Greg had referred briefly to sibling rivalry, but had tried to dismiss it as nothing out of the ordinary. It sounded like there might be more to it. 'Did she say what the argument was about?'

'She told me she didn't hear.'

'Okay,' said Raven. 'So it's not all happy families at the brewery. We'll follow that up and see what we can find out. Tony, how did you get on?'

'I spoke with the head brewer, sir. Gavin Thompson. He showed me around and talked about how the business had changed over the years. He seemed quite nostalgic for the good old days. From what he said, I gathered he was one of the founders of the brewery, alongside Greg. Reading between the lines, I don't think he likes the direction that the two brothers want to take things.'

'Okay, so there are tensions within the business,' said Raven. 'This is definitely something we need to learn more about.'

'There's something else, sir.'

Raven could tell from Tony's eagerness that he had found something important. 'Yes?'

'Gavin mentioned the former finance director, a man

called Jeremy Green.'

'What about him?'

'It seems that he died in an accident a year before Sam was run over. He slipped and fell while out walking at Flamborough Head.'

'Slipped and fell?' Raven was familiar with the nearby beauty spot. Flamborough Head was a wild and rugged coastline of chalk cliffs battered by the sea. He recalled a school trip there involving windswept clifftops and screeching gulls. The wind had driven rain into his face and the class had retreated into the coach to eat their packed lunches. Raven had taken the opportunity to enjoy a quick snog behind the lighthouse with his first girlfriend, Donna Craven, while Darren Jubb, his erstwhile schoolfriend, had scribbled obscenities in the condensation on the window of the coach. As for the intended educational purpose of the trip, Raven had no recollection.

'Jeremy was a keen walker,' said Tony, 'but he strayed too close to the clifftops. Went over the edge, apparently.'

'Really?' It was a small miracle that none of Raven's classmates had vanished over the cliffs during that long-ago excursion, but the likelihood of such an outcome happening to an experienced walker seemed slim.

'Gavin described it as an accident. He said the firm had gone through a run of bad luck, first with Jeremy's death, then with Sam ending up in hospital.'

'Bad luck, eh?' Raven was reminded of what Dr Kirtlington, the hospital doctor, had said about Sam – that he was lucky to have survived the hit and run and to have woken from a coma. *Good luck, bad luck.* There was something going on at Salt Castle Brewery all right, but Raven didn't think luck had any part in it. 'Dig out the coroner's report for Jeremy Green and let me know what you find,' he told Tony.

'Sir?' It was Jess. 'I know we already have our hands full interviewing everyone at the brewery, but do you think it's worth talking again to the taxi driver who found Sam in the road? He was interviewed at the time, but since he's such a key witness, it wouldn't hurt to speak to him again.'

'You're right.' Raven liked it when his team showed initiative. 'Why don't you go and do that? Tony, you chase up that coroner's report. I'm going to go and speak to the eldest son, Marcus. I want to find out what this argument between the brothers was all about.'

# CHAPTER 7

Woodland Ravine was a wide, tree-lined road with large detached houses on one side and a grassy bank on the other that sloped down to Peasholm Beck. Raven parked his BMW behind a Lexus SUV, then climbed the sloping path up to a double-fronted house that looked down on a well-tended garden. A thorny rose, bare of foliage at this time of year, framed the redbrick porch. The finance director of Salt Castle Brewery wasn't doing too badly for himself.

A woman in her early thirties opened the door. She was a slim brunette dressed casually in baggy jeans and a checked shirt, her hair tied back in a ponytail. Her face was pretty but clear of makeup.

Raven introduced himself. 'Mrs Earnshaw, I was hoping to have a word with your husband. Is he in? I spoke to Greg Earnshaw this morning and he said that Marcus was working from home today.'

'Yes, he is. Do come in, Chief Inspector.'

She led the way to the rear of the house where a modern extension housed a shiny kitchen-diner and family room. The open-plan space was as big as the entire ground floor of Raven's house. Bigger. The island unit alone approximated to the size of his own kitchen floor. Bifold doors gave onto a paved patio while natural light streamed through a lantern roof in the ceiling.

Raven's thoughts turned to Barry and his promise to rip out the rest of the kitchen that day. Raven had no idea what kind of hellhole he would find when he returned to Quay Street, but he knew it would be the complete opposite of this perfect incarnation of design chic.

A chubby-faced baby boy sat in a high chair at the breakfast bar, sticking his fingers into a bowl of unidentifiable orange mush. He looked up at Raven and gurgled in a friendly way.

'Sorry, I'm just giving Freddie his lunch. What a mess you've made, little man!' Marcus's wife cooed and fussed over the baby who laughed and tried to stick his orange fingers in her face.

'Don't worry, Mrs Earnshaw. I'm sorry to bother you at home.'

'Please, call me Olivia. I'll let Marcus know you're here.' She disappeared off to another part of the house, leaving Raven alone with Freddie. Greg had said he was nine months old. Raven wouldn't have had a clue, he was hopeless with babies.

The baby chuckled and stretched out his gooey fingers. Raven kept his distance, trying to remember if feeding time had been as messy as this with his own daughter. The trouble was, he'd hardly been around when Hannah was growing up, too busy trying to put the world to right, solving crimes and banging up criminals. And what did he have to show for all those long days and hours of overtime? A broken marriage, a daughter who barely spoke to him, and a kitchen that was as far removed from the one he was standing in as it was possible to imagine.

Olivia returned. 'Marcus is just on the phone, but he'll be with you in a minute. Would you like a coffee while you wait?'

'I wouldn't say no, thank you.'

While Olivia inserted a capsule into a fancy built-in machine, Raven asked her if she'd been at the party the night Sam was run over.

'Yes, I was there. But I was six months pregnant at the time, so I couldn't drink any of the beer that was on offer.'

Raven would have put Olivia down as more of a white wine drinker than a beer enthusiast, but perhaps a taste for hops was compulsory in this family.

She set a tiny cup of espresso down in front of him. Raven sniffed appreciatively, savouring the aroma. He'd take roasted beans over hops and malt any day. 'What do you remember about that night?'

Olivia turned away to wipe Freddie's face and hands. 'It was just a small party. A private gathering for family and employees. I sat with Naomi most of the evening – that's Anthony's wife. Denise, our mother-in-law, joined us.'

'You didn't spend the evening with your husband?'

'The boys were circulating, making sure to spend time with everyone. That was the purpose of the evening. To keep the staff happy.'

'And was everyone happy?'

'I'm not sure I understand your meaning.'

'What do you know about the argument that took place between the three brothers that day at work?'

'Argument?' She turned to face him full-on. 'Marcus didn't say anything about an argument. If it took place earlier that day, I can assure you that whatever it was about, it had all blown over by the evening.'

'Sorry to keep you waiting, Chief Inspector.' A tall, blond-haired man with a neatly-trimmed beard breezed into the kitchen. He was dressed casually in jeans and a rugby shirt. Raven easily recognised him from the photo Greg had shown him of his eldest son. Marcus Earnshaw gave Raven's hand a vigorous shake. 'Look, I can only spare you ten minutes or so, so let's go through to my office and get away from the chaos of the kitchen.' He laughed, although Olivia didn't seem to find his comment very amusing.

In any case, Raven felt Marcus was being unfair. The baby had been contented and well-behaved, and the only mess was confined to his high chair. The rest of the kitchen was immaculate. Raven thanked Olivia for the coffee and followed her husband through to his office.

★

'Pull the door closed behind you, Chief Inspector.' Marcus Earnshaw's home office overlooked the front garden, well out of earshot of his kitchen and his wife. He seated himself in an executive leather chair behind a large, mahogany desk and invited Raven to make himself comfortable on a low sofa opposite. 'You'll be here about Sam. Dad said you might drop by for a quick chat.'

With a period fireplace, a high ceiling, and oil paintings of Scarborough Castle and Whitby Abbey adorning the walls, it was certainly a grander place to work than the functional office at the brewery where the brothers shared a space with other staff. From what Raven had observed, Marcus was simply using the baby as an excuse to work from home and didn't actually do any hands-on childcare.

'I spoke to your father this morning. I understand you're his eldest son.'

'That's right.' Marcus leaned back in his chair and folded his hands behind his head. His manner was confident, bordering on arrogant.

'Tell me a little about yourself. How long have you been finance director at the brewery?'

'Two years now. Can't believe how the time has flown. I qualified as an accountant and started my career working for one of the Big Four in Leeds. I wanted to position myself at the cutting edge of finance, to see how the best companies operated. But I reached a point when it felt right to join the family firm. We were starting to grow fast and Dad wanted someone with the right skills to take the company forward.'

'So you've worked for your father for two years?'

'Three actually. When I started, the previous finance director was still with us. I worked alongside him for a year before stepping into his shoes.'

'The previous finance director would be Jeremy Green.'

'That's right. Good old Jeremy.' Marcus smiled fondly as if recalling an amusing but bumbling old uncle. 'He'd done the accounts since the day Dad set up the company, but he didn't have the formal qualifications of a chartered accountant. "Qualified by experience" is how he liked to describe himself. Dad trusted him to do the job, and he did his best, but there comes a time with every business when you need someone who really understands finance.'

'And that person was you?'

Marcus smiled. 'Of course. Dad always intended to hand over the running of the company to the next generation. He saw it as his legacy. And I felt that the family firm would be the right vehicle for me to make best use of my skills.'

'So you had no particular interest in beer when you joined the brewery?'

Marcus sniffed. 'There's no need to be churlish. I'm interested in profit, and if there's profit in beer, then I'm interested in beer.' He unfolded his hands from behind his head and drummed his fingers on the desk. 'Was there anything in particular you wanted to ask me about Sam?'

'Actually,' said Raven, hoping to throw Marcus off balance, 'I'd like to ask you about Jeremy's death.'

But Marcus must have been expecting the shot. He remained outwardly cool. 'Very sad. He was Dad's best friend. They'd known each other since school. But Jeremy had no family to miss him, and luckily I was perfectly positioned to take over the reins, so there was no harm done to the business.'

'Lucky for you.'

An affronted look appeared on Marcus's face. 'What are you suggesting? That I pushed him off the cliff? Don't be absurd.'

'I'm not suggesting anything, Mr Earnshaw. You just made that suggestion yourself.'

Marcus looked ruffled but kept his mouth firmly shut. Raven tried a different angle. 'What's it like working so closely with your family?'

'It works well enough. We have a close bond. We understand each other.'

The setup sounded rather nepotistic to Raven, but maybe that was the point of a family firm. 'How does it work when making decisions about the business?'

Marcus shrugged noncommittally. 'We hold board meetings to discuss any significant matters. Dad always likes to hear our opinions.'

'But he makes the final decision.'

'Well, he founded the company, so that's only to be expected. But he won't be around forever.'

Raven wondered whether Marcus was thinking about his father's retirement, or something more final. 'I expect you're in a good position to take over, being the eldest son, and in charge of finance.'

Marcus didn't rise to the bait. He dismissed Raven's suggestion with a wave of the hand. 'No one in this family is talking about Dad stepping down anytime soon. He's still got a few more years left in him. And he's certainly not expressed any intention to name a successor, other than making it clear that he wants control of the firm to stay with the family.'

Raven wasn't convinced that Marcus would be content to stand aside while one of his brothers seized the reins of power. Everything about him – from the mahogany desk to his talk of wanting to work with the biggest and best companies – spoke of a deep well of ambition. He'd already taken over Jeremy's job. Raven had no doubt he would waste no time pushing himself into Greg's role as soon as an opportunity presented itself.

'Tell me about the night Sam was run over. There was a private party at the brewery, for the benefit of the staff?'

'Yes. These sorts of events are good for morale. It's

cheaper to throw a party every now and again than it is to recruit and train new workers.'

'And were you there the whole time?'

'Yes. Olivia would have liked to go home early – she was expecting Freddie at the time and said she was tired. But it was important for the directors and their wives to show their faces. I told her she'd just have to stay awake a bit longer.'

'Did you spend the evening with her?'

'No, I was doing the rounds, making sure I said something nice to everyone. It's not like I don't see enough of Olivia in private.'

Marcus hardly sounded like a man deeply in love with his wife. But perhaps he simply wasn't very good at expressing his feelings. Plenty of men were like that. Raven wasn't much good with emotions himself, although he hoped he didn't come across as quite so crass as Marcus Earnshaw.

'Did you speak to Sam that evening?'

'I bumped into him once or twice,' said Marcus evasively.

'And what did you talk about?'

'Nothing much. I really don't remember.'

'Did you see him leave?'

'No.'

'Did you see anyone else go outside?'

'No.'

'And did you go outside yourself?'

'Why would I?' Marcus stared defiantly at Raven across the desk. 'At least, not until the taxi driver gate-crashed the party and raised the alarm.'

'So you had no idea what had happened to Sam until then?'

'Of course not. I'd have called for an ambulance myself if I'd known.'

Raven watched Marcus carefully. 'A witness has reported seeing an argument between you and your brothers during the day. What was that about?'

Marcus's mouth twitched. 'Who said that?'

'Just answer the question.'

Marcus leaned back in his chair, his fingers interlaced behind his head. He was trying to demonstrate a carefree, relaxed posture, yet everything about his pose revealed the tension in his limbs. 'Well, whoever said it was an argument is exaggerating. It was just a discussion. Brothers don't always see eye to eye on everything, that's family life for you. Do you have a brother? If you do, then you'll know what I'm talking about.'

'I don't have a brother,' countered Raven, 'and I'd like to know precisely what this discussion was about.'

'If you must know, it concerned the future direction of the business. The company is in talks over a possible merger with a large national brewery. I can't say any more, it's confidential.'

'I see. And what is your position on this possible merger?'

Marcus spread his palms wide as if the answer was obvious. 'Naturally, I'm in favour of it. It would be a great opportunity for us to grow, to expand into new markets, to attract more investment. Anthony agrees with me.'

'But not Sam?'

'Sam's young. He doesn't understand business properly yet.'

'But he looked after your existing customers. He must have understood why they continued to do business with you. Maybe he had their best interests at heart.'

Marcus laughed heartily. 'We're not here to serve our customers, Chief Inspector, we're here to make a profit for ourselves. There's no room for sentimentality in the corporate world. Businesses grow, or else they die. Anyway, I don't see what any of this has to do with Sam's accident.'

Raven fixed him with a stare. 'Accident? What happened to Sam was no accident.'

'I don't know what you mean.' For the first time in their conversation, Marcus was visibly thrown off kilter.

'Then it would seem that your father hasn't been entirely candid with you, Mr Earnshaw. I didn't drop by today for a "quick chat". I'm investigating an attempted murder.'

'What?'

'Sam didn't simply stumble into the path of a speeding vehicle that night. He was pushed.'

'You must be joking!'

Raven fixed him with a cold stare. 'Do you think it's a laughing matter?'

'No, I–'

'So, this is why I'm interested in the argument that took place between you, Anthony and Sam. It would seem that Sam was an obstacle to your plans, and that someone may have taken the opportunity to remove that obstacle.'

'That's an outrageous accusation!'

'Just as Jeremy was an obstacle to your advancement. Yet he too met with an unfortunate turn of events.'

Marcus gripped the edge of his mahogany desk in cold fury. 'How dare you! If anyone wanted Jeremy out of the way...'

'What?'

'Forget it.' With obvious effort, Marcus calmed himself down, letting go of his desk and sitting back in his chair. 'I was just letting off steam. I didn't mean anything.' He rose to his feet. 'I think we're done here. I'd like you to leave now.'

# CHAPTER 8

The office of the taxi firm was just off the busy thoroughfare of St Thomas Street, behind the site of the old opera house and next door to a pizza takeaway. It was a short walk from the police station, and Jess was glad to stretch her legs and get some fresh air after a morning in the brewery. She wondered if she would ever get the smell of malted barley out of her nose.

'Ricky should be back in about ten minutes, love,' said the receptionist, a middle-aged woman who sat behind the desk of the cramped booking office, turning the pages of a celebrity magazine as she waited for the phone to ring. 'He's just dropping a customer off at the spa. You want to wait for him?'

Jess agreed to do that and took a seat in the tiny waiting area. To pass the time, she pulled out her phone and started scrolling through Instagram. She liked and commented on a couple of posts – some of her friends had gone out to a bar in town at the weekend and then on to a nightclub. From the pictures they'd posted, they'd had a raucous time, knocking back drinks and becoming less inhibited as the evening progressed. She could have gone with them, but she'd declined, giving work as an excuse. In truth, she'd spent the evening quietly with Scott, the youngest member of the CSI team, who she had recently started dating. They'd gone to see a film and then shared a bag of chips on the seafront. She wondered when she might introduce Scott to her friends, but it was still too soon for that. Scott was shy and needed careful handling. He had a trauma in his past that meant he was wary of committing to new relationships, afraid of being hurt. Jess was happy to take things slowly for the time being. There was no rush. She was hoping she'd be able to persuade him to spend Christmas at Rosedale Abbey with her family. But she hadn't broached the topic yet. Scott could be easily scared off.

The door opened, letting in a blast of icy air and a waft of pepperoni. A man entered: mid-thirties, clean-shaven, with a single earring in his left ear, wearing a padded jacket zipped up to his chin against the cold. 'You said there was a police detective here to see me.'

'Over there.' The receptionist glanced up briefly from her magazine and pointed in Jess's direction. 'This is Ricky Potts, love,' she told Jess. 'He's the one you want.'

Jess stood up, pocketing her phone. 'Nice to meet you, Mr Potts.'

'You're the police?' Ricky looked at her suspiciously, as if unable to believe that someone as young as Jess could be a detective.

'DC Jess Barraclough.' Being just twenty-one years old, not to mention a woman, Jess was used to encountering scepticism from members of the public from time to time. She tried not to let it bother her. The problem would get less with time, she supposed. She showed the taxi driver her warrant card and although he looked surprised he seemed to accept the evidence of his own eyes.

'Is there somewhere private we can talk?' she asked him.

'You can go through to the back,' said the receptionist without lifting her eyes from the article she was reading.

'There's no one else in.'

Jess followed Ricky through to a poky kitchen where there was just room for a kettle, a microwave and a fridge. He took a seat on a wooden stool, offering Jess a slightly less battered chair. 'All right then, what's this about?'

'We're revisiting a hit and run incident that took place last year near Salt Castle Brewery. The victim's name was Sam Earnshaw. I understand that you were the person who found him and raised the alarm.'

'Aye,' said Ricky. 'I did. But I told the police everything I knew at the time.'

'Some new evidence has come to our attention, so we're reviewing the case. Can you tell me exactly what happened that night?'

'I certainly can,' said Ricky, beginning to visibly relax and settle into a story-telling mode. 'Now, I don't remember all the fares I take – they start to blur into each other over the years. But I remember that night like it were yesterday. Trish – that's our receptionist – contacted me to say we had a call from the brewery. I happened to be out that way and she asked if I could handle it.'

'Do you often go to the brewery?'

'Oh, aye, a fair bit. Usually running visitors to the train station, that sort of thing. Occasionally one of the bosses. It's a family affair, so everyone's related. Now, the other brothers can be a bit off-hand, always too busy on their phones to talk to the likes of me, but Sam, he was happy to chat, so I got to know him quite well. He were a nice lad. Anyway, this were late in the evening – about ten or so – and it were pissing down, excuse my language.'

Jess smiled to show she didn't mind him swearing. She was happy that Ricky had overcome his initial reluctance to talk and was now making up for it with a vengeance.

'So, I were driving slowly with m'windscreen wipers going ninety to the dozen. Visibility were shite. But there were this thing in the road. I couldn't make it out at first. Well, you don't expect to find bodies lying around, do you? Good job I were only doing twenty miles an hour, otherwise I might have run the poor bugger over a second time. Not that it were me what run him down the first time,' he added hastily.

'Don't worry,' Jess assured him. 'You're not under any suspicion. So what did you see?'

'There were an umbrella blowing about the place. It hit m'windscreen. I slammed on the brakes, then I realised that the thing in t'road were a body. Bloody hell, I thought. I jumped out and went to see what were what. I recognised Sam, the punter I were supposed to be picking up. He were out cold, soaked to the skin. Wonder he didn't die of hypothermia. So I didn't waste time. I would have dialled 999 and called for an ambulance there and then, but it were raining and I realised there were something going on in t'brewery. So I ran inside and shouted for help. That's about it. I told the police what I've just told you.'

'And you didn't see any other vehicles or anyone else hanging around outside?'

'Nah, it were too wet to be out on a night like that.'

Jess was frustrated that she hadn't learned anything new. She found it inconceivable that no one at this so-called party had seen or heard anything more.

'There is one thing,' said Ricky, 'that I didn't remember until afterwards. It had all been such a shock at the time. I meant to go to the police with it, but it were mad busy in the run-up to Christmas and I never got round to it. And then, well, it seemed a bit late to bring it up.' He gave Jess a sheepish glance.

'Go on.'

'As I were on m'way to the brewery, still maybe a quarter of a mile off, I saw this white van speeding in the opposite direction. I mean, that's van drivers for you, they're a law to themselves, but I noticed this one because one of its lights were out.'

'Just the one?'

'Aye. The one on the passenger's side.'

'You're sure about that?'

'I notice these things.'

Jess beamed at him. 'Do you remember anything else about the van?'

'Just the lights and the speed it were going. Like it were trying to get away in a hurry, you know? Then again, that's how all van drivers drive. There ought to be a law against it. Well, I suppose there is.'

'Thank you,' said Jess. 'You've been really helpful.'

'And I won't get into trouble for not mentioning the van sooner?'

'Not this time, Mr Potts.' Jess did her best to adopt a stern expression. 'Just be sure it doesn't happen again.'

★

'Mum's got all these big ideas for Christmas,' said Becca. 'She wants to do a huge turkey with all the trimmings, and she's talking about inviting your parents and your brothers and their wives, not to mention my grandparents. And Liam, of course, mustn't forget about him!'

Sam smiled at Becca and squeezed her hand. She squeezed his back. It was so good to feel his touch again, to feel his hand gripping hers with more strength each passing day instead of the limp, lifeless appendage she had held onto for so long.

'But if you're not up to it, then just say. I'd rather spend Christmas here in the hospital with you than have a huge crowd round at the guest house. Anyway, I daresay your mum and dad have their own plans. But Mum's so used to catering for large numbers of people, she doesn't think anything of inviting the world and his wife to dinner.'

Becca was getting quite exhausted listening to Sue going on about Christmas. She'd already started putting her plans into action, asking Liam to bring home a Christmas tree from one of his mates who was selling them at a knock-down price that seemed too good to be true. She'd sent David up into the loft to dig out all the lights and decorations ready to put up. And it was only the first day of December. Becca knew that her mum just wanted to make up for last year when Christmas had effectively been cancelled after Sam's accident, but it was getting a bit much.

'Tell Sue she's very kind,' said Sam. 'I'd love to spend Christmas at your place if I'm up to it. I'm not so sure about everyone else though. Mum likes to host Christmas for the family at home. Besides, Marcus and Olivia have got their hands full with the baby. They might prefer to be alone.'

'Have you met the baby yet?' Becca had only met Marcus and Olivia a few times before the accident and she hadn't seen either of them since. Nor had she seen Sam's other brother, Anthony or his wife. Throughout the entire year that she'd spent coming to see Sam at the hospital the only visitors she'd encountered had been Greg and Denise.

'Marcus popped in once on his way from work. It was just him though. I haven't seen Freddie yet.'

'What about Anthony?'

'He's away on business.'

Becca bit back the comment that was on the tip of her tongue, namely that she didn't think Sam's brothers were making much of an effort to visit him in hospital. She couldn't understand it. After twelve months of sitting beside Sam in his comatose state and talking to him without a flicker of a response, it was a joy to talk to him now and hear him respond, to see his smile. His voice was getting stronger by the day. He'd started a course of physiotherapy to help him regain strength in his limbs.

It was still early days yet, and Dr Kirtlington had warned that recovery would be slow. There might be setbacks along the way, or "bumps in the road", as he called them. The hospital consultant liked to speak in metaphors. "A long road ahead" was one of his favourites, followed closely by "one step at a time".

But for the first time in ages, the future looked positive.

'So what have you been up to?' It was the question Sam always asked her, hungry for information about the world outside the hospital, perhaps trying to make up for his own blank days by substituting Becca's supposedly action-packed ones. It must be hard to wake up after a whole year and wonder what you'd missed. What world events had passed you by, what had your partner been doing in your absence? But when Becca looked back on the past twelve months, she realised she'd done very little except work and sit by Sam's bedside. The world outside had passed her by too.

'I went to Pickering today.'

'Pickering's nice.'

'I didn't go to the nice part. Crime always seems to happen in the grotty end of town.'

Sam smiled. 'Criminals ought to have better taste. If I ever commit a crime, I'll be sure to do it somewhere smart and fancy. Then the detectives will have a more pleasant time investigating it.'

Becca laughed. It was good to hear Sam making jokes again. In the old days he had always been able to cheer her up. It was one of the things she loved most about him.

'So,' he asked, 'are you working for DI Dinsdale at the moment?'

Dinsdale was Becca's other boss, the one she usually reported to when she wasn't assigned to Raven.

'I'm actually working on my own at the moment. Seems I don't need a boss at all. Who knew?'

He grinned at her.

'Dinsdale's on holiday, thank goodness,' she continued, 'taking a two-week break in the winter sun.'

'You should have told me. I could have bought a plane ticket and joined him. I've got nothing on right now.'

This time his joking failed to raise her spirits. Becca and Sam had often talked about travelling together. Before the hit and run, they had even considered jacking in their jobs and buying a round-the-world ticket. Seeing it all, while they were still young. Now Sam couldn't even leave the hospital. Maybe they should have done it when they still had the chance.

Sensing her mood slip, he quickly changed the subject.

'What about Raven? Give me the skinny on him.'

'There's not much to tell. I haven't known him that long.' For some reason, Becca felt reluctant to talk about her new boss.

'Well, what's he like to work for? You used to moan about Dinsdale all the time.'

'Everyone moans about Dinsdale.'

'But Raven's not a bit like him. When he came to interview me, he seemed... I don't know... focussed? Like what I was telling him was somehow personal.'

Becca wondered how much she ought to reveal about Raven's past. 'I think it is personal. Raven's mother was killed in a hit and run accident when he was a teenager. I think it's fair to say that he took it badly.' *And left Scarborough, not to return for over thirty years.* But Becca didn't think it was fair to reveal that, even to Sam. Raven was such a private person. He went to so much trouble to keep his personal life a secret that sharing the few facts that she had gleaned about him seemed like an intrusion.

The DCI had walked into Becca's life one rainy day back in October, dressed in a black suit, black tie and black coat, having come straight from his father's funeral. His coal black hair and dark eyes had completed his forbidding appearance. He'd said nothing about what he was doing in Scarborough, simply that he had worked for the Met in London. She had discovered for herself the fact that he'd left the army after being injured in battle and had been awarded the Conspicuous Gallantry Cross in acknowledgement of his bravery. He hadn't even divulged the fact that he was living in a wreck of a house down by the harbour in Quay Street – it had been Liam who had found that out. Her brother was always sniffing out opportunities to buy up old properties to convert into holiday accommodation. But Raven showed no interest in selling his house, nor returning to London. He seemed to be here to stay.

'Is that why you told him what happened to me?' asked Sam. 'Because of his mother?'

'No. I asked him to speak to you because I trust him to do his job. If anyone can get to the bottom of it, Raven can.'

'I hope you're right. I told him everything I could remember.'

'I know,' said Becca. 'But there's something I've been wondering. Do you remember any of the things I talked to you about while you were in the coma? Dr Kirtlington encouraged me to talk to you as much as possible. He said you might be able to hear my words even though you couldn't respond.'

Sam's face fell. 'Not really. Sorry. I do remember voices, but I can't remember what they were saying. It might have been you talking to me, or they might have been dreams.'

Becca felt a pang of disappointment. All those words she had poured out, all her hopes, her fears, her longings… Sam had heard none of them. It seemed like a colossal wasted effort, except that in the end he had come round.

'Don't worry about it. You woke up, that's all that matters.'

Their light-hearted chatter of earlier seemed to have slipped away and been replaced by a mood of melancholy.

Sam's voice grew serious. 'There was one dream I kept having… over and over. It was really vivid at the time, but since I regained consciousness, I just can't remember anything about it. But it feels important, like it's a memory of something that really happened, not simply imaginary.'

'Something that happened on the night of the party, perhaps?'

'I don't know.' Sam screwed his eyes shut. 'It's just no good, it won't come back to me.' He sank back into his pillow and let go of Becca's hand. He looked drained, and she worried she'd worn him out with all her questions and wittering on about Sue's plans for Christmas.

He was still very weak and she needed to take more care. Dr Kirtlington had warned that any over-exertion would delay Sam's recovery and might even prevent him returning to full health.

She watched over him for a minute longer while he lay in the bed, his eyes closed, his chest gently rising and falling. Then she leaned over and planted a soft kiss on his cheek. 'I'll see you again tomorrow, Sam.'

But he was already fast asleep.

# CHAPTER 9

*I*t's a cold, dark night in late November. Becca's in her car,
wishing she could leave her engine running, the heater
blasting out hot air, but she's supposed to be incognito, not
drawing attention to herself, on the off chance there's some truth
in their tip-off that the gang they've been tracking for the best
part of three months really is operating out of a lock-up garage
in this back street behind the old Dean Road cemetery.

She glances at her watch. Dinsdale's supposed to be here by
now, relieving her so that she can go and meet Sam when he
gets away from the party at the brewery. Becca would have liked
to go to that party herself, but that's police work for you.
Antisocial hours, unplanned overtime, cancelled leave. Not that
she's ever noticed Dinsdale have to cancel a holiday. She drums
her fingers on the dashboard, hoping that something will
happen. Either a show by the gang – suspected of importing
counterfeit goods from overseas – or else Dinsdale's arrival. She
really needs to get away soon if she's going to meet up with Sam
as planned.

There's movement up ahead and she strains her eyes in the
dark to see. A young lad is sauntering down the lane, hands in
pockets, hoodie turned up against the cold, doing his utmost not

*to look dodgy. Well, he's not making such a good job of that. He's caught Becca's eye for starters.*

*She watches him as he approaches the garage. Go inside, she urges him. Open the door.*

*But he carries on past, whistling nonchalantly, and turns into the street beyond, vanishing just as quickly as he arrived.*

*Damn it. Looks like no one's going to show, maybe not even Dinsdale at this rate. Becca's willing to give it another half hour before shooting off. The weather's turning nasty and it looks like that storm's finally about to hit. Sure enough, the pitter patter on her windscreen begins, and soon it's a deluge. Water lashes the bonnet, the wind rocking the car from side to side. The Jazz is so tiny it might take off if it blows any harder.*

*Where the hell is Dinsdale? Becca's about to give him a call when her phone goes. This is probably him now with some lame excuse, but no, it's Sam's dad.*

*She picks up. 'Hi, Greg, how's the party going?'*

*He tells her, but his words make no sense.*

*Sam in an accident. Rushed into hospital. Critical condition.*

*She listens, but can't absorb what he's telling her. None of it can be true.*

*His voice comes down the phone again. 'Becca? Are you still there?'*

*Thoughts swirl in her head, refusing to form into any clear pattern. She needs to get her brain in gear, take some action, but time is frozen.*

*Finally she manages to get some words out of her mouth. 'I'll be there now, Greg. I'm on my way.'*

*A car appears at the opposite end of the lane and trundles towards her. Dinsdale, at last. His door opens and he trudges out into the rain, grappling with an umbrella. He approaches her car, coming to tell her what's kept him no doubt, but Becca no longer cares. She starts the engine, slips the gear into reverse and drives away, leaving him stony-faced and dripping in the lane.*

*Five minutes later she's at the hospital, and her world is falling down around her.*

★

Barry had lived up to his promise. The old kitchen units were now piled up in the skip outside Raven's house, leaving nothing behind but four bare walls and some sad-looking pipework rising up out of the floor. A thin coating of dust covered every surface in the house, even in Raven's bedroom. The downstairs bathroom next to the kitchen was still functional, but Raven knew that it would be next on the builder's hitlist and that very soon his house would be rendered almost uninhabitable. He ought to have given some thought to how he was going to manage with nowhere to cook, but he had been blocking the idea from his mind, clinging instead to a vision of a perfect kitchen some way in the future. A kitchen like Marcus Earnshaw's, perhaps, though on a vastly smaller scale.

Now, rising early to avoid any possibility of encountering Barry and his incessant banter, Raven slipped out of the house before first light and made his way to the harbourside café he suspected was going to become his regular eating place for the duration of the building work.

The wind of the previous few days had abated, and the sea was calm. A warm glow along the horizon heralded the beginning of a better day. Already the fishermen were gathering along the harbourside, preparing their nets and loading their boats. Gulls swooped low above their heads, also ready for a day's fishing.

Raven disappeared inside the café and took a seat by the window. In London, under Lisa's direction, he had endured a strict regime of continental-style breakfasts. Cereals, yogurts and croissants spread with honey or preserves – perhaps a paper-thin wafer of prosciutto if he was lucky. Now he was free to indulge his true tastes and recreate the kind of breakfast that his mum had cooked for him as a boy. A bowl of porridge. Eggs, bacon and fried bread. Sausages at the weekend. Raven perused the menu for a moment before deciding to order the lot.

The fact that his father had died of a heart attack while staggering home on the very pavement that Raven had just sauntered along wasn't enough to deter him. It wasn't sausages that had killed his dad and he was pretty confident that his shunning of alcohol would go a long way to counter the ill effects of a full English breakfast.

By the time he had finished, the sun had risen and the first boats were leaving the harbour, the gulls in their wake. Raven walked back to Quay Street and collected his car, driving the short distance to the police station on Northway along empty streets. He knew he would be the first in – apart from Gillian possibly – but he had jobs he needed to do.

\*

By the time everyone arrived at work, Raven had commandeered a spare office as a private incident room. It wasn't ideal, being on the small side, but at least he and his team could pursue the investigation in confidence without worrying about Becca eavesdropping on their conversations or ferreting through their findings.

He rounded up Jess and Tony as soon as they were in, leaving Becca sitting at her desk in the main room looking rather forlorn. He hoped he would soon have something he could share with her.

Once they were assembled, Raven turned first to Jess. 'How did you get on at the taxi firm?'

Jess was her usual enthusiastic self and seemed keen to give her report. 'Good. I spoke to the driver, Ricky Potts. He confirmed everything we already knew. But he had some additional information he hadn't mentioned to the police at the time. He said that as he was on his way to the brewery to collect Sam, he noticed a white van speeding in the opposite direction. The van's passenger-side headlight was out. I think he only remembered about it afterwards, and he was going to tell the police but you know how it is, he didn't get round to it and then just forgot. Of course, it might not be relevant. The van may have nothing to do with Sam's accident.'

'Still,' said Raven, 'Sam told me that the vehicle that hit him was a van. He couldn't be sure of the colour because it appeared orange under the glow from the streetlights. But that's exactly how a white van would look in that kind of lighting, and this is the first piece of evidence we've had regarding a suspicious vehicle in the area that night. Tony, do you think you could get a list of all the white vans in Scarborough?'

'That would be a long list, sir,' said Tony without any trace of sarcasm. 'But I'll see what I can do.'

'Good man. Did you manage to dig out the coroner's report into Jeremy Green's death?'

'Got it here,' said Tony, holding up a manila folder. He opened it up. 'It's a pretty straightforward report. Jeremy was out walking along the clifftops at Flamborough Head. It was a walk he took regularly it seems. It was winter, so there was no one around to witness what happened. The post-mortem found no signs of foul-play. His injuries were entirely consistent with a fall from a height. And nothing was found at the crime scene to indicate that anyone else might have been with him when he fell. Therefore, since there was no evidence to the contrary, the coroner ruled that it was accidental death.'

'It sounds like a somewhat unlikely accident,' remarked Raven. 'And in light of what happened to Sam, it seems even less likely. What was it that Oscar Wilde said about company directors? To lose one may be regarded as a misfortune, to lose two looks like carelessness.'

'Something along those lines, sir.' The corners of Tony's mouth curled upwards in polite response to Raven's weak witticism. 'But still, coincidences do happen. And there have been a number of similar deaths at Flamborough Head over the years.'

Even though it was Tony who had first alerted Raven to the former finance director's death, when faced with a process that appeared to have been done by the book, he seemed unwilling to cast doubt on the coroner's official verdict. Tony was Raven's go-to man when it came to trawling through mountains of paperwork for a detail that someone else might have missed, but he was a stickler for rules and procedures.

'All the same,' said Jess, 'how likely is it that any sensible walker would fall to their death while strolling along the clifftops?'

That was more to Raven's way of thinking. Question everything, leave no stone unturned, make up your own mind based on the facts. 'I think there's only one way to find out.'

'You fancy going for a walk, sir?'

Raven scooped up the manila file that Tony had given him. 'Get your coat on,' he said to Jess. 'We're going on a field trip.'

# CHAPTER 10

Becca watched through the window of the police station as Raven and Jess headed out to Raven's car. She wondered where they were going and whether they were making any progress with the investigation. Raven wore his usual stern expression, giving nothing away, but Jess looked quite excited, as if the pair were going on an adventure. She saw them get into Raven's car and drive off. Whatever they were up to, Becca wished she could be going with them, even if it meant being driven around at breakneck speed in Raven's BMW.

But that wasn't going to happen. Instead, she returned to her allotted task of investigating the theft of laptops from the warehouse in Pickering, wishing she had Tony's patience for mundane jobs. Her thoughts turned to Mr Owens, the warehouse owner, who had invested his hopes in her ability to solve the case. She owed it to him to do her best, however distracted she might be by Sam's state of health and thoughts about who had tried to kill him.

Faced with no real leads following her visit to Pickering, she decided to look into similar thefts in the area, going back over the past two years. It didn't take her long to find several unsolved burglaries that bore marked similarities to the one she was investigating.

One of the burglaries involved a break-in at a warehouse on a trading park near Whitby where a quantity of mobile phones had been taken, and another in Eastfield to the south of Scarborough, where the thief had made off with a dozen brand new televisions from an electrical retailer. In the first case the warehouse door had been forced open with a crowbar. In the other, a bolt cutter had been used to remove a padlock.

In the first instance a white van had been captured on CCTV at the time of the break-in, though not well enough for an identification. However, in the case of the theft of the televisions, an eyewitness had reported seeing a van in the vicinity with a number 12 on its number plate, dating the vehicle registration to between March and August of the year 2012.

Becca was reminded of the white vehicle she had glimpsed on CCTV at the warehouse in Pickering. Could it be the same one in all three cases?

Her phone vibrated with an incoming message and she picked it up, pleased to see Sam's name on the screen. He had sent her a selfie, taken after his morning's physiotherapy session, with the caption, *Sign me up for the Yorkshire marathon!* Becca smiled at the joke, but it also broke her heart. Sam was working hard to regain the strength in his wasted muscles but he could still barely walk unaided, let alone run twenty-six miles. The best she could hope for was that he would be strong enough to join her family at Christmas. She replied to say she'd see him later that evening, adding a smiley face and a row of kisses. Then she refocussed her attention on her computer, determined to make some real progress before lunch.

★

Flamborough Head was a forty-minute drive from Scarborough, or thirty the way Raven took the roads. He hated driving slowly. What was the point? If you had somewhere to go, it was better to get there quickly. Going fast was more fun.

Jess seemed to enjoy the journey too. Or at least, she raised no objections to his motoring style, and he decided to take that as a thumbs up.

They passed through the settlements of Osgodby, Cayton Bay, Gristhorpe and Flamborough itself before arriving at their destination. The weather had worsened since the start of the day, becoming overcast and blustery, and Raven's thoughts went to the fishermen he had watched setting out to sea. If they had any sense, they'd be back in the harbour by now.

The final approach to Flamborough Head was a straight narrow road, and as Raven neared the end, the lighthouse that guarded the cliffs rose up before him. The lighthouse was still active and had replaced a much older chalk tower that was no longer in use. Raven had often glimpsed the light at night, just visible down the coast from Scarborough, blinking its distinctive warning signal to ships at sea. Four white flashes every fifteen seconds.

He pulled into the car park at the end of the road next to a café and restaurant which was open for business despite the time of year. Stepping out, he looked up at the clean white tower of the lighthouse. Just shy of a hundred feet, its cylindrical form was topped by a double balcony and glass windows that housed the electric light and rotating lens. To working fishermen like Raven's father and grandfather, its beacon had been a lifesaver.

The promontory of Flamborough Head stuck out into the North Sea like an indignant bent elbow making a gesture of defiance at the forces of sea and wind. To the north lay Filey and to the south Bridlington, both quiet seaside towns with long, gentle curves of golden sand where families could relax on the beach, paddle in the sea or stroll along the promenade. But here, the chalk cliffs were high and treacherous, the coastline aggressively rugged, the clifftop walks only really suitable for serious hikers and birdwatchers. In retrospect, it had been reckless to bring a bunch of badly behaved teenagers here.

Leaving the lighthouse behind, Raven and Jess continued on foot, following a path that cut a line through rough scrub towards the tip of the headland. The place was even bleaker and more desolate than he recalled from his school visit. At least that trip had taken place during the month of May, although it hadn't been a particularly good day.

He remembered now what the purpose of that visit had been – to look at birds. During spring and summer, the cliffs around Flamborough were packed with visiting seabirds – fulmars, gulls, kittiwakes, guillemots and puffins – and birdwatchers and tourists flocked there to see them nesting on the cliffs. Now, in early December, the sky hung low and threatening, heavy with dark clouds. The sea was a forbidding gunmetal grey, a strong easterly wind tore at Raven's hair and coat, and there was no one else to be seen.

Jess set the pace and Raven struggled to keep up with his younger and considerably fitter colleague. With the hood of her red parka up and her feet encased in a pair of stout walking boots, she was clearly in her element out here in this wilderness. Raven turned up his collar and hunched his shoulders. His right leg protested at the effort it was being asked to make as he trekked along, his head bowed down against the wind.

The path took them as far as the fog signal station located close to the furthest tip of the headland. The station consisted of two squat buildings, positioned between a pair of metal masts. Tony had marked a map showing the spot where Jeremy Green had fallen to his death, and Raven studied it, wrestling with the wind that was doing its best to pluck the paper from his grasp, and trying to work out exactly where they needed to go.

'It's this way, sir,' shouted Jess over the gale. She pointed south and set off across a grass track worn flat by countless hikers and bird-watching enthusiasts. Raven gritted his teeth and followed in her wake.

Jess came to a stop, seeming confident of her position. 'It was right here. By the drinking dinosaur.'

Raven looked out towards the sea and saw what she was pointing at.

A narrow peninsula, formed over centuries, protruded from the coast, ending with a sea arch. It was easy to see how the outcrop had acquired its nickname. The thin ridge that connected it to the coast was the dinosaur's tail. The rising bulk of land in the middle resembled the body of the beast, whilst the elegant arch looked like the long neck of a Brontosaurus. The dinosaur's head was a bulge of rock at the opposite base of the arch to the body. It was a striking natural feature, the sort of thing that would attract visitors.

The grass leading down to the clifftop sloped steeply away. Raven moved close to the edge and peered down at the rocks below. The tide was in, crashing against the shore, churning angrily around the dinosaur's feet, steadily eating away at the base of the sheer white cliffs. The coastline of Yorkshire's East Riding was under relentless attack. More than a dozen villages had been lost to the sea since Roman times, their existence recorded only in ancient documents and in the names of roads that once led to them. A thousand years from now, these cliffs and the peninsula that reached into the seething waters might all be gone.

'Be careful, sir,' called Jess. Her voice sounded distant and far off, snatched away on the wind.

Raven edged even closer, the leather soles of his shoes sliding across the slippery surface. He grabbed at a tuft of grass, anchoring himself to the ground, and leaned out as far as he dared. A hundred feet below him the water swirled, throwing itself against the chalky cliffs, pulling back between each wave before surging forwards once more for a fresh assault. White flakes of foam drifted up from the maelstrom, bringing with them the taste of salt.

A sudden gust threw him off balance and his feet slipped out from under him.

Jess cried out. 'Oh my God. Sir!'

Raven twisted around, clinging to the sturdy tuft of grass. If it gave way now he was a gonner. But the grass was made of stern stuff. It had to be to survive in these conditions. He hauled himself away from the precipice and clambered back up the slope to Jess, who looked relieved.

'Don't worry,' he reassured her. 'It's not my turn to go. Not yet.'

It would be doing something like this, though, of that he was certain. He couldn't imagine himself growing old like his father, dying of natural causes at the age of seventy-five. Nor could he picture himself like DI Dinsdale, who would no doubt retire before long and live a quiet life, pottering in his garden, reading the newspaper and taking off-season trips to the Algarve, or whatever it was that Dinsdale aspired to do once his career was behind him. No doubt the retired detective would live to a ripe old age until he was found one day, having passed away peacefully in his bed.

No. When Raven's time came, he would die in action, in the line of duty, or because of some mad, reckless stunt like this. He didn't know how, where or when. But he sensed it coming, like a dark dot on the horizon.

'So what do you reckon?' he asked Jess. 'How easy would it to be fall off the cliff edge?'

'Very easy if you were stupid enough to do what you just did, sir.'

He liked how she tacked "sir" onto the end of her rebuke, to make it sound more like the kind of thing a junior officer would say to their superior. He grinned at her, enjoying the way her face glowed almost as red as her parka when she blushed.

'But if you were a sensible person. A keen walker. Would you go that close to the edge?'

'No way. I'd keep a safe distance. Particularly on a day like today.'

The wind whipped again at Raven's hair, raising white crests on the waves that swept towards the shore. He wondered what had made him do such a reckless thing, venturing so close to the cliff edge. Something was driving him, pushing him on, and it wasn't simply his promise to Becca to find out who had tried to kill Sam. Was it too simplistic to say that in trying to find out who had pushed Sam under the van he was trying to atone for his own mother's death?

Probably. But it explained a lot.

He started to walk back towards the signal station. 'According to the coroner's report, Jeremy was an experienced walker. He would be unlikely to take unnecessary risks.'

'Then you don't agree with the verdict of accidental death?' said Jess. 'You think Jeremy was murdered? By the same person who tried to kill Sam?'

'I think it's plausible, don't you?'

'And yet the post-mortem found nothing suspicious about the death. "Injuries consistent with a fall from height."'

Raven grinned at her. 'A bit like the injuries I very nearly sustained just a minute ago.' But Raven couldn't believe that a middle-aged finance director would act the way he'd just done. 'This was no accident. Jeremy was pushed. Taken by surprise without a struggle. That means the killer was someone he knew and trusted.'

They trudged back to the car in silence. It would be difficult after all this time to prove it. But the idea that Jeremy Green had been murdered felt highly probable.

'Of course, there is another possible explanation,' said Raven, leaning against the car.

'What's that, sir?'

'Suicide.'

# CHAPTER 11

Becca continued to sift through witness statements for the rest of the morning. It was laborious work but it had to be done.

DI Dinsdale had been responsible for investigating two of the burglaries she had identified as being similar to the one at Pickering. No suspects had been interviewed in either case, and no arrests made. No surprise there. The only wonder was that Dinsdale hadn't found some poor mug to stitch up for the crimes.

Becca managed to find several other instances of unsolved burglaries in the area that involved the theft of electronics goods from warehouses, retailers and similar types of business. In several of them a white van had been reported or captured on CCTV. There was nothing too unusual about that, of course. Most commercial vans were white, for some reason that Becca had never fathomed. That tended to make them all look the same, and so far she had found no witness statements or images that identified the make or model of the vehicle in question.

But eventually she found a statement relating to a burglary that had taken place just over a year earlier at a small family-owned electrical store in Scarborough. In that case, a dozen Sony PlayStations had been taken, and a white Ford Transit Connect had been reported leaving the area at speed. It had been spotted by a late-night dogwalker who suffered from insomnia.

Becca loved late-night and early-morning dogwalkers. They were a police detective's best friend.

Now, where had she put that statement from the eyewitness who reported seeing a van with a 2012 registration plate? She rummaged through the piles of papers on her desk and eventually pulled out the relevant document.

She laid the two statements side-by-side and read through both again.

Two separate burglaries on two different dates in two nearby towns. In one a Ford Transit van had been spotted leaving the scene. In the other, someone had been observant enough to note the year of registration of a suspicious vehicle. Two different vehicles, or the same one?

A hand plonked a mug of tea on the desk in front of her, making her jump. 'Bloody hell, Tony, you gave me a fright!'

'Sorry.' Tony stepped back, looking bashful. 'I just thought you might like a cuppa. You haven't moved from your desk all morning.'

'Well, thanks.' Becca appreciated Tony's kind thought. She knew she wasn't the only one who had been left behind when Raven and Jess dashed off. 'What are you up to at the moment?'

Tony looked uncomfortable. 'I'm not really supposed to say anything about it. Raven said to keep it quiet.'

Of course, he was working on the investigation into Sam's attempted murder. Becca was glad that Tony was on the case, even though she knew he wouldn't be able to share the details with her. 'I know. Sorry for asking.'

But Tony seemed to appreciate a chance to chat. Perhaps he was feeling cheesed off at having been left behind. 'I'm trying to get a list of all the white vans in the Scarborough district. Hell of a job. I don't think Raven has any idea how many vans there are. It's more than two thousand!'

'White vans? Funny you should say that. I've been trying to identify a white van that may have been used in a number of burglaries.'

'Maybe I can help you. What have you got to go on?'

'The model and the date. A Ford Transit Connect registered in 2012.'

'Hang on, let me get my list.' Tony disappeared into the meeting room that was being used as an incident room and returned with a handful of printouts. He paged through the sheets of paper, running his finger down the right-hand column. 'You're in luck. 2012 is pretty ancient for a commercial van to still be on the road. There's only one vehicle matching that description still registered in the Scarborough area. Here you go.' He gave her the registration number.

'That's great, Tony, thanks.' This was one of the things Becca enjoyed most about her job – teamwork. 'So why has Raven got you checking white vans? Do you think it was a white van that hit Sam?' Sam had told her about the van that ran him down, but he hadn't been sure of the colour. But it was a fair bet that it had been white.

'It's a possibility,' conceded Tony. 'Based on something the taxi driver said.'

'What was that?'

'He saw a white van with one headlamp missing as he was approaching the brewery to pick up Sam.'

'Hang on.' Becca started sifting through the various files and reports she had scattered across her desk. 'Here!' She held up the file on the theft of the PlayStations. 'This burglary took place on the night that Sam was run over. The eighteenth of November last year.'

She caught Tony's eye and could see that he was thinking the same thing she was. That the van involved in the spate of burglaries was the same one that had hit Sam.

'Let's do a search for that van, then,' he said. 'See who owns it.'

Becca typed the registration number into the police database. The owner of the van was registered as a plumbing supply company. The address of the company sent a shiver down Becca's spine. 'That's just around the corner from the brewery!'

'Blimey,' said Tony. 'Do you think–'

Becca rose to her feet. 'Yes, I do.'

'Maybe we should wait for Raven to get back.'

'I'm not waiting a single second.' Becca grabbed her coat and car keys. 'Get your coat on, Tony, we're going to check out bathroom and kitchen supplies.'

# CHAPTER 12

When Raven reached the main road that led back to Scarborough he put his foot down, glad to be heading back to civilisation. The visit to Flamborough Head had been useful, but bracing. As the BMW's heaters began to thaw his numbed face, he considered what his next steps would be.

'I'm going to have a chat with Greg and Denise,' he told Jess. 'See what I can find out about Jeremy. If he and Greg were best friends, Greg will know as well as anyone what state of mind he was in when he met his death.'

'What would you like me to do, sir?'

'Why don't you track down Ellie Earnshaw? She's Sam's cousin and she's been doing his job at the brewery for the past year.'

'Happy to, sir.'

After dropping Jess at the station, Raven drove straight on to the Earnshaw family home. The house on Scalby Mills Road overlooked the North Cliff Golf Club. It was a substantial detached property, dating from the 1970s, with a large flat-roofed extension. But although it was big it wasn't in any way showy, and looked quite dated next to some of its whitewashed neighbours. However, it did enjoy a fabulous view across the bay to Scarborough Castle on the headland.

Salt and castle. The location seemed apt.

Raven rang the bell and the door was opened by a tall woman dressed casually in a long-sleeved top and trousers. With a long neck, striking green eyes and slender frame, Denise Earnshaw exuded a natural chic, although the strain of the past year had clearly taken a toll on her. Her hair, cut simply above her shoulders, had been allowed to turn silver and there were worry lines etched across her brow, the sign of a face that had spent too long trapped in a state of anxiety.

'Hello. Can I help you?'

'I'm DCI Raven, here to see your husband.'

'Ah yes, come in. Greg's just through here.'

Denise led the way through a wide hallway and into the room beyond. Unlike Marcus's house, which was dominated by its designer kitchen, the heart of Greg and Denise's home was a large open-plan living room, arranged over two levels. On the lower floor, armchairs and sofas were grouped around a huge TV screen fixed to the wall. Steps led up to a raised level, which was just as big, with floor-to-ceiling glass doors leading to the rear garden.

Greg was seated in a reclining chair on the upper level, a laptop resting on his lap. He looked up. 'Raven, I wasn't expecting you.'

'No need to get up,' said Raven, as Greg started to rise to his feet.

'Nonsense. It's only common courtesy to welcome a guest into your home. Would you like some tea or coffee?'

'If you're sure it's not a problem.'

'Of course it isn't,' said Denise. 'What would you like?'

'Coffee, please. Black, no sugar.'

'I'll make it for you.' She disappeared through a second door into the kitchen.

Greg set his laptop on a coffee table and came to the top of the steps.

'You're catching up on some work at home?' said Raven.

'Catching up?' Greg chuckled. 'When you run your own business, work never stops. It becomes your life.'

'I thought you might begin to slow down, now that you have Marcus and Anthony to lean on.'

'And Ellie,' said Greg. 'She's been a godsend, stepping into Sam's shoes while he's been in hospital. But I'm still the boss. I need to stay on top of things. I can't afford to let anything slip.'

'Not much chance of that happening,' said Denise, returning with a cup of coffee and handing it to Raven. 'I keep telling him that it's time to step aside and take it easy. Greg's hardly taken a day off in his life.'

'I'll step aside when I'm ready,' insisted Greg. 'Besides, what would I do with myself if I retired?'

'There's a golf club just across the road. You enjoy a good game of golf.'

Greg snorted. 'When I'm relaxing. But I can't spend the rest of my life playing golf!'

It was clear that Greg's retirement – or otherwise – was a longstanding subject of debate in the Earnshaw household.

Greg adopted a more conciliatory tone towards his wife. 'I will retire one day, darling, I promise. Just as soon as I can be certain that everything's in hand.' He strode over to a nearby sideboard and lifted a silver-framed photo. The image showed a baby boy who Raven recognised as Freddie, Marcus's son. Greg gazed at it wistfully. 'At the end of the day, that's what it's all about, isn't it? Having something to pass on.'

Photographs of Greg and Denise's three sons – Marcus, Anthony and Sam – at various stages of childhood and adolescence were arranged above the fireplace and on shelves. This was clearly a home where children had grown up in a loving environment, well cared for and valued by both parents. The contrast with Raven's own childhood was striking. While his mother had done her best to provide a good home for him, her efforts had been undermined by his father's drinking and violence. A single punch was enough to shatter a child's sense of security forever. Raven's had been shattered on more than one occasion.

Greg descended the steps that linked the two halves of the room and invited Raven to take a seat on one of the sofas. He and Denise sat down opposite. 'Anyway, enough talk of retirement, what can I do for you?'

'Actually, I wanted to speak to you about Jeremy Green.'

Greg raised an inquisitive eyebrow. 'What about him?'

'I understand that he died in an accident a couple of years ago.'

'That's right. Over at Flamborough Head.'

'Is it true that he'd worked for you from the beginning?'

'Right from the start,' said Greg. 'Me, Jeremy and Gavin, my head brewer. We were best mates at school. When I suggested starting a brewery, the other two thought it was a grand idea. Jeremy knew a bit about finance, Gavin knew a lot about beer, and I knew how to sell, or thought I did. When I look back, sometimes it amazes me that we managed to pull it off. The odds were stacked against us. Did you know that one in three new businesses fail within their first three years? And two in three fail within the first ten years. The thing is, we didn't know how little we knew about starting a brewery.' He smiled at the memory. 'But we made up for our inexperience with hard graft and bloody-mindedness. I was on the road a lot in those early days, building our customer base, and Jeremy kept everything running on the ground. He was the rock I could depend on. I couldn't have done it without him.'

'It must have been a huge loss when he died.'

'It was,' admitted Greg. 'I lost a close colleague and my best friend.' On the sofa beside him, Denise squeezed his hand. 'But fortunately for the business, Marcus had been working alongside him and knew all the ropes.'

'I realise that this is a sensitive matter,' said Raven, 'but I have some questions I need to ask about Jeremy.'

'All right.'

'Were you aware of any personal problems in his life?'

'None at all. He was very contented, as far as I know.'

'No money problems?'

'Certainly not.'

'And family?'

Greg's mouth turned down. 'Jeremy had no family.'

It was Denise who explained. 'Jeremy lost his wife to cancer at a very young age. They had no children and he never remarried.'

'I see,' said Raven. 'So he lived alone? What was Jeremy's state of mind prior to his death?'

Greg knitted his eyebrows together. 'You're suggesting he might have taken his own life? The coroner ruled accidental death.'

'But what do you think?'

Greg mulled it over for a moment before responding. 'I see no reason why he would have wanted to kill himself. He was happy enough and his death was a tragedy. Jeremy was my best friend, and there isn't a single day that I don't think about him.'

Denise nodded, tears making her eyes shine. 'We both miss him terribly. He was more than a friend, he was like family.'

'But as you say,' said Raven, 'it was fortunate that Marcus was so well positioned to take over.'

Greg frowned. 'That's right. And one day I'll hand over the reins completely. But I'm not ready to go yet.'

'I heard,' said Raven, 'that there was talk of a takeover.'

'I think you mean a merger.'

'There's a difference?'

'A merger is a mutual decision between two companies to become one. A takeover can be hostile.'

'There's no hostility involved in this case?'

'None whatsoever. But there is a difference of opinion between board members about how to proceed.'

'When I spoke to Marcus, he seemed keen.'

'Aye, Marcus is the driving force behind the merger, and Anthony supports him.'

'But you don't?'

Greg sighed. 'You've got to understand, Raven, that I built this business with my own hands. I made sacrifices along the way.' He glanced sideways at his wife, who lowered her gaze to her lap. 'This has always been a family firm and it should stay that way. I don't want to see it pass into the control of some faceless organisation.'

Raven guessed this was the root cause of Greg's unwillingness to retire. He was worried that his life's work would be swallowed up by some large corporate entity. He would no longer be able to point and say, 'I created that!'

'And what was Jeremy's view on the matter?'

'Jeremy was an old-timer like me,' said Greg. 'He would have wanted us to stay independent.'

'And Sam feels the same way?'

'Sam's still got a lot to learn when it comes to business, but he does understand the importance of maintaining our independence.'

'Sam's always been the one who takes most after you, hasn't he?' said Denise.

Greg grunted his assent. 'The thing is, Raven, I want to ensure that the business will endure after I'm gone.' His eyes wandered the room, resting on the many photographs of his sons and grandson. 'When you build your own business, you think it's all about you – and it is, at first – but in the long run, you come to realise that what matters most is the gift you can pass on to the next generation.'

His eyes returned to Raven's face and seemed to harden with resolve. 'Legacy. That's really what it's all about.'

# CHAPTER 13

Coleman's Plumbing Supplies appeared to be doing a brisk trade. A number of vans – all of them white – were coming and going or were in the process of being loaded up with roll top baths, shower trays and lengths of copper piping. You could say one thing for Scarborough folk – they liked to keep themselves clean. Becca squeezed her Honda Jazz into a tight parking slot between two vans and got out.

'I don't see our vehicle,' said Tony, checking number plates as they made their way inside.

'Could be out on a delivery,' said Becca. 'Or round the back.' She asked a passing member of staff if the boss was around and he pointed at a balding, middle-aged man who was strutting around the warehouse, a mobile phone pinned to his ear, giving grief to someone on the other end of the line about a delayed consignment of toilet cisterns. As soon as he'd ended the call with a threat never to do business with the supplier again, Becca approached him.

'Mr Coleman?'

'Yeah?' The man wasn't in the best of moods. He gave Becca and Tony a disdainful look. 'We don't serve members of the public here, love. This is trade only. You want to try somewhere in town.'

Becca pushed her warrant card in his face. 'We're not customers.'

Coleman looked even less pleased than when he thought they were there to browse fixtures and fittings for a new bathroom. 'What's it about this time? If someone's complained that I don't pay my bills, they should read the terms and conditions. Payment after sixty days. It's there in black and white.' He waved a clutch of papers at them as if to prove his point.

'It's nothing to do with unpaid bills, Mr Coleman. We're here about one of your vehicles.'

'You won't find a problem there either. MOTs, insurance, I got it covered.' He turned away from her to check his delivery note.

'We believe that one of your vans may have been involved in a series of thefts in the area.'

Coleman lifted his chin and directed a hard stare at her. 'You got proof of that?'

'Perhaps we could step into your office?'

The manager looked like he was about to refuse, but Becca squared up to him, making it clear that he had no choice. Tony took a step closer, offering silent support.

After a moment, Coleman gave in. 'All right, but it better not take long. I've got a business to run here. As you can see, we're very busy today.'

Becca followed him into his office where he took a seat behind a desk littered with order forms and receipts. She was reminded of the office at the warehouse in Pickering. How could anyone run a business with such sloppy paperwork?

'Mr Coleman, is this vehicle one of yours?' Tony showed the manager a print-out with the details of the van.

Coleman glared at it angrily but said nothing.

'We already know that it is,' said Becca. 'What do you use it for?'

'Picking up supplies and delivering them.'

'Who was driving the vehicle on the eighteenth of November last year?'

He threw up his hands in disbelief. 'Are you kidding me? I have twelve people working for me, it could have been any one of them. Look, why do you think the van's been used to steal stuff?'

Becca ignored his question. 'Don't you keep proper records?' She glanced again at the chaos on the desk. 'If you can't tell us who was driving the van on that date, we'll have to take all this lot back to the station, along with any electronic records.'

Coleman gave a loud sigh and turned to his computer. 'All right, give me a minute.' He began tapping at his keyboard. 'November eighteenth, that was Billy Buxton.'

Becca referred to her notes. 'What about August the tenth this year?'

Coleman bashed keys for a second time. 'Billy again.'

'And the sixteenth of September?'

'Billy.' Coleman's voice remained defiant, yet even the belligerent manager seemed to be having doubts about his delivery driver's innocence.

Tony cleared his throat. 'After Billy used the van on November eighteenth, was there any damage to the vehicle?'

'Aye. It needed a new headlight. Billy told me he'd hit a deer out on the road.'

Becca needed no further convincing. She knew in her gut that not only had she found the person responsible for the thefts at Pickering and elsewhere, but that she'd put a name to the driver who had left Sam in a coma.

When she spoke, her mouth was dry. 'Where is this Billy now?'

A van pulled up outside, clearly visible through the office window, its engine rattling loudly. A white Ford Transit Connect. Becca didn't need to see the registration plate to know that it contained the number "12".

'That's Billy now,' said Coleman. He put his hands against his head in a gesture of defeat. 'What has that great wazzock been up to?'

# CHAPTER 14

When Jess turned up unannounced at the brewery, Sandra, the secretary, gave her a welcoming smile. 'Back again, dear! Shall I put the kettle on?'

'Thanks,' said Jess. Sandra clearly seemed to think that at least half of her role here at the brewery was to mother the staff and visitors. 'I won't say no to a cuppa. And is Ellie here? I was hoping to speak to her.'

'Yes, it's just me and her today,' said Sandra. 'The men have all swanned off.'

Jess looked across the office to a young woman who was seated at a desk by the window, busily typing on her laptop.

'Go and introduce yourself,' said Sandra. 'I'll bring the tea and biscuits over.'

Ellie looked up as Jess approached. She was a few years older than Jess, maybe twenty-five or twenty-six, and sported a pixie haircut with purple highlights. She held out her hand. 'Hi, you must be from the police.'

'That's right. DC Jess Barraclough.'

'Nice to meet you, Jess. Pull up a chair.'

Jess wheeled a vacant chair over, noting that Ellie's desk

was clean and uncluttered, unlike Sandra's, and that the young woman appeared to be relaxed. She sat down. 'I'm just here to ask you a few questions about Sam. Is that all right?'

'Fine,' said Ellie. 'Greg told me that the police would want to interview me.'

'I understand that you're doing the job Sam used to do, is that right?'

'Yes. I'm now the account director for my sins!' Ellie shook her head, as if she was still surprised that she'd ended up in such a role.

'You didn't expect to be offered the job?'

'I wasn't even working for the brewery when Sam was run over.'

'So how did you end up here?'

'Uncle Greg came to me after Sam was taken into hospital. He needed someone to step in and take over. I was between jobs at the time and thought, why not? It'll probably just be for a few weeks, maybe three months or so, until Sam recovers. But that was a year ago, and here I am.' She indicated the neat piles of paperwork on her desk.

*Uncle Greg.* Jess was reminded just how insular the brewery was. Every single one of the directors was a direct blood relative of Greg Earnshaw. When he had run out of sons to appoint, he had turned to his niece.

Sandra returned with two mugs of steaming tea and a plate of biscuits on a tray. She unloaded them onto Ellie's desk. 'Give me a shout if there's anything else you need.' She returned to her own desk.

Ellie pushed the plate of biscuits towards Jess. 'I'd better not touch these. I swear I've gone up two dress sizes since working here, and it's not just because of the beer.'

Jess was starving after a morning spent tramping across Flamborough Head with Raven. She helped herself to a shortbread.

'So your father is Greg's brother, is that right?'

'Yes, Dad's his younger brother. That makes me Sam's cousin.'

'And your father's name is?'

'Keith Earnshaw. He runs a restaurant in the centre of Scarborough.'

Jess made a note of the name. 'He must have been pleased for you when you joined the family business.'

Ellie pulled a face. 'Not really.'

'No?'

She dropped her voice so that Sandra wouldn't hear. 'Actually, Dad cautioned me against taking the job. He really didn't want me to do it.'

'Why was that?'

'He has this thing about not mixing family and business. I think it's something personal between him and Greg.'

'The two brothers don't get on?'

'They had a bit of a falling out years ago, but I don't know what it was about. It's one of those taboo subjects that's never mentioned around the dinner table. Dad won't even stock Uncle Greg's beer in his restaurant. You can imagine that Uncle Greg sees that as a betrayal. For him, everything's about family. He even offered Dad a discounted rate, but Dad still refused.' It was clearly all Ellie could do to stop herself rolling her eyes in despair at her father's pig-headedness.

'But you took the job anyway?'

Ellie grinned. 'Why not? I thought, it's a wonderful opportunity. I like working with people and I'll be doing Uncle Greg a favour. I don't have a grudge against him. Besides, I've always liked Sam. I did it mainly for his sake. My hope is that he'll be able to walk in here one day, and I'll be able to show him how well I've looked after all his customers.'

'You think he'll come back to work, then?'

'I hope so.'

'And what will happen to you if he does?'

Ellie shrugged. 'I'll find something. Maybe I'll stay on with the brewery, maybe I'll look for something new. I'm still young. I've got plenty of time to decide what I want to do with the rest of my life.'

Jess smiled. She had taken a quick liking to Ellie and her cheerful, happy-go-lucky ways. The young woman was clearly trying as hard as she could to fulfil the role that life had thrust her way, but equally happy to hand it over to someone else when – or if – the time came.

'You said that you weren't working for the brewery at the time of Sam's accident,' said Jess. 'So, does that mean you weren't here that night?'

'Actually, I was. Uncle Greg's always been very kind to me even though he and Dad don't speak to each other. So he invited me to come, and since I'd just lost my job and was feeling a bit sorry for myself, I thought I might as well tag along. Besides... free beer, how could I refuse?' Her mouth broadened into a grin before turning down again as she recalled what had taken place.

'Your father wasn't there?'

'No. But I remember talking to Sam that night. He seemed really happy, like he had no cares in the world. He was planning to go and meet his girlfriend later.'

'Becca,' prompted Jess.

'Yes, but then...' Ellie's voice trailed off. 'I can't believe anyone would want to hurt him.'

Ellie had clearly been told – by Greg or someone else in the know – why the police had reopened their investigation into the incident.

'Do you have any idea why someone might have pushed Sam?' asked Jess.

Ellie shook her head. 'No.'

'Did you see him arguing with anyone?'

'No.'

'And did you notice anyone go outside around the time Sam left the building?'

'No, I didn't even see him leave.'

Jess folded away her notebook, feeling like her session with Ellie had been a waste of time. Apart from the tea and biscuits and a friendly chat, she was no better off for having visited the brewery. 'Is there anything else you can tell me that might help to explain what happened to Sam?'

Ellie hesitated, glancing over at Sandra, who was busy typing, engrossed in her work. She lowered her voice once more so that Jess had to strain to hear her words. 'The only thing I can say is that the three brothers never got on.'

'Sam, Marcus and Anthony?'

Ellie nodded. 'I don't know what was going on, but I'm pretty sure they all hated each other.'

*

Dr Kirtlington stood at the end of Sam's bed, studying his notes. As always, his expression remained inscrutable. Sam could never tell whether the hospital consultant was pleased with his progress, or gravely concerned.

'What do you think, Doctor?'

The doctor finished reading through his notes before replying, clearly in no hurry to express an opinion. 'I think you're doing well, Sam, all things considered. The physiotherapist seems happy with your progress so far. You're steadily regaining your strength, the signs are good, however...'

'However what?'

Dr Kirtlington fixed a professional smile to his face. 'You're at the very beginning of your road to recovery, Sam. There's still a long journey ahead. Full rehabilitation from a coma can take months or years, and usually proceeds in phases. It's often a case of two steps forward, one step back.'

Sam was growing tired of the doctor's platitudes. He was hungry for information and eager to be back on his feet. He desperately wanted to leave the stifling environment of the hospital and return to normality. He'd give anything to be able to sleep in his own bed and to eat his mum's home-cooked food again. 'When do you think I'll be well enough to go home?'

'We'll cross that bridge when we come to it, shall we?'

Sam shook his head. 'I'd really be much happier at

home, Doctor. I'd sleep better in my own bed. It's always so noisy here.'

Dr Kirtlington sighed, considering his patient with ill-concealed frustration. 'For the time being, I think you'll be safer here.'

'Safer?'

'More comfortable. Is there anything I can get you?'

'No. I think I'll just have a nap.'

The doctor seemed pleased by that. 'Good idea. You need to rest as much as you can.'

Sam shut his eyes as the doctor closed the door behind him. It was staying in the hospital he found most exhausting of all. The endless round of doctors, nurses, physios, cleaners, the staff who brought his food... he just wanted to be alone with Becca.

He wondered what she was doing now. Chasing criminals around Pickering, no doubt. She was clearly just as frustrated by her situation as he was. He knew how much she wanted to be searching for the person who'd pushed him into the path of the oncoming van.

His eyes shot open.

He could see the van clearly. The orange cast of streetlights reflected in the road... cold rain stinging his face... the wind tugging at the golfing umbrella.

The umbrella.

Why had he forgotten about the umbrella?

It was the first time for him to remember that detail, but he could picture it vividly now. Enormous, with green and white stripes. He'd taken it with him to wait for the taxi. He'd wrestled with it in the wind, and it had blown away after he'd been pushed.

Was this what he'd been struggling to remember for so long?

The umbrella wasn't his. He'd picked it up from somewhere before leaving the brewery. He'd been in a rush to leave, and not just because he was eager to see Becca. There had been some reason why he'd been hurrying away.

Why had he taken that particular umbrella? The answer was just out of reach.

And then it came to him. The umbrella belonged to Marcus.

But why was that important?

# CHAPTER 15

Becca led the way out of the office of Coleman's Plumbing Supplies, Tony at her heels.

A young man with short dark hair, and tattoos running up his neck was at the wheel of a grubby white Transit van. He pushed open the door with his foot and scrambled out: slouch, faded denim jacket, an unlit cigarette dangling from the corner of his mouth.

Becca checked the number plate of the vehicle. 'This is it,' she said to Tony.

She closed in on the man with the van, who was now struggling to light his cigarette, flicking his lighter and cupping his hand against the wind. 'Billy? Can we have a word? We're from North Yorkshire Police, based in Scarborough.' She held out her warrant card.

Her words had a magical effect on Billy.

He took one look at her police ID, dropped his cigarette and lighter and took off at breakneck speed towards the road, narrowly avoiding another van that was coming into the car park. It swerved to miss him, letting out a long blast on its horn.

'Shit.' Becca ran after him, but the van that had just

arrived was blocking her path and she couldn't see which way Billy had gone. She dodged around it in frustration. When she reached the road, she looked left and right and caught a glimpse of bleached denim running like the devil was in pursuit. She set off again, Tony behind her.

She passed the brewery on her right, keeping pace with the fugitive. Becca wasn't as fit as she'd like to be – all those cooked breakfasts tended to pile on the pounds – but neither was Billy. Too many cigarettes, too many hours stuck behind the wheel of his van. He puffed and panted, twisting his head every now and again to see if she was still following.

She was. There was no way she was letting him get away.

He ran out of the business park where the brewery and plumbing supply depot were situated and onto the main road leading into town. He crossed it with barely a glance at the oncoming traffic, causing a car to screech to a halt. Becca followed, taking care to check for traffic before setting into the road.

A bus pulled up and passengers alighted onto the pavement – a youth plugged in to his headphones, ignorant of everyone and everything around him; an old lady dragging a tartan shopping trolley; a young mother with a pushchair and a stroppy toddler refusing to sit in it. Billy darted around the bus, causing the old woman to shake her head in indignation.

'Police! Stop!' called Becca. The old lady twitched her trolley briskly out of the way and the mother managed to wrest her son into his seat. Only the guy with the headphones continued to saunter along the pavement, oblivious to the chase. Billy shoved him roughly out of the way and turned down a side road.

Becca put a spurt on, a stitch stabbing her in the side. She really needed to lose some pounds and get back to the gym. She'd had no time this last year, spending all her free hours at Sam's bedside.

'Fucksake,' complained headphone guy as Becca sped

past him.

They were in a narrow street now between two rows of redbrick terraced houses. Blue and green wheelie bins lined the pavements like a homage to waste. In one of the cramped front yards, a dog barked furiously at the commotion. A fat lot of good that did. Some canine teeth clamped around the runaway's leg would have been a lot more use.

Billy was almost at the end of the road and gaining ground. Becca didn't know how much longer she could keep this up. Her heart was straining to burst free from its cage. She was gasping for breath, almost doubled over in pain. She should have called for backup before giving chase. But she'd been so desperate to nail the hit and run driver herself.

'I can't... go on,' she gasped.

Just then, a refuse lorry reversed into the street, beeping loudly. Men in orange coveralls appeared from around the corner and started grabbing wheelie bins to empty into the back of the truck. Billy's exit was blocked. He turned and in desperation grabbed hold of the nearest bin. He shoved it into Becca's path. It was a last-ditch attempt to thwart his capture, but it did little more than delay his arrest by a few seconds.

The wheelie bin toppled over onto its side, spilling its contents of glass, cardboard and recyclable plastics into the road, and earning Billy a hail of abuse from the bin men.

'Hey,' shouted Becca. 'Stop! Police!'

The refuse collectors paused in their work to watch the show. Billy looked frantically around him, a trapped animal. But there was nowhere left to run. The bin men closed on him from behind, grabbing him by the arms.

'Let me go!' shrieked Billy, but his captors didn't look like they were going to give up so easily.

By the time Becca arrived, she could tell from the look in the man's eyes that he knew it was over. She snapped a pair of handcuffs over his wrists, pinning his arms behind his back. 'Billy Buxton, I am arresting you on suspicion of burglary, resisting arrest, causing serious injury by dangerous driving, assault occasioning actual bodily harm, and failing to stop at the scene of a road traffic collision.' She paused for breath, then read him his rights, although she'd gladly have tipped him in the back of the rubbish bin along with all the other discarded waste.

The bin men gave her a round of applause and a cheer. 'Nice one, luv,' said one of them. 'Put him away for a long time.'

# CHAPTER 16

Raven had been assured by Greg that the person he wanted to speak to next would shortly be returning from his business trip to Edinburgh. So after leaving the Earnshaw family home in Scalby, he drove the two and a half miles across town to the Esplanade where Greg's middle son Anthony and his wife Naomi owned an apartment. The Esplanade was at the posh end of Scarborough, built above the south cliffs and the spa, close to the Italian Gardens and – quite literally – looking down at the harbour and the old streets where Raven lived. According to Denise, the apartment enjoyed spectacular views across the South Bay. But today the sea was an unappealing grey sludge, the sky no better, and the castle on the headland a wraith, half lost in the mist sliding in from the sea. The beach itself was empty, save for one middle-aged couple trudging stoically across the sands.

It was half past three and already nearly dusk.

December in Scarborough. Barely seven hours of daylight. Raven was still trying to get his head round how much farther north his new home was than London. Sometimes Yorkshire felt like a different country.

He left his car on a side street and walked the short distance to the address Greg had given him – one of a row of five-storey white stucco townhouses with wrought iron balconies on the first and second floors.

As he approached the entrance to the terrace, the gate swung open and a familiar figure stepped onto the pavement. Their encounter was unavoidable.

'Afternoon, Marcus.'

Anthony's older brother was dressed in a suit rather than the casual outfit he'd been wearing when Raven had visited him at home that morning. Perhaps he was heading into the office, or on his way back. He shot Raven a look of surprise. 'Chief Inspector! What are you doing here?'

'I was hoping to have a word with Anthony. Is he in?'

'Not yet. He was held up in traffic. Roadworks near Newcastle. He should be back any minute.' Marcus checked his watch, seeming eager to be off. He was already moving away from Raven, pulling his car keys out of his pocket.

'Don't you want to wait for him?' asked Raven. 'Since he's almost home.'

'What?' Marcus appeared flustered by the suggestion. 'No need. I just called by to, er, drop off the end-of-year financial report. Naomi will let you in. Goodbye.' He scurried away down the road like a man with a train to catch.

Or one hoping not to be caught himself.

Raven rang the bell marked *Earnshaw* and waited for the intercom to crackle into life. 'Hello, this is DCI Raven, Scarborough CID. I'm here to see Anthony Earnshaw.'

A short silence ensued.

'May I come in?' asked Raven.

A woman's voice answered. 'This is Naomi Earnshaw. Anthony isn't back.' Her tone wasn't exactly welcoming.

'Do you mind if I come inside and wait?'

There was a pause during which he half expected to be told to go away, but then a buzzer sounded and the door clicked open. He entered the building and began to climb the staircase that greeted him.

*Steps*, he thought as he dragged his leg up to the second floor. Why did there always have to be steps?

He was met on the landing by a glamorous brunette. Naomi Earnshaw was nothing like Marcus's wife, Olivia. She hadn't skimped on the lipstick or eye shadow, and there were no mum-jeans in sight. Long wavy hair tumbled over her shoulders, and her skin was flawless. She wore a loose silk shirt over skin-tight trousers.

'Sorry to trouble you.' Raven pulled out his warrant card to confirm his identity, but Naomi had already turned away. He followed her into the apartment.

'Anthony should be back soon.' She indicated the lounge. 'You can wait in here.'

The room was large, smartly furnished in a minimalist style and conspicuously child-free. Three tall windows looked out onto a balcony. In the distance, lights were already twinkling in the harbour. Naomi strode over to close the curtains, shutting out the gloom.

'Would you like a coffee?' The offer was made grudgingly, but Raven accepted it regardless. He never refused the offer of a coffee, and if he was going to wait he might as well do it in comfort.

While Naomi busied herself in the kitchen he folded his overcoat over a cream sofa and sat down, giving his leg a rest after the climb and letting his eyes roam the room. Everything from the furniture and the curtains to the walls and floor was a subtle off-white. Raven guessed that the colours had fancy names like jasmine, ivory and alabaster. A few black accents provided contrast. There were no books in sight, and no family photos, apart from one of Naomi with her husband on their wedding day.

She returned with a cup of black coffee and passed it to him without comment before glancing at the watch on her slim wrist.

'I was hoping to speak to you anyway,' he said, forestalling any attempt for her to leave.

His reluctant hostess had little choice but to sit down

opposite him. She kicked off her heels with a sigh and tucked her long legs under her, waiting for him to speak.

'We're looking into the incident that took place last year, when Sam was hit by a vehicle.'

'Yes, I know.' Naomi's tone gave nothing away. 'Marcus did mention it.'

*Marcus*. Was that what he was doing here? Warning Naomi that the police were likely to make an appearance? Or had he popped in with other thoughts on his mind?

'We're speaking to everyone who was there that night.'

'I see.' She sounded as if she couldn't imagine anything duller to talk about.

'So, were you there that night? At the party?'

'Yes. Everyone was.'

'Tell me what you did.'

'Did? I didn't do anything very much at all. I spent the entire evening with Olivia – that's Marcus's wife – and Denise, my mother-in-law. There wasn't even anything to drink.'

Raven raised a puzzled eyebrow.

'Except for beer.'

He suppressed a smile. 'I take it you're not a big beer fan.' The way Naomi described the evening, it sounded like she'd been bored out of her mind. 'And what did your husband do?'

'As far as I know, Anthony drank beer and chatted to his guests. He isn't actually very interested in discussing birthing plans and debating the benefits of breast feeding versus bottles.' It was clear that Naomi had no interest in those topics of conversation either. It was hard to imagine that she had much in common with the homely Olivia, except that they had both married into the same family. 'We ladies hardly saw our husbands all night.'

Raven was willing to bet that Anthony had received a right earful afterwards as a result. He sipped his coffee. Not bad, but it didn't quite match the cup Olivia had produced for him. The quality always came down to the freshness of the beans. 'Does Anthony do a lot of travelling for his work?'

'Yes, it's his job to sell beer to new customers. He travels all over the country. He's been in Edinburgh for the past few days.'

Long enough for Marcus to drop in more than once, Raven figured, especially with the unsuspecting Olivia tied up at home with the baby. He recalled the way the older brother had scurried off after leaving the building. 'And how do you find that? Anthony being away so much, I mean.'

'Me? I'm quite capable of enjoying life without the continual presence of my husband.'

'I'm sure you are. So, does Anthony enjoy working for the family firm? Does he mind the fact that there's no distinction between work and family?'

Naomi shrugged, as if she didn't see the point of his question.

'Take Marcus, for instance, calling by to drop off the end-of-year accounts just now. That kind of thing must happen all the time.' He paused. 'Perhaps even when Anthony is away.'

Naomi's eyes blazed with anger. 'If you're suggesting that Marcus was here for some other reason…' She gestured towards the kitchen. 'The accounts are in there. You can go and check if you don't believe me.'

'That won't be necessary. I was simply interested in how Anthony feels about the arrangement.' Raven waited politely, leaving it unclear precisely what *arrangement* he might be referring to.

Naomi opened her mouth to speak, but before she could reply, there was the sound of a key turning in the lock. Visibly relieved, she jumped to her feet. 'You can ask Anthony yourself how he feels. That'll be him now.'

# CHAPTER 17

Billy Buxton had declined his right to free legal representation, saying he didn't need it because he "hadn't done owt" and "didn't want to hang about" waiting for a lawyer to turn up. That suited Becca just fine. She didn't want to hang about either. She knew that if she waited too long, Raven would come back and immediately take over. Right now, this was her collar and she intended to conduct the interview herself. The idea that she was about to question the jerk who had run over Sam and left him for dead in the middle of the road gave her such an adrenalin boost that she could barely sit still. As soon as she got a call from the custody sergeant to tell her that her suspect was ready to be questioned, she and Tony proceeded to the interview room.

She found Billy sitting nervously, fiddling with the frayed cuffs on his denim jacket. He ducked his head as Becca scraped back a chair and sat directly in front of him. She took a moment to assess his appearance, noting his tussled hair, his hunched, defensive posture and the way he scratched nervously at the tattoos on his neck.

*Furtive*. That would be a good word to describe his

appearance. *Guilty*. That was another.

She opened her file and quickly re-read the briefing summary that Tony had put together for her.

Billy Buxton, aged twenty-one, a native of Scarborough. He'd left school at the age of sixteen to do a plumbing course at the local college of further education before moving on to a job at Coleman's Plumbing Supplies. There, he'd become a delivery driver after passing his driving test. He had no previous convictions.

But that was only because he'd been lucky.

Today, his luck had run out.

Tony switched on the tape recorder and ran through the preliminaries of the interview, reading the suspect his rights. When he'd finished, Billy lifted his eyes nervously to Becca. 'Can I have a cigarette?'

'No. Let's get started.' She turned to her notes. 'The van you use for your job is a white Ford Transit Connect. Is that right?'

'Yeah,' said Billy.

'The vehicle that you were driving today – is that the van you always drive?'

'Yeah.'

'Can you tell me what exactly you do for your job?'

Billy scratched his nose, pondering the matter as if he'd never considered it before. 'I help prepare customers' orders. Sometimes I go out on pick-ups and deliveries.'

'How far do you travel in your work?'

'All over North Yorkshire.'

'I see. Can you tell me where you were on the night of Saturday the twenty-sixth of November?'

Billy shrugged. 'Out wi' me mates?'

'Is that a guess, or a statement of fact?'

'Dunno. Can't remember what I were doing that night.'

'Let me see if I can refresh your memory.' Becca retrieved two images from her file, taken from the CCTV footage that Mr Owens of Pickering had helpfully provided. One showed a figure dressed in a dark hoodie and wearing a baseball hat wheeling a trolley stacked with cardboard boxes out of a warehouse. The other showed the same scene with a slightly later timestamp. The corner of a white vehicle was just visible at the edge of the frame. 'Is this you? Is that your van?'

'No,' said Billy without even glancing at the photos.

'Take a closer look.' Becca slid them across the table until they were right under his nose. 'These images show the theft of a consignment of fifty brand new laptops from an electronics wholesaler in Pickering.'

Billy stole a quick look, swivelling the photos around before studying them more closely. A glimmer of hope entered his eyes. Perhaps he thought this was all they had on him. 'Hard to say. Could be anyone, really. Could be any van.'

Becca removed the two photographs. 'And where were you on the night of August tenth?'

A smirk appeared on Billy's face. 'Out wi' me mates again?'

Becca showed him another photo, a blurry shot of a white van moving past a different warehouse. It was the trading park in Whitby, where a quantity of mobile phones had been stolen. 'Is this your vehicle?'

Billy was growing in confidence. 'Nah, don't think so. I don't even know where that place is.'

'Really?' Becca retrieved the photo. 'Where were you on the night of the sixteenth of September?'

It was all Billy could do now not to grin openly. 'Me mates again?'

Becca wanted to slap him. 'I don't think so, Billy, because on that night a break-in took place at an electronics retailer in Eastfield. A bolt cutter was used to remove a padlock, and a dozen brand new televisions were stolen. An eyewitness reported seeing a white van with a number "12" on its registration plate leaving the scene. That's the same year as the van you use for your job.'

Billy sat up a little straighter, the nonchalant attitude sliding off his face. His plastic chair creaked. 'That weren't me.' His eyes flicked from Becca to Tony and back again. 'Loads of white vans like that around.'

'Not so many,' said Tony. 'In fact, do you know how many 12-registered white Ford Transit Connects there are in the Scarborough district?'

'No.'

'One.'

The word seemed to hang in the air as Billy considered its implications. 'Still proves nowt,' he said, but without much conviction.

'Do you know what else all these burglaries have in common?' Becca asked him. 'In each case the premises were forced open using either a bolt cutter or a crowbar. Do you own either of those tools?'

'I dunno, I...'

'We found a bolt cutter and a crowbar in your van,' said Tony.

Becca leaned forward. 'Where were you on the night of November the eighteenth last year?'

Billy hesitated, wondering what answer he could give that might get him off the hook. There was no more bluster about being out with his mates. 'That were ages ago,' he whined.

'Just over a year. But on that night a burglary occurred at a family-owned electrical store in town. A dozen PlayStations were taken, and a white Ford Transit Connect was spotted at the scene.'

'I dunno what I were doing that long ago,' said Billy miserably. 'How could anyone remember that far back?'

'Your employer has confirmed that you were making use of the van that day,' said Tony. 'As you were on all the other dates that have been mentioned.'

'Well, it's m'job.' Billy tugged at his shirt and scratched the back of his hands. A light sheen of sweat glistened on his forehead. Maybe he was beginning to wish he'd accepted the offer of a lawyer.

Becca drove home her advantage. 'Later that same night, a hit and run incident occurred outside the Salt

Castle brewery, at the same business park as the plumbing supply depot where you work. The victim reported being hit by a white van.'

'That weren't me!' Fear had spread over Billy's features now. The look of an animal sensing the hunter closing in for the kill.

Becca's heart was galloping so loudly in her chest she marvelled he couldn't hear its rhythmic drumbeat. She carefully removed the final photo from her folder. A photo of Sam, taken after he'd been rushed into hospital, the gash on his head clearly visible, the bruising on his face like purple fingers pressing into his skin. She couldn't bear to look at it herself, but pushed it roughly in front of Billy. 'Do you recognise this man?'

Billy couldn't bear to look at the photo either. He shoved it away like it was scalding hot. 'I never seen him before!'

'A credible witness reported seeing a white van with a missing headlight speeding away from the scene of the hit and run. Your employer told us that you reported a broken headlamp on your vehicle the very next day.'

'I hit a deer!'

'Do I look like I'm going to believe a stupid story like that?' Becca leaned forwards and was gratified to see Billy pull away from her. He looked as if he wanted to crawl into a hole. 'You've already been arrested on suspicion of a number of serious charges. Would you like to add attempted murder to that list?'

The colour drained completely from Billy's face. 'I didn't... I mean, it wasn't... I dunno...' He was gabbling incoherently now.

Becca watched him, devoid of all pity. Usually it was DI Dinsdale who played bad cop in these interviews. This time it was her.

She seemed to be pretty good at it too. Maybe Dinsdale had taught her a thing or two after all.

'There's only one way out for you now, Billy. Don't imagine that you can get off the hook for the burglaries you committed, because you can't. There's more than enough evidence here to convict you. You're looking at a community order or a prison sentence for sure. However, in the case of the hit and run…'

'Yeah?' A huge weight of desperate hope rested on that single word.

Becca crushed that hope. 'The evidence there is overwhelming too. You ran a man down and left him lying in the road. It'll be a custodial sentence for that. But the charge of attempted murder… that's the big one. It carries a maximum sentence of life imprisonment.' She paused for a second to let him absorb that thought. 'Tell us what happened that night and maybe there's a chance a jury will be sympathetic.'

She let him ponder the situation, watching as his hands trembled and his mouth formed soundless words. A lawyer would have told him that the evidence was circumstantial, that he should keep his mouth shut or say "no comment". But Billy had turned down the offer of a lawyer. He was alone with his misery.

Eventually he slumped onto the table, his head in his hands. 'All right, all right!'

Becca waited for him to gather himself together. When he lifted his head, his eyes were red. He wiped his nose on the sleeve of his jacket. 'Okay. I admit it. I did hit someone that night. But it weren't my fault.'

'Tell us exactly how it happened, Billy. Take your time.' Knowing she'd broken him, Becca softened her voice, made it easy, coaxing.

She didn't want revenge, just answers.

'It weren't my fault,' he repeated. 'Someone pushed him in front of the van. I saw it wi' me own eyes.'

'What did you see? Who pushed him?'

Billy gave another of his infuriating shrugs. 'Dunno. The guy I hit were carrying a big umbrella so I couldn't see. But he didn't just walk out in front of me. Someone pushed him. That's the person who caused the accident. You should be going after them.' A self-pitying whine had crept into his voice as he sought to shift the blame to someone else.

'Who pushed him, Billy? A man? A woman? Can you describe them?'

But Billy couldn't help. 'It were dark. It were raining. I couldn't see a thing! It weren't my fault!'

Becca knew that she had reached a dead end. She would get nothing more out of Billy Buxton. He had to be one of the most useless witnesses she'd ever interviewed.

But at least she had caught the driver who'd put Sam in hospital. With the help of Billy's own confession, he would serve time for the harm he'd done. And she could go to Sam this evening and tell him that his version of events had been corroborated. Neither Dr Kirtlington nor anyone else could continue to cast doubt on his story.

She had done as much as she could. Now it was up to Raven and the team to get to the truth.

# CHAPTER 18

Anthony Earnshaw was a clean-shaven, slimmer and more athletic version of his older brother, but unmistakably from the same gene pool. He breezed in through the hallway, a suitcase behind him and a suit-bag on one arm, and gave his wife a kiss.

'You're back at last, darling,' said Naomi. 'Was it an awful journey?'

'Terrible. I'm glad to be home.'

Raven rose to his feet. 'Sorry to intrude, Mr Earnshaw, but your father said I'd find you here. It's DCI Raven, North Yorkshire Police.'

Anthony dropped his suit-bag over the arm of the sofa and advanced into the room, his right hand outstretched. 'Good to meet you.' He gripped Raven's hand and shook it warmly in the way that only a professional salesman or a politician could. 'How can I help? Has something happened?'

'DCI Raven is here to ask some questions about Sam,' explained Naomi.

Anthony looked puzzled. 'Sam? I thought the police inquiry into that was all done and dusted.'

'We've reopened the inquiry in light of new information,' explained Raven.

'I see,' said Anthony. 'Well, naturally I'll be happy to help you in any way I can.' Glancing towards Raven's empty cup of coffee, he said, 'I see that Naomi has been looking after you, but can I offer you a proper drink? I could certainly use one.'

'Not while I'm working.'

'Well, I'm sure you won't mind if I have one myself.' Anthony opened a glass cabinet and took out a crystal tumbler and a bottle of whisky.

Not beer.

Perhaps he'd had his fill of the brewery's products while out on his sales trip, or perhaps like his wife, Anthony wasn't a natural fan of the product he sold.

Or maybe he just needed something stronger right now.

He poured himself a generous measure. 'Roadworks at Newcastle – what a nightmare! And there was the usual snarl-up at Middlesbrough.' He shuddered.

'You travel that way regularly?' enquired Raven.

'I travel everywhere regularly,' said Anthony with a grin. 'Always out on the road.' He turned to Naomi. 'Isn't that right, darling? I don't know how you put up with me being away so much.'

Raven suspected he knew perfectly well how Naomi managed to cope when her husband was away. Although Anthony was leaner and fitter than Marcus, with fewer years on his bodywork, Marcus had the distinct advantage of availability. On these cold, lonely December evenings, the attraction was clear.

Naomi picked up a sports bag from the hall. 'I'm off to the gym, darling. I've already spoken to DCI Raven.'

Anthony regarded her with surprise. 'You're going out?' He seemed disappointed that his wife was leaving just as soon as he'd returned from his trip. 'Will I see you later?'

'Of course. I'll be back in an hour or so.' She kissed him again and disappeared into the hallway.

Anthony gestured for Raven to sit down, and took a

seat opposite on a matching sofa. He dropped his car keys – embossed with the Porsche logo – onto a side table and folded one leg casually over the other, taking a sip of the whisky. 'God, that's what I need!'

'You've had a stressful trip,' remarked Raven, 'but a successful one, I hope?'

'Great, thanks for asking. I managed to sign two new contracts and persuaded another customer to double their existing order.' He took a second mouthful of the whisky and leaned back, one arm reaching casually over the back of the sofa.

The front door of the apartment opened and closed. Naomi had gone out.

'Your wife,' said Raven, 'is she involved in the business too?'

'Naomi works from home doing freelance PR. She's done some projects for the brewery, but she has lots of other clients too. She's very good at her job.' Anthony's eyes flicked to the wedding photo on the side table. 'We've been married seven years. No kids, as you can see' – he indicated the pristine, clutter-free room – 'and that's the way we like it. We enjoy our careers too much.'

'You enjoy working for your father?'

Anthony crossed his legs the other way. 'Dad's good to have around. He built the business from scratch, so he knows exactly how it works. In fact, he used to do the job that I do now. Who knows, one day I might be sitting where he is.'

'At the head of the company?'

'Why not? It'll either be me or Marcus. And Marcus lacks... flair. He's an accountant. Good at his job, but he doesn't have the vision to take the firm to the next level.'

Raven nodded sagely.

It seemed clear, however, that Marcus wasn't lacking in flair or vision when it came to his love life, and had already taken it to the next level. It was remarkable that Anthony was blissfully ignorant of the situation. Then again, Raven had been oblivious to the fact that Lisa was sleeping with a rival behind his back. Come to think of it, Lisa's new partner was also an accountant. Raven needed to try not to let that colour his opinion of Marcus. The guy might be a first-rate prick but that didn't make him a killer.

Not necessarily.

'How do you get on with your brother?'

'Great. That's the beauty of working in a family business. We know each other so well. Trust is never in doubt.'

It was all Raven could do to stop himself from telling Anthony what was going on right under his nose.

'Do you always agree with each other?'

Anthony smiled. 'Of course not. What brothers ever do? But when we disagree, we always work it out.'

'I understand that there's a merger in the offing.'

'Right, yes.' Anthony put his whisky aside and sat up straighter, growing animated as he outlined his views on the subject. 'It would be good for the brewery to be part of something bigger. We'd have a broader distribution network' – he spread his arms wide – 'and more opportunities to grow and invest.'

Anthony's opinion sounded remarkably similar to the case Marcus had made in favour of the merger. Which brother was pushing the agenda, and which tagging along behind? Each seemed convinced that they were leader in waiting, all set to step into their father's shoes.

But there was only room for one at the top.

'Your father doesn't agree.'

Anthony shrugged dismissively. 'Dad will come around eventually. He's got to think about the future. He can't do it his way forever. Marcus is behind me – as finance director he can see that the numbers make sense.'

'And what about Sam?'

At mention of his younger brother, Anthony's ebullient manner faltered. 'Well, Sam was more cautious. He needed more convincing.'

'Have you spoken to him since he recovered consciousness?'

'I still need to pop round. I've been away.'

'Of course you have. Tell me, how do you think Sam fits into the future of the company?'

Anthony spread his hands in a gesture of ambivalence. 'He's still in hospital. Ellie's doing his job now, and doing it very well.'

'But Sam is your brother. Surely Greg will want him involved again? Surely Sam will want his old job back?'

'I'm sure he will, just as soon as he's back on his feet.'

'And if he continues to oppose the merger?'

Anthony swirled the rest of the whisky in his glass and downed it in one. Gone was the affable salesman, doing his best to please. His next words were tinged with unmistakeable hostility. 'I don't really know what you're getting at, Chief Inspector. I thought you were here to talk about Sam's accident. All you seem to be interested in is whether there are any disagreements within the family.'

It was time for Raven to lay his cards on the table and see how Anthony reacted. 'You and Marcus were seen having an argument with Sam the day he was hit by a speeding vehicle. Perhaps you aren't aware of this, but the hit and run was no accident.'

'What do you mean?'

'Sam was pushed into the road.'

Anthony levelled Raven with a measuring stare. 'That's preposterous! Nobody would want to kill Sam. I can't believe what you're telling me.'

'Nevertheless,' said Raven, 'that's what happened.'

Anthony stood up, the empty glass in his hand. 'If you're suggesting that Marcus and I tried to kill Sam because he disagreed with us on a matter of business, that's completely ridiculous.'

'Do you have any other ideas about who might have wanted him out of the way?'

'Of course not.' Anthony began to pace the room, circling the sofa and moving over to the windows.

Raven waited for him to work off some of his energy before he spoke again. 'I'd like to ask you about the night of the party. Did you speak to Sam that evening?'

Anthony took his empty glass over to the drinks cabinet and poured himself another large measure. He returned to the sofa, but there was nothing relaxed about his posture now. He leaned in towards Raven, the crystal in his hands splitting the light, the whisky like liquid amber. 'Sure I did. But not about work or anything. I think we talked football.'

'Who else did Sam talk to?'

'Everyone. Sam's good at mingling. He chatted to all the staff. But he had to leave early to meet his girlfriend.'

'At the time Sam left,' said Raven, 'did you notice anyone else go outside too?'

Anthony thought for a moment, taking a long sip of his drink. 'I didn't see anyone go out...'

'But?'

He shook his head. 'This is absurd. It doesn't mean anything.' He lifted the glass to drink again.

'What doesn't?'

Anthony froze, the glass suspended beneath his lips. 'Marcus. He must have gone outside at some point during the evening because I remember noticing that his hair was wet. But he would never have done anything to hurt Sam. They're brothers.'

'Sometimes,' said Raven, 'the ones who hurt us most are those closest to us.' He stood up to signal that the interview was over. 'Oh, by the way. Speaking of Marcus, he was here earlier. While you were out.'

'What?' Anthony gave a short shake of his head. 'What was he doing here?'

Was that irritation? Anger? Outright denial? Or merely resignation? It was difficult to gauge.

'He called by to drop off the accounts,' said Raven mildly.

'But Marcus already e-mailed me a copy of the accounts. There was no need for him to call by.'

Raven shrugged. 'I expect he was just being helpful. Anyway, thanks for your time. And please thank your wife for the coffee. Don't get up, I'll see myself out.'

He left the apartment, glad he had no brothers of his own, or family of any kind, and braced himself to resume battle with the stairs.

For some reason, going down was always twice as hard as coming up.

# CHAPTER 19

When Jess returned to the station, she found the incident room dark and deserted. Raven wasn't back, and there was no sign of Tony either. Becca's desk in the main office was also empty, and Jess couldn't blame her for slipping away early on a Friday evening. Becca had put in plenty of extra hours in her time, and it must be so frustrating being confined to burglary cases when she obviously wanted to help the rest of the team find out what had happened to Sam.

All the same, Jess had to concede that Becca's loss was her gain. With Becca excluded from taking part in the investigation, there was more opportunity for Jess to get involved. She'd been thrilled when Raven had asked her to accompany him to Flamborough Head – despite the strap-in-tight-and-hold-on ride to get there and the heart-stopping moment when her boss had nearly tumbled over the edge of the cliff.

You never knew what might happen when you were out with Raven.

Jess couldn't wait to catch up with Scott and tell him all about it. He had confessed to being a secret admirer of

Raven. *Brave*, he'd called him. *Fearless*.

Well, yeah. But he was also a bit *bats in the belfry*.

She switched on the lights and closed the door behind her, taking advantage of the empty office to give Scott a call. He answered on the third ring. 'Hey, Jess.'

'Hi, what are you up to? Finished work yet?'

'Just wrapping up some stuff for Holly. I can't leave until that's done.' Holly Chang was head of the CSI team, and Scott's boss. It was never a good idea to get on her wrong side.

'I've just got to type up my notes from this afternoon, then I'll call it a day. Want to meet up afterwards?' Jess took care to keep her voice casual, not wanting to put Scott under any undue pressure. He could be like a startled squirrel, bolting for cover if he felt under the slightest threat. Slow and steady, that was the way to handle Scott.

'For a drink?' Scott's natural environment was outdoors, much like Jess. Neither of them really liked noisy bars, but Scarborough boasted some good traditional pubs, and at this time of year you could pass a pleasant hour or two in front of a roaring log fire. Their favourite haunt was Old Scalby Mills. It was a bit of a trek to get there, being at the far end of the North Bay, but that was part of the attraction. They would be able to sit together in the warmth, looking back towards the castle headland and plan a nice long walk for the weekend.

And maybe they would sample a pint or two from the Salt Castle range. They could call that research. Maybe she could even claim it on expenses.

'Sure, okay? See you in half an hour?'

'Cool.'

She ended the call, smiling to herself. Scott might need some careful handling, but she still found him adorable.

She was pulling on her parka when Raven's phone started to ring. With a sigh she walked over to his desk and answered it.

It was the duty sergeant. 'Is DCI Raven around? There's a visitor here to see him.'

'He's out at the moment. I'll come down and deal with it myself.' Jess headed downstairs hoping this diversion wasn't going to take up her whole evening.

A well-groomed blonde was waiting in reception. Early forties perhaps, with immaculate makeup magicking away any wrinkles. She wore a camel woollen coat teamed with a cashmere scarf and black knee-length boots. A stylish tote bag was looped over one shoulder.

'Can I help you?' asked Jess.

Haughty blue eyes took her in at a glance. 'I'm here to see Tom. Tom Raven.' The woman's voice was crystal cut and pure home counties.

'I'm afraid that DCI Raven's not here right now. But if I could take a name and contact details...'

The woman sighed. 'I've been trying his mobile but he's not answering.'

'I expect he's busy working,' said Jess in Raven's defence. Who on earth was this woman who had swanned into the police station expecting a senior detective to run around after her? Out of the corner of her eye Jess could see the duty sergeant trying to keep a straight face.

'If you do see him,' said the woman, 'could you tell him that Lisa's here? I've booked myself into a hotel on the Esplanade. I'll be staying for a few days.'

'What surname shall I give?'

'Raven,' snapped the woman as if it were obvious. 'I'm his wife.'

★

Becca drove straight to the hospital, determined that Sam would be the first person to hear her news. She hadn't even told Raven yet about the arrest of Billy Buxton. She'd tried calling him but had just got his voicemail. Typical. Well, if her boss couldn't be bothered to take her call, he would have to wait.

She hurried along the all-too-familiar corridors, smiling and nodding at nurses whose faces had become like those of old friends. When she arrived at Sam's room she found him sitting up in bed, eating his evening meal from a plastic tray – some unidentifiable pasta gloop. If she'd thought, she could have brought him a takeaway to celebrate. But she'd been too excited to think about that.

He smiled at her as she burst into his room. He looked stronger than at any time since waking from the coma. 'You look like you've just won the lottery,' he said.

'Better than that.' She gave him a quick hug and kiss then pulled up a chair and sat down.

'Go on, then, don't keep me in suspense.'

'I made a breakthrough!'

Sam's mouth fell open as she related her story, outlining the way she'd tracked down the driver of the van, his escape attempt and subsequent arrest, and best of all his admission that he had been behind the wheel of the hit-and-run vehicle.

'So you caught him,' said Sam once she'd finished. 'And he's been arrested?'

'He'll get a prison sentence for sure.'

'And he confirmed that someone pushed me?'

Becca nodded, knowing that for Sam this was perhaps the most important piece of news. Now that an independent witness had backed up his version of events, Dr Kirtlington and the doubters could go screw themselves. Sam had been right all along.

She held his hand tightly. 'I know it's horrible to think that someone wanted you dead, but now Raven's investigation can crack on without any risk of it being pulled. It's real evidence.'

'I have the most amazing girlfriend in the world.' He kissed her hand. 'But I've got news for you too. I finally remembered the thing that's been bugging me. It came back to me this afternoon. I've been waiting to tell you.'

'You remembered?' Becca could hardly believe that another breakthrough had followed so closely on the heels of her own. 'What?'

'It was the umbrella that was the key. I remembered

that I'd been holding it just before I was run over.'

Becca nodded encouragement. Previously, the events of the evening had been a bit of a blank to Sam. He'd been able to describe the hit and run itself, but not what preceded it. 'Billy said you were carrying a big umbrella. It's what hid the attacker from view.'

'It was Marcus's golfing umbrella. Once I'd remembered that, other things started to come to me. Events that happened at the party.' A shadow passed across his face and Becca felt cold hands squeeze her heart. What new horror was he about to reveal?

'Go on,' she whispered.

He started to speak as if he didn't know how to tell her. 'The reason I'd gone outside in the rain to wait for the taxi was because... because I'd just seen something I wasn't supposed to see.'

'What?'

He closed his eyes as if reliving the scene in his head. 'After Sandra called a taxi for me, I went looking for an umbrella to take with me. I popped upstairs to the office to borrow Marcus's. The office should have been empty. Everyone was down in the tap room. But I saw a light coming from beneath the door of Dad's office. I didn't know what to do. I was sure I'd seen Dad downstairs. I worried that someone had got in and was looking at confidential files or something. But it was nothing like that.'

He told her what he'd seen.

'Oh my God,' said Becca, reaching for her phone. 'I need to tell Raven.'

# CHAPTER 20

O n his left, the neon signs of amusement arcades, mirrored in wet pavements. On his right, the sea stretching black and endless, the breeze lifting spray above the railings of the promenade.

Raven drove along the seafront, chewing over what he'd learned.

Marcus. An adulterer. A liar. A murderer?

His own brother had seen him with wet hair – proof that he'd been out in the rain the night Sam's attacker had struck. But when questioned, Marcus had categorically denied going outside.

It wasn't enough evidence to arrest him, but Raven was pretty sure that the eldest brother would be receiving another police visit the next morning to talk through the inconsistency in more detail. Maybe Raven would invite him down to the station for a formal interview. It was time to tighten the screws and see if the cool accountant would crack under pressure.

Raven's phone had been on silent all the time he'd been talking to Naomi and Anthony and he hadn't checked it until after leaving their apartment. Along with a missed call from Becca, to his irritation he'd found half a dozen calls from Lisa. She hadn't left a voicemail, clearly expecting him to answer his phone when it suited her. He had no idea what she wanted but had no intention of calling her back until he'd got home, changed out of his work gear and had something hot to eat. He needed sustenance before he was capable of dealing with his estranged wife.

As he neared Quay Street, he also wondered with some trepidation what Barry might have done while he was out. A whole day with a sledgehammer and a wrecking bar and anything could have happened. Would Raven even have a bed to sleep in?

He dropped his car in the pay-and-display at the end of the road and headed towards his house. There was no light on inside and no sign of the builder's van, so at least he was saved some idle wisecracks and a doom-and-gloom report on the state of the building's disrepair.

He was about to put his key in the lock when his phone rang again. If this was Lisa he would call her back when he was ready. But it was Becca. He answered immediately.

'Hi, what's up?'

She sounded breathless. 'News. I've arrested the driver of the van that hit Sam.'

'You have?' Now Raven regretted not returning her call from earlier. He really ought to make a point of checking in more often with his team. Then he remembered that Becca wasn't supposed to be part of his team and shouldn't have gone anywhere near the van driver. But it seemed churlish to point that out right now.

'Yeah, yeah.' She sounded impatient, as if this was some minor detail. 'The driver admitted hitting Sam and confirmed that he was definitely pushed in front of the vehicle. But the important thing is that Sam's remembered what happened on the night of the party.' She was breathing heavily as if walking quickly at the same time as talking. He heard the bleep of a car remote and then the slam of a car door.

'Tell me what he remembered.'

'It's Marcus. He's having an affair with Anthony's wife.'

'I know.'

'You do? But the thing is, Sam found them together at the party. They were having sex on the desk in Greg's office.'

'Classy.' There was no accounting for other people's fantasies. Sex with your brother's wife in your boss's office. But Raven had heard of worse.

'And Marcus saw Sam, so he had a motive for wanting to shut him up.' Becca paused to draw breath. 'Do you understand what I'm saying?'

'Yes, I do. And Marcus had another motive – Sam was opposed to a company merger that Marcus was trying to push through. So that gives him two reasons for wanting Sam out of the way.' Raven was already walking back towards his car. 'I'm on my way to his house right now.'

★

Clunk, click. Raven swung the BMW out of Quay Street and back onto Sandside, setting off the way he'd just come.

Sea to his left this time, nightlife to the right. At the west pier he jumped an amber light and took a sharp turn into Eastborough, shooting past gift shops, joke stores and a place selling Scarborough rock – TEN STICKS FOR A POUND. A touch on the brakes and a yank of the steering wheel and he was roaring up the hill into town. Body piercing and a tattoo parlour now: the old town really liked to show off its attractions.

A little further on and the street went high-end. A shellfish bar, an art gallery and a place that sold fossils, crystals and minerals. Then came the ubiquitous bars and pubs. Crowds spilled out onto the pavement, causing Raven to honk his horn and slow down. But soon he was on Newborough and it was all fashion retailers and banks. The gradient levelled off, the road widened and the crowds thinned. He followed the road round into St Thomas

Street, an eclectic mix of furniture shops, cafés and taxi firms, and then he was onto Dean Street, location of the old workhouse, prison and cemetery. A wide, straight road where he could really put his foot down.

He pulled up at Woodland Ravine a mere six minutes after having set off – he may have been a little cavalier with the rules of the road – and found Becca's Honda Jazz already parked outside Marcus's house. She'd got here quicker than he'd expected. But if she'd driven straight from the hospital after speaking to Sam, it was only up the road.

She jumped out of her car and ran to meet him.

'You really shouldn't be here,' he told her.

'Looks like I am.'

Arguing was pointless, they both knew that. 'Okay, but leave the talking to me.'

A warm light glowed behind the curtained windows of the downstairs lounge, otherwise the house was in darkness. The entrance porch was a black well of shadow, and the clambering rose that framed it made jagged spurs against the brickwork.

A security light clicked on as they approached, and Raven pressed his thumb against the bell.

Olivia answered the door. She was wearing a casual top, baggy jogging pants, and a pair of fluffy slippers. Comfortable clothing for relaxation.

The contrast with Anthony's wife was more marked than ever. Raven was willing to bet that Naomi didn't own any fluffy slippers. Or baggy pants, for that matter.

'Hello?' Olivia was clearly surprised to see Raven and Becca on her doorstep so late in the evening.

'Sorry to disturb you, but is Marcus in? We need to speak to him.'

'He's not here. He went into the brewery to finish a job.'

'At this time?' said Raven.

Olivia shrugged and gave a sad little smile. 'Sometimes he doesn't get back until much later. He told me not to wait up.'

'I see,' said Raven. 'Thank you.'

The sordid truth about where Marcus really spent his late nights would emerge before long, and it would be almost impossible to keep it from Olivia. Besides, she deserved to know what her husband got up to when he stayed late at work and when his brother was away on business.

However painful that knowledge might be.

Raven recalled his own hurt when Lisa left him. It had been deep and bruising but had quickly given way to questions and a need to understand. And to her credit she'd been upfront and honest with him. *You're never here, Tom. You work all kinds of crazy hours. At least Graham comes home in the evenings.*

It was as simple as that. He had no one to blame but himself.

He walked back to the car. 'What do you reckon?' he asked Becca. 'Is Marcus really likely to be at the brewery?'

'It's worth a shot. If he's not, then I don't know where we'll find him.'

Raven nodded and got back into his car. There was no point telling Becca not to follow him. She would anyway.

\*

When Raven reached the brewery he found the building in complete darkness. If Marcus had come here to work this evening, he had certainly finished now.

And yet a Lexus SUV was still in the car park, its lights off.

Becca pulled in behind him and clambered out. She pointed to the Lexus. 'That's Marcus's car. What's it still doing here?'

'Good question,' said Raven, pulling on a pair of blue nitrile gloves. He checked the doors of the car, but it was locked and empty.

Could Marcus have gone somewhere on foot, or was he

still inside the darkened building?

Raven had a bad feeling, and it got worse when he tried the door to the brewery and found it unlocked.

He switched on a torch and stepped inside.

There were no lights on inside the building, but the various instrument panels fitted to the brewing equipment bathed the place in a low glow. Stainless steel vats flashed briefly as Raven's torch swept across them, but were quickly swallowed again by darkness. He checked the door to the tap room, but it was locked.

Discreet safety lighting set into the risers of the stairs illuminated the way up to the office.

Raven motioned for Becca to follow him.

The staircase snaked around the walls of the building, turning a corner before reaching the office level. The glass door at the top showed no lights within.

Raven took the steps one at a time. No sense making this harder on his leg than it needed to be.

At the top of the stairs he tried the door and found it unlocked.

The larger of the two offices was empty. A computer on one of the desks had been left on, gently humming to itself, a tiny white light flickering on its front panel.

Raven moved across to Greg's private office and turned the handle. The door swung open, but like the main office it was unoccupied. Raven's torch picked out the surface of the desk and an image flashed through his mind of two bodies locked together in the throes of passion. He quickly put a lid on that.

'There's no one here,' said Becca.

They proceeded to the brewing hall.

'Marcus?' Raven's voice reverberated through the cavernous space. The only response was the bubbling and gurgling of the vats, like living, breathing beasts. He swung his flashlight and the beam reflected off the steel tanks, deepening the tall shadows on the far wall. He lifted the torch towards the metal walkway near the roof, but the light failed to penetrate the gloom.

They began to circle the perimeter of the hall, their feet scraping and echoing on the concrete floor. Raven thrust his torch into the ink-black spaces between the vats, around the backs of the steel pipes, along the dials and levers that governed them. Up close, the machinery radiated warmth. The rich, yeasty smell of fermenting malt was almost overpowering.

'What's that?' whispered Becca. She clutched his arm and pointed to the narrow space between two of the steel cylinders.

A sweep of the torch picked out a dark mass on the floor.

At first glance it could have been a sack of hops, but Raven knew it wasn't.

He approached cautiously until there could be no doubt. A body lay on the floor of the brewing hall in a crumpled heap, one leg splayed out, one arm bent at an impossible angle. The light from the torch slid along the body to the upturned face but Raven's gut already told him what he was going to see.

Marcus Earnshaw, eldest brother of Sam, and finance director of Salt Castle Brewery. His eyes gazed unseeingly into the void.

Raven knelt at his side and held two fingers to his neck, checking for a pulse. But there was no sign of life. The faithless husband, father and lover, was dead.

# CHAPTER 21

Raven took his journey to the brewery the next morning at a more sedate pace than the evening before. After the discovery of Marcus's body, he'd stayed there late into the night, securing the crime scene with Becca's assistance, and setting various processes in motion – arranging for the family to be informed, calling in the CSI team, notifying the coroner's office, and informing Gillian that he was no longer investigating an attempted murder, but the real thing. She hadn't been best pleased to hear that, but at least now she couldn't threaten to take him off the case.

When he'd eventually got home, he'd been so tired he couldn't even be bothered to be shocked by the devastation Barry had wrought. His kitchen was gone entirely and the bathroom was just a toilet and a temporary tap in the wall with a bucket underneath. Gone too were half the floorboards, leaving the downstairs little more than a shell. He'd seen more homely building sites.

Seriously, he couldn't continue to live there.

He'd been so exhausted that all he'd been capable of doing was hauling himself up the stairs and collapsing onto his bed, still in the shirt he'd worn that day. Yet sleep had been broken and fitful and he'd woken at the crack of dawn, dragged himself upright, changed into a clean shirt and tie, and headed out, unable to face the arrival of his builder or take another look at the carnage he had unleashed.

He'd rather face a murder scene than spend any more time in what remained of his home.

The cloud cover of the previous day had cleared, taking the mist with it and leaving only a sparkle of dew on the cold pavements. Raven trudged as far as the café, but only stopped long enough to pick up a bacon butty and a coffee in a styrofoam cup. He could eat in his car just as well as at a table, and with a comfier seat too.

He placed his drink in the cup holder, took a bite out of his sandwich, and slid the car into gear.

His phone rang as he was pulling up outside the brewery. He checked the caller display to see if he wanted to answer it. He didn't.

It was Lisa. Again. She was nothing if not persistent.

He considered letting the call go to voicemail, but knew that if he did she would keep on trying to reach him throughout the day. He couldn't hide from her forever. Whatever she wanted, it was best to get it out of the way so he could put her out of his mind.

He answered the call warily.

'Lisa.'

'Tom, at last! You've been avoiding me.'

He tried to gauge her tone. Mock annoyance. An undertone of playfulness. She wanted something from him.

'You know how it is. Work.'

'Work.' She held the word on her tongue, treating it with disdain. 'I guessed it would be. You haven't changed, Tom. Always the same excuse.'

Excuse? There was no need to give her excuses anymore. It was simply a reason. 'Well, I'm actually at a crime scene right now, so if there's something you want?'

'Just to talk, Tom. Is that too much to ask? Especially since I have just travelled all the way to the wilds of North Yorkshire to see you!'

In his astonishment he almost dropped the phone. 'You've done what?'

'I thought you knew. Didn't your colleague tell you I was here in Scarborough? Blonde, slim, quite pretty. Looked the sporty type. A local girl, judging from her accent.' Lisa couldn't keep the condescension from her voice even when she tried. She'd always made fun of Raven's northern roots.

'You spoke to Jess? Don't tell me you went to the station to look for me?'

'Well, where else was I supposed to find you? It's not like you left me a forwarding address.'

With good reason.

'Well, I can't talk now.'

Two uniformed officers were stationed outside the entrance to the brewery, and the CSI vans were lined up outside. One of the investigators was going into the building, all suited-up in white coveralls, a metal box of tricks under his arm. Holly Chang, the CSI boss, would probably be inside and Raven didn't want to keep her waiting. No doubt she would be complaining about missing her kids' swimming competition or some such thing and would hold Raven personally responsible for ruining her weekend. He didn't need a Yorkshire terrier snapping at his heels on top of everything else.

'I need to see you, Tom. When can we meet?' That was so like Lisa – demanding to know *when* they could meet, not *if*.

'Look, what is this about?' He knew she wouldn't have left London and travelled hundreds of miles to a part of the world she detested – the North – just because she missed him. Was something wrong? His thoughts turned suddenly to his daughter. 'It's not about Hannah is it? Is she all right?'

'Hannah's fine, don't panic. No, this is all about us.'

*Us.* Nice.

Except that there was no "us" anymore, only "him" and "her".

So perhaps this was it, the announcement he'd been expecting for some while. A divorce. Well, might as well get it done and dusted. Then he could put Lisa behind him and move on. Though why she hadn't simply got the lawyers to handle all the correspondence impersonally, he couldn't imagine. Did she really want to drag the process out?

'We could do dinner,' he offered. 'But I'll be busy all day.'

'Dinner would be lovely. I suppose I can keep myself entertained with a bracing walk along the seafront.' She made it sound like a punishment. 'Although the weather is a bit – what do you say in Yorkshire? *Parky?* I'll reserve a table at my hotel.'

'No.' Raven was determined that Lisa wasn't going to have everything her way. It would do her good to be at his beck and call for a change. 'I'll meet you at Quay Street at seven o'clock.' He gave her the house number. 'Now I really do have to go.'

★

As Raven slid the phone back into his jacket pocket, a rickety old Land Rover that looked like it would be more at home on a farm track turned into the car park and drew to a spluttering halt alongside Raven's BMW. The M6 may have been seventeen years old, but the Land Rover was even more ancient. Jess jumped out, giving the door a good slam behind her. 'Sir.'

As ever she was bright and cheerful, even though she'd been dragged into work unexpectedly on a Saturday morning.

'Morning, Jess. Good of you to give up your weekend. Hope you didn't have anything planned?'

'Nothing important, sir. Just a long walk with a friend.'

Her attention drifted to the line of CSI vans parked outside the brewery. 'I needed to talk to you anyway. A woman came to the station last night looking for you.' A pink flush crept into the young detective's cheeks. 'That is... I mean, your wife, sir. She said–'

'No worries,' said Raven, saving her from any further embarrassment over the matter. 'I've already dealt with it.'

'Okay, good.'

That ought to have ended the discussion, yet Jess stood waiting, her manner suggesting more than a passing interest in the arrival of the mysterious stranger from the South. Not to mention a curiosity to explore the uncharted waters of Raven's marital status.

She would have to stay curious, however. Raven was done talking about Lisa.

Another vehicle came into the car park. A blue Ford Focus, with Tony at the wheel. He parked neatly behind the Land Rover and got out.

'Morning, sir.'

Raven nodded his greetings. He now had a full complement of his team, such as it was. It was time to go inside and start work. The three detectives pulled on their crime scene coveralls and went into the brewery.

There, the CSI people were busy, moving around the ground floor and along the walkway that spanned the upper level. Holly Chang was standing by the body and Raven decided it was best to tackle her before he did anything else. He'd already dealt with his wife that morning. How much worse could an encounter with the diminutive head of CSI be?

Quite a lot worse, if previous experience was anything to go by. Even though Holly reached scarcely five feet in her head-to-toe one-piece, the CSI boss packed a punch much greater than her physical stature.

He braced himself for some well-directed sarcasm or a round of complaints.

She looked up as he approached. 'Ah, DCI Raven. Good morning. Or I daresay it would have been if this hadn't happened.' She indicated the body of Marcus Earnshaw, which was still lying where Raven had found it. Photographed, searched and examined, but otherwise undisturbed. 'Buggered up my weekend lie-in, that's for certain.'

'Well,' parried Raven, 'I'm sure he's having a worse day than either of us.'

'So far,' returned Holly darkly from behind her face mask.

Raven knelt down beside the body. As he'd observed the previous night, Marcus had apparently fallen from the metal walkway that spanned the upper level of the brewery. Part of the safety railing had come away and was lying underneath the body. A tangle of steel and flesh.

'He's made a proper Jackson Pollock of the place, hasn't he?' remarked Holly. 'I don't envy the poor sod who has the job of scrubbing this floor afterwards.'

The concrete flooring around the body was stained a dark cherry red, pooling where the skull had fractured, running in tiny rivulets into the pocks and cracks of the floor. Not to mention the spots and splashes forming a halo for several feet around.

'Hydrogen peroxide and a good hard scrubbing brush,' said Holly. 'But it'll be a right bugger to get the last of it off.'

Raven decided to accept her cleaning tip as a gesture of conciliation. 'What have you found so far?' he asked.

'Mobile phone, wallet, car keys. Plenty of cash in his wallet, so doesn't look like robbery, but I guess you'd already worked that out.'

Raven pointed to the metal walkway running overhead. 'What have you found up there? Any signs of a struggle?'

'Let me show you.'

Raven allowed Holly to lead him up the steps and onto the overhead platform. It was no more than three feet wide, just enough to accommodate them single file. The plastic coverings over Raven's shoes dulled the sound of his footsteps, but even so, the metal sang as he climbed. From the top, he could see right across the brewery to an internal window in the offices opposite. Bright sunlight poured in through glass panels in the roof.

He grasped the metal railings that lined each edge of the walkway. They reached to waist height even on him, and seemed solidly fixed. It wouldn't have been easy to dislodge them.

But when they reached the spot from which Marcus had fallen, it quickly became obvious that along a length of several metres the safety barrier had come away completely, leaving an unprotected drop to the floor below.

'Someone deliberately removed the screws that were holding this in place,' said Holly. 'Any weight against this part of the barrier, and you'd have toppled straight over the side.'

Raven peered down at the bloodstained floor below.

'We've dusted the railing for prints, obviously,' said Holly.

'But if someone took the trouble to remove the screws before luring Marcus up here,' Raven reasoned, 'they probably had the sense to wear gloves while they did it.'

'Well, you're a real glass-half-empty kind of person, aren't you?'

Was that a hint of grudging approval from the CSI boss? It was impossible to tell from behind her face mask. But Raven sensed a thawing of relations between the two of them. Maybe she wasn't quite the dragon he'd first thought.

'Anything else?' he enquired.

Holly pointed across to the internal window opposite. 'My tech guy Scott is in the office now, checking for camera footage. You know, just in case the killer posed for a photo before going about their business.'

Raven grinned. 'Just in case.'

It seemed that there was little more for him to do at the crime scene itself. He ran his eyes one last time along the shiny metal pipes and cylinders and the dials and displays that monitored their operation. The system was still running, uninterrupted by the drama that had unfolded here. The finance director of the brewery may be dead, but the brewing of beer continued unabated.

*

Raven found Scott in the company of Jess. Scott was seated in one of the office chairs, Jess leaning over him, stray wisps of her long golden hair brushing his cheek. The two of them jumped apart as he entered, reinstating an invisible force field between them. Raven paused by the door. 'Not interrupting anything am I?'

'No, sir.' Jess blushed again in that fetching way she did, the pink climbing up the back of her neck. 'Scott was just showing me what he'd found on the CCTV.'

'Was he, indeed?' Raven had encountered the quiet CSI tech guy before, but had never spoken to him. It was, admittedly, hard to get a word in when Holly was in full flow but even so, Scott seemed to be an unusually quiet chap.

So much the better. That was fine with Raven.

He took a closer look at the young techie, reassessing him in the light of what he'd just observed. It was impossible to see Scott's face in the crime scene getup he was wearing, but he was clearly a tall guy, youthful and languid in his movements, a whisper of blond hair curling out from beneath his white hood.

'So, what have you got for us, Scott?'

'Nothing, I'm afraid.'

'Nothing? There's always something on camera, however insignificant.'

'Not in this case, sir,' said Jess. 'Scott was just explaining it to me when you came in. The footage has been deleted.'

'Someone deliberately erased it?'

'That's right,' said Scott. 'All the files are gone. Whoever did it knew the passcode. We dusted the computer keyboard for prints, but that was wiped clean too.'

'And there's nothing you can do to recover the data?'

'Sorry, no.'

Raven hadn't been expecting much from the CCTV. Whoever had pushed Marcus off the walkway clearly knew their way around the brewery and would know where the cameras were placed and how to avoid them. But he was still disappointed to find zilch. 'So they wiped the CCTV footage and then they cleaned the keyboard and the railing. They seem to have covered their tracks rather well. Holly doesn't think they left any trace behind at all.'

'Unless,' Jess suggested, 'the post-mortem uncovers something on the body itself.'

'Good thinking. Why don't you call the pathologist and get the PM fast-tracked?' Not too likely on a Saturday, especially when the local pathologist seemed to have taken a strong personal dislike to him on a previous case.

But you never knew. Maybe for once the glass would turn out to be half full.

One of the CSI juniors entered the office. 'DCI Raven? There's someone to see you outside.'

'I'm on my way.'

There was nothing more for Raven to do inside the building. So far all his hopes of finding a lead had been thoroughly dashed. Perhaps this newcomer would have something to offer.

★

'I want to see him. Let me see my son.' Greg Earnshaw's booming voice was clearly audible as Raven approached the exit of the brewery.

The grieving father was being held back by the two police constables on duty outside the building. 'Please calm down, sir. The officer in charge is on his way.'

When Raven stepped outside, Greg stopped his struggle. He locked eyes with Raven. 'Is it true what I've been told? Is Marcus dead?'

Raven motioned for the constables to release Greg from their grip. 'I'm afraid so. Come with me. Let's go somewhere more private.'

But Greg stood still as a rock. 'I want to see him, Raven. I have a right to see my son.'

'We'll need you to identify the body, but not until it's been taken to the mortuary.'

'No! I want to see him now.' Greg faltered. 'I need to. I have to know it's him. Don't you understand?'

Raven softened his voice. 'I understand perfectly well. But this is a crime scene now and there are procedures that have to be followed. I can't allow you inside until the CSI people have completed their work. The mortuary van should be here any moment. I'll ask one of my constables to drive to the hospital with you, and you can view his body there. Believe me, it will be better that way.'

Greg swallowed a sob. 'I can't believe this has happened. Not after what happened to Sam.' He looked like a man who was utterly defeated. 'You can't imagine what this has done to my poor wife. Denise will never get over this.' He pressed his thumb and forefinger into his eye sockets and tried to control his breathing which was coming in ragged gasps.

When he had composed himself, Raven took him gently by the arm and led him away from the entrance. Greg came like a lamb, all anger spent.

They started to walk together around the perimeter of the car park. 'Greg, we need to understand what happened here last night. Why was Marcus working late at the brewery?'

'It wasn't so unusual. Marcus worked from home a lot of the time, but would often come to the brewery for a meeting or if he needed to do something.'

'Did you see him yourself last night?'

'Yes, I was here when he arrived, late afternoon. He was busy with the year-end accounts. We were due to have a board meeting to discuss them. That will have to be postponed now.'

'And who else was in the office yesterday afternoon?'

'Well, Sandra, of course, and Ellie.' His brow darkened. 'And Anthony came in later too.'

That must have been after Raven had interviewed him. 'Were you expecting Anthony to show up yesterday?'

'Not really. He'd only just got back from his trip to Edinburgh.'

And he was at least a couple of whiskies worse for wear when he did show his face. 'How did he seem?'

Greg stopped walking and turned to face Raven. 'Why are you asking me about Anthony?'

'I need to know what happened, Greg. Step by step. Who was present, what they did. That's how we're going to get to the bottom of this and find out who killed your son.'

Greg nodded his understanding. He took a deep breath before continuing. 'Anthony was in quite a state. I could hear his voice from inside my office, so I came out to see what was going on.'

'And what was going on?'

'All hell was breaking loose.'

'I think you'd better explain.'

With a visible struggle, Greg mastered his emotions again. 'Anthony had clearly been drinking. I could see it in the way he behaved. Dammit, I could even smell it on his breath. He told me he'd come to see Marcus. He demanded to speak to him outside. He wouldn't say what it was about. I said no and told him to go away and calm himself down, but Marcus insisted on going with him. They went outside and had a blazing row. Bloody awkward it was, I can tell you, in full view of anyone who cared to watch.'

'What was the argument about?'

Greg looked away from Raven, unable or unwilling to maintain eye contact. 'No idea. I'm not an eavesdropper.'

'Could it have been about Naomi?'

Greg turned back and gave him an appraising look. 'I

can see you've got your sources, Raven.' He lifted his gaze to the distant peak of Oliver's Mount, his eyes searching for something far away, or perhaps within himself. 'It's not something I'm proud to say about my own flesh and blood, but as the eldest, Marcus always had a sense of entitlement, as if he thought he could have whatever he wanted.'

'In this case, his brother's wife.'

Greg sighed. 'I thought they were going to come to blows. They're both fine men, big and strong. I was all ready to go out and pull them apart. But once he'd said his piece, Anthony stormed off. Ellie went home, and so did I. Marcus insisted on staying behind. He said he'd lock up. That was the last I saw of him.'

By the time they finished talking, a black-liveried ambulance had arrived and Marcus's body was being loaded into the back. Raven called one of the constables over. 'Take Mr Earnshaw to the hospital. He needs to be with his son.'

# CHAPTER 22

Although Raven had identified himself over the intercom, the door to Anthony's apartment opened on a short chain, and Naomi didn't remove it until she'd made certain it was Raven and that he was alone.

'I was afraid it might be Anthony,' she murmured as he entered the apartment.

She had obviously heard the news about Marcus and feared what her husband might do to her.

Naomi appeared greatly changed from when Raven had first met her, only the previous afternoon. Shock and grief had robbed her of her beauty. Devoid of makeup she was much plainer, more vulnerable looking. Her hair was dishevelled, her skin sallow. The dark rings under her eyes told him she'd had a sleepless night. She wore a long, loose-fitting cardigan, the sleeves pulled down low over the backs of her hands.

'Come through,' she said in a listless voice as if she had no fight left in her. She sat down on one of the sofas, tucking her feet under her, hugging her cardigan around her thin frame.

'Where's Anthony?' asked Raven, taking the sofa

opposite.

Naomi shook her head. 'I don't know. He didn't come home last night.' She tugged at the sleeves on her cardigan, pulling a loose thread. 'I got a call from Denise about ten o'clock to say that Marcus had been... been found d... dead.' She stuffed her fist into her mouth, her shoulders shaking. 'God, sorry, it's just so awful. I can't take it in.' She grabbed a handful of tissues from a box beside her.

Raven waited patiently while she dabbed her eyes and blew her nose. 'When did you last see him?' he asked once she'd composed herself.

'When I left the apartment to go to the gym. By the time I returned, he'd gone out. I haven't seen him since.'

'Have you tried phoning him?'

She shook her head. 'I... I didn't...' She regarded Raven through teary eyes. 'I don't have anything to say to him.'

'Do you know where he might have gone?'

'No idea. There's no shortage of hotels in Scarborough, is there? Or he could be miles away by now. He took his car with him, and he's used to travelling.'

Raven would have to call Tony and ask him to notify the ports and airports to look out for Anthony. They'd need to put a watch on the ANPR network to locate his car if he was on the road. And they'd also have to start checking local hotels and guest houses. They were facing a monumental task and he would need to speak to Gillian and request more resources.

But right now he was dealing with a grieving woman who was also an important witness. 'Tell me about you and Marcus. How long had the affair been going on?'

Naomi heaved a great sigh. 'A couple of years. I never intended it to happen. I love my husband, or at least I did.'

Raven waited for her to go on, in the knowledge that silence was often the best way to make a witness open up. After a while Naomi spoke again, as he'd known she would.

'Anthony was always away, travelling on business. I was

lonely here on my own. God, that makes me sound pathetic, doesn't it? But I'm being honest with you. I wanted Anthony to get a job that didn't involve so much travelling, but he was dedicated to his role in the *family firm*.' She spoke the last two words with a passion. 'It was as if his job was more important than our marriage. But Marcus was sympathetic. And he had his own problems too.'

'Such as?'

'You've met his wife, Olivia? All she ever wanted was kids. For her, it was like Marcus was just a means to an end. The perfect home, the perfect family... all of his money went on paying the mortgage for their big house, on buying the latest kitchen appliances, on things for the baby. But Marcus didn't really want children, and he certainly didn't want his wife to turn into a mumsy creature more interested in puréed carrots than in him. I think she may even have tricked him into having a baby. You know they hadn't slept together since Freddie was born?'

Raven listened dispassionately as Naomi listed her grievances and justifications for her behaviour. Growing up with an alcoholic father had prepared him well to understand such self-pity. The whole world had been Alan Raven's enemy – everyone to blame but himself. In Naomi's mind, she and Marcus had no doubt been lonely, misunderstood victims trapped in loveless marriages. She would probably say anything to excuse her actions. Yet from the very beginning she must have understood the hurt the affair would cause when it came to light, as it inevitably would. Her protests now were a smokescreen, intended to deceive herself just as much as him.

'A year ago, on the night of the party,' said Raven, 'Sam saw you and Marcus together.'

She had the decency to look abashed, casting her eyes down. 'That was a mistake. It should never have happened. We'd been so careful until then. But that night... well, I guess we'd both had too much to drink.'

'When I asked you about the party before, you told me

that you'd spent the whole evening sitting with Olivia and Denise.'

'I spent *most* of the evening with them,' she shot back defiantly. 'But I needed to get away and have a break, and that was when I bumped into Marcus, and… he just pulled me inside the office for a quick kiss.'

'It was more than a quick kiss, from what I gather.'

She squirmed in her seat, unwilling to say a word.

'You must have known that Sam had seen you.'

A blush infused her pale cheeks. 'Of course I did. I pulled my clothes back on and went downstairs. Marcus went looking for Sam. He wanted to explain, to put things right. But he couldn't find him anywhere. He didn't know that Sam had gone outside in the rain.'

'Anthony told me that Marcus *did* go outside. He said he'd seen him with wet hair.'

Naomi looked shocked. 'Anthony said that? But no, it was Anthony who went outside. I saw him coming back through the door. He thought no one had seen him.'

'When was this?'

'Some while before the taxi driver arrived with the news about Sam.'

Raven stared at her, trying to gauge who was telling the truth: Naomi or Anthony. Was it Marcus, her lover, who had gone outside that night, or Anthony, her husband? What possible motive could she have for protecting Marcus, now that he was dead? It seemed more likely that Anthony was lying – that he had been trying to point suspicion at his brother.

'Anyway, it wasn't really Sam you had to worry about, was it?' pressed Raven. 'It was Anthony. When did he find out about the affair?'

'That was also the night of the party. I don't know if he saw us, or if Sam said something to him before he disappeared, but… Anthony found out that night.'

'What was his reaction?'

'What do you think? We had a blazing row when we got home. I promised to stop seeing Marcus, and I did for a while... but then it started again after Freddie was born.'

'Does Olivia know about the affair?'

Naomi looked stricken. 'No! She lives in her own baby-filled world, she doesn't see what's going on around her. You won't tell her, will you? What good would come of it now that Marcus is dead? Olivia's a good person – I never meant to hurt her.'

Raven was making no promises about what he might have to tell Olivia. Secrets had a way of finding their own way to the surface once a murder inquiry began. He paused a moment before asking his next question. 'In your opinion, is Anthony capable of killing Marcus?'

Naomi pursed her lips thoughtfully. The fact that she hadn't responded with an immediate denial, coupled with the fear that had been evident in her behaviour when he arrived spoke volumes. 'It's not something you want to believe of the person you're married to, but...' She left the words unspoken. 'You will find him, won't you? I... I'm afraid of what he might do if he comes back here.'

He could see the fear in her eyes. Even though she'd been unable to say it out loud, she clearly believed that Anthony had killed Marcus. Now she feared for her own life.

'Is there anyone you can stay with, until Anthony is found?'

She shook her head. 'No, I'll be fine. I'll stay here and keep the door locked and I won't go out. If Anthony shows up, I won't let him in. I'll call you.'

*

Raven was on the phone to Tony the instant he left Naomi's apartment. 'Tony, grab a pen and write this down. I need you to start a search for Anthony Earnshaw.'

'Sir, I was just about to call you. I have news.'

'Tell me in a moment, Tony. Listen, start by notifying the ports and airports in case he tries to travel abroad and then–'

'Sir? There's no need for that. I know where Anthony is.'

Raven ran to a stop, his list of tasks forgotten. 'You do? Where?'

'I just got a call from Gavin Thompson, the head brewer. Anthony is currently on his sofa, sleeping off a hangover.'

Well, that was easy. Raven's glass was turning out to be half-full after all. 'Text me the address,' he told Tony. 'I'll meet you there. And while you're at it, arrange for a couple of uniforms to get over there too. We'll bring Anthony in for questioning.'

He slipped the phone back into his jacket pocket and returned to his car. The sun had risen fully now, and the day looked like it was going to turn out glorious. A blue sky and a calm sea, waves gently lapping against the shore. Sunlight brushed the empty beach, turning dull sand into gold.

Yes, perhaps this would be the day his luck finally turned.

The address Tony texted was on Longwestgate, halfway up the steep hill that rose from the harbour up to St Mary's Church near the castle. Raven approached it from above, turning down the steep street of Tollergate. The cobbled road was about as wide as his car, and he prayed he didn't meet another vehicle coming up. He bumped his way down to the junction with Longwestgate, then nosed the long wheelbase of the M6 around the ninety-degree turn, almost scraping the paintwork against the bricks of the corner house. These old streets were a nightmare for driving round, and worse for parking, even off season.

He managed to squeeze the car into a tight spot between two other vehicles before getting out and proceeding on foot. At moments like this he could almost understand Becca's desire for a pocket-sized car like the Honda Jazz.

Almost.

As its name suggested, Longwestgate was indeed very long. Raven passed row after row of charming – if in some cases dilapidated – fishermen's cottages, interspersed with occasional views of the sea. Gavin Thompson, however, didn't live in a cottage but in a ground-floor flat in a four-storey block set back from the road and reached, inevitably, by a flight of steps.

Raven paused for a quick rest, then took the steps slowly, careful not to put undue weight on his bad leg. The marked police car was parked discreetly in the street and his DC was waiting for him outside the door to the flats.

'Good work, Tony. Have you been in yet?'

'Just to check he's still here, sir. He hasn't woken up yet.'

'Must be one hell of a hangover. Come on, let's go and have a word with the brewer first.' Raven signalled for the uniformed officers to wait outside the entrance to the flat, then followed Tony inside.

It seemed that not everyone who worked at the brewery was receiving the lucrative rewards that Greg, Anthony and, until very recently, Marcus were enjoying. Gavin's flat was small, barely big enough for one person, let alone two. It was tattered too, and could have used a fresh coat of paint, not to mention some new carpets. Then again, as everyone had said so often, the business was all about family. Gavin Thompson may have been right at the heart of the company since it was founded, but he wasn't a blood relative.

And in any case, Raven was hardly in a position to point out scuffs on the paintwork and stains on the carpet. At least Gavin's place wasn't missing half the floor.

He found the brewer in the tiny kitchen at the back of the flat, sitting at a Formica-topped table, cradling a mug of coffee in his big hands, smoking a cigarette. He seemed too large for such a small room, with broad shoulders, a high domed head and a big nose that looked to have been broken at least once. This morning he was unshaven and dressed in a baggy grey T-shirt over black jogging pants.

The slogan on his mug read, "Sod this. I'd rather be drinking beer." He looked up as Raven entered. 'Coffee?'

'Please.' There were no fancy gadgets on display in Gavin's kitchen. Instead, the brewer flicked on the kettle and heaped some granules into a Leeds United mug while Raven took a seat.

'How d'you take it?'

'Black, no sugar.' Raven waited for the kettle to rumble and shake itself to the boil while Tony watched from the kitchen doorway.

Gavin filled the mug and brought it over, resuming his place at the small table. He tapped his cigarette on a glass ashtray that looked like it had been pinched from a pub. In the days when smoking was still allowed in pubs.

Raven inhaled, the sharp aroma reminding him of the bad habit he'd kicked a long time ago. He could never quite decide if he missed the acrid smell, or if it disgusted him. Maybe both. Either way, he was well shot of it. 'So,' he said, 'can you tell me how Anthony ended up here?'

Gavin sucked at the cigarette, making the tip glow orange. He blew smoke at the ceiling. 'I bumped into him on the way to the pub. Or, more accurately, he bumped into me. He'd already had a few. To be honest, I was surprised to see him at this end of town. It's not his usual haunt, down by the harbourside. But he offered to buy me a beer and so we got chatting.'

'What time was this?'

'About ten. I'd just popped out for a quick pint before bed.'

'Live alone, do you?'

'Aye, it's just me here.' Although worn, the kitchen was clean and tidy, everything in its place, much to Raven's approval.

'So, what did the pair of you talk about?'

Gavin tapped ash into the ashtray and took a sip of his coffee. 'I asked him about his trip to Edinburgh, and he told me how it had gone. But then he started talking about personal stuff. It was a bit awkward, but I've known

Anthony ever since he was a kid, so I suppose he trusts me. Anyway, once he'd started there was no stopping him. He told me his wife was having an affair with Marcus.' Gavin took a final drag on his cigarette before squashing it into the ashtray. 'Of course I knew about the bust-up between the two brothers at the brewery yesterday. A very public way of letting off steam. But understandable, I suppose, when your brother's been sleeping with your wife. Anthony was still very emotional – angry one minute, in tears the next. He told me he'd thought the affair was over, but he'd just found out it was still going on.'

Raven nodded glumly, knowing that it was his own intervention that had tipped off Anthony about what was happening between Marcus and Naomi.

'Did he tell you what he'd been doing since the argument with Marcus?'

'Getting tanked up.' Gavin stared into his coffee mug. 'I tried to get him to pace himself, but he seemed intent on drinking himself into oblivion. He was mad, absolutely furious with Marcus. He kept saying, "He's a dead man!" I told him to calm down, but he kept repeating it. At the time, I didn't think anything of it. It's just a turn of phrase, right? But when Greg called me this morning and told me about Marcus, I started to wonder if there was more to it. That's when I decided I'd better call the police.'

'You made the right call,' said Raven. 'How did Anthony end up back here?'

'By chucking-out time, he was in no state to go anywhere. I could have called him a taxi, but it was obvious that he didn't want to go home to his wife. So I brought him back here to sleep it off. He's been out like a light ever since.'

Raven took a sip of his coffee. It was stale and musty, not a patch on what Olivia or Naomi had provided for him. But it was hot and black, and a man with no kitchen of his own could hardly grumble. 'You've been working with Greg since the beginning, haven't you?'

Gavin seemed glad of something new to talk about.

'Aye. The good old days. It was just me, Greg and Jeremy back then. Plus Sandra, of course. Sandra was there from the start.'

'And you know the Earnshaw family well?'

Gavin cracked a smile. 'Me, Greg and Jeremy were at school together. We always said we'd do something together. I never imagined we actually would. It was all down to Greg, really. He was always the boss, even when we were kids. So, yeah, I'd say I know Greg and Denise as well as anyone, and I've known the boys since they were babies.'

'Were there any difficulties between Anthony and Jeremy?'

Gavin wrapped his fingers around the now empty coffee mug, his bald head creasing into a frown. 'Now why are you asking me about Jeremy?'

Raven didn't answer him directly. 'When I spoke to Marcus about Jeremy, he told me that if anyone had a reason for wanting Jeremy dead it was – but he didn't say who.'

'I don't know what he meant.'

Raven persisted. 'You've known Jeremy and Anthony for a long time and you worked with them too. Perhaps they had an argument? Or there were rumours about some kind of disagreement at work?'

'I don't know what you're getting at, but I long had suspicions there was bad blood between those two. Money, was my guess.'

'Something to do with the proposed merger?'

'No. Jeremy died long before the idea of a merger was put forward. But anyway, I don't get involved with the business side of things. I just make the beer.'

A door off the hallway creaked open and a bleary-eyed Anthony emerged. He staggered into the hallway, a hand pressed to his head. He was still in the clothes he'd been wearing when Raven had interviewed him the previous afternoon, but the clean-cut and suave sales director had been transformed into an ashen-faced wreck of his former self. 'Hey, Gavin, got any Paracetamol?'

He lumbered down the hallway, one hand groping for the wall, the other shading his bloodshot eyes from the morning light. He could barely stand up straight and didn't appear to have registered the presence of two police detectives in the kitchen.

Raven moved to intercept him. 'Anthony Earnshaw, I am arresting you on suspicion of...'

He got no further before Anthony lurched into the bathroom off the hallway. Violent retching sounds ensued as he proceeded to chuck his guts up. He dropped to his knees on the linoleum floor and chundered away, succeeding in getting most of it in the toilet pan.

Raven stood back, arms folded, waiting for it to come to an end. He had witnessed the same scene a hundred times over as a child, watching as his father emptied himself of the previous night's drink, sometimes filled with remorse for his behaviour, sometimes ready for more of the same.

Raven had no sympathy for drunks. How could he? He had seen what they could do.

When it was over, even the flushing of the toilet and the running of the bathroom tap couldn't mask the stink of bile and vomit. The two uniforms stepped forward gingerly and seized Anthony by the arms.

'Take him to the police station and give him something to settle his stomach,' said Raven as they hauled the arrested man to his feet. 'We'll interview him as soon as he's sobered up.'

He watched as Anthony was led away.

'Chuffing hell,' said Gavin, rising from his chair. 'That's the thanks you get when you bring drunks home.' He lifted one meaty hand to signal farewell to Raven. 'Bet you're glad he's not going in your car.'

# CHAPTER 23

It ought to have been a day of celebration. Becca had been looking forward to it for so long, imagining the smiling faces, the fond farewells from the nursing staff, the moment when she would have Sam beside her in the car. He was going home at last, back to his parents' house, after more than a year.

Dr Kirtlington had done his very best to dissuade him from leaving, but Sam was adamant and eventually even the doctor had decided sensibly to stand aside. Sam would need to return to hospital for regular physiotherapy sessions, but he was finally being discharged as a patient.

The hospital consultant had taken Becca to one side before allowing Sam to leave. 'You understand that this is against my clinical advice. I would prefer Sam to remain in hospital for a while longer so that he can be given the care he needs. If he goes home, he will need close monitoring, and a great deal of support.'

'I understand that, Doctor, but he'll be in the best possible place, with people who care for him.' Yet even as Becca spoke the words, a heavy weight tugged at her. Someone had tried to kill Sam, and the day that should have been one of joy had been completely overshadowed by the shocking discovery of Marcus's body on the floor of the brewing hall. A killer was out there, and maybe it would be better to keep Sam in the safe environment of the hospital.

Yet one look at his face told her how desperate he was to leave, and she wasn't going to stand in his way.

She put on a brave front as she thanked the nurses for everything they'd done. Some of them were quite emotional seeing him go. He'd clearly become a favourite. There were hugs and kisses and more jokes about running the Yorkshire marathon. And then it was just the two of them, Becca wheeling Sam down the corridors that had become as familiar to her as her own home.

Outside, it was cold but sunny, with a crisp edge to the light that sharpened everything into focus. Becca knew she would remember this day for the rest of her life.

She had parked the Jazz as close as possible to the hospital entrance. She'd even cleaned and tidied it in readiness, and lowered the back seat so that they'd be able to accommodate the folding wheelchair that Sam would rely on until he had fully recovered the strength in his limbs.

She helped him into the passenger seat, folded the wheelchair and loaded it into the back, and then climbed in beside him. Only then did she turn to him and say, 'I'm so sorry about Marcus.' She took his hand in hers.

For a moment, they sat there, neither of them speaking. What was there to say? Sam's brother was dead. How did you move on from such a tragedy?

*One day at a time.* Exactly how Becca had kept herself going since the night of the hit and run. Had it got any easier as time went by? Not really – just more routine.

Eventually, Sam said, 'Do you know how he fell? Did someone push him?'

So far the official police position was that they were treating the death as suspicious. But Becca had seen the crime scene for herself. It was more than suspicious. It was murder.

'Raven's leading the investigation,' she told him, taking refuge behind formal police language. 'We'll have to wait for the results of the post-mortem and for forensics to report their findings.'

She could tell from his face that she'd misjudged her reply. 'I'm not some member of the public, Becs. Marcus was my brother.'

She nodded, knowing that he deserved more from her. 'The truth is that we can't be certain yet, but it looked to me as if someone pushed him to his death.'

'The same way someone pushed me.'

He'd said out loud exactly what she'd been thinking ever since discovering the body at the brewery. But who would do such a thing, and why?

'You know,' said Sam, 'I told you that I was carrying Marcus's umbrella when I was pushed into the road. I had my back to the brewery, I didn't see the face of my attacker and they didn't see mine. In the dark and the rain, they might easily have mistaken me for Marcus.'

This was another of the thoughts that had been nagging at Becca since Sam had told her what he remembered. 'Do you think Marcus was the intended victim all along?'

'Don't you?'

There was no point denying it. The facts were staring them both in the face. Two attacks on two brothers, one of whom could easily have been mistaken for the other. And now one of them was dead.

In a way the thought was comforting. If Marcus had been the target all along, then Sam wasn't in any danger. Right?

'Anthony's been arrested,' said Sam. 'Hasn't he? Don't try to hide it from me.'

'I'm sorry,' said Becca. 'I really am.' She knew how much Sam loved his brothers. The idea that one was now dead at the hands of the other and that Sam had been pushed into the path of a speeding vehicle by that same brother was too awful to contemplate. She turned the key in the ignition. 'Come on, let me take you home.'

\*

It took time for a drunk to sober up, but by the afternoon Raven judged that Anthony was in a fit state to be interviewed. He sent Tony off to the custody suite and arranged for the solicitor to be notified.

The delay had given him time to do some housekeeping. His first action had been to phone Naomi and reassure her that Anthony was in custody and that she was safe. Greg had confirmed that the body in the mortuary was indeed that of his eldest son and Raven had sent Jess to the hospital. He was hoping to hear back from her to find out when the autopsy was likely to take place. While it certainly looked like Marcus had been pushed from the walkway, it would be good to know for sure.

The phone on his desk rang as he was waiting for Anthony's solicitor to arrive. 'Raven.'

A stern feminine voice proceeded to give him a good telling off. Raven recognised the icy articulation of Dr Felicity Wainwright, Senior Pathologist at Scarborough Hospital. 'DCI Raven, I understand that you have put in a request for a post-mortem to be carried out as a matter of urgency.'

'Yes, that's right.' After a previous encounter with the misanthropic pathologist, Raven had walked away very much the worse for wear, and he girded his loins in preparation for another bruising skirmish.

'On a Saturday. Do you not understand the meaning of the term "working day"?'

Raven grimaced. It was tempting to remark that he was spending his own day off behind his desk, and that the pathologist must have known that because she'd dialled his work number, but he bit back his tongue. Confrontation wouldn't help. He aimed for a more placatory tone. 'I know that it's short notice, but—'

'Don't bother to grovel,' snapped Dr Wainwright. 'I

hate it when men grovel. Anyway, I've already done it.'

Raven's mouth opened in astonishment. 'You have?'

'Death at a brewery. Never had one of those before. I was intrigued. A pity the corpse wasn't found headfirst in a butt of malmsey wine.'

The reference was lost on Raven. 'Sorry?'

'The Duke of Clarence,' said Dr Wainwright witheringly. 'Accused of plotting treason against his brother, King Edward. Didn't you study Shakespeare at school? *Richard III*. "Now is the winter of our discontent."'

'I must have missed that lesson,' said Raven. Fortunately a knowledge of English literature hadn't been required to join the army. Or the police for that matter.

'Anyway, our man didn't drown in a vat of wine. He came to a much more mundane end. I explained it all to the detective who attended.'

That would be Jess, presumably. 'I haven't spoken to her yet,' said Raven. 'Would it be possible to summarise your findings for me?'

After her brief bout of loquaciousness, Dr Wainwright returned to her clipped, acid syllables. 'It'll be in my written report.'

'And when will that be ready?'

'Two working days.'

Raven grimaced. Why had the pathologist bothered to phone him if she had nothing useful to tell him? Had it all been to show off her superior education? Or did she simply enjoy tormenting him? He strongly suspected the latter. 'I'm about to go into an interview with a suspect. Perhaps you wouldn't mind running over the main points for me now?'

'Very well.' Raven detected a grudging willingness to be helpful. 'The body displays injuries consistent with a fall from height. Fracture of the thoracic spine along the thoracolumbar junction. But that wasn't fatal. Neither was the internal bleeding, although it probably would have been, given time. No, it was the blunt trauma to the skull that finished him off. Cracked his head open on the concrete floor.'

The cause of death was pretty much what Raven had already surmised. Marcus had fallen off the walkway and died of his injuries. 'I was particularly interested in whether there was anything that might help to identify his attacker. DNA traces under his fingernails, for example?'

'You think he was pushed?' Dr Wainwright's interest picked up. 'I'm sorry, but there was nothing to indicate that.'

Another dead end. And given the meticulous way that Marcus's killer had wiped away all physical evidence and video recordings that might have identified them, he couldn't say he was surprised.

'Is there anything else I can help you with?' Was that a hint of morbid curiosity in the pathologist's voice? Dr Wainwright might display a strong contempt for the living, but her interest in the deceased was unhealthily strong.

'There is something, actually,' said Raven. 'Did you carry out the post-mortem on Jeremy Green?'

'The walker who fell off a cliff. I remember it well. Do you have a problem with my conclusions?'

'No, not at all,' said Raven hurriedly, not wanting to antagonise Dr Wainwright now that she was showing signs of cooperation. 'I simply wanted to ask your view on the coroner's ruling.'

'Accidental death. The coroner had no choice. There was no evidence to the contrary.'

Exactly what everyone kept telling him. 'Okay, but were you surprised by that?'

Dr Wainwright sniffed dismissively. 'DCI Raven, in my profession, I'm *never* surprised. Death, as you must surely realise by now, is an inevitability.'

'So it didn't bother you that an experienced walker, who fell to his death while walking a familiar route, was ruled to have done so accidentally?'

When the pathologist delivered her final reply, the scorn in her voice was back to full throttle. 'Chief Inspector, you haven't been paying attention to my words.

What I said was that the coroner *had no choice* in ruling accidental death. I didn't suggest for a moment that I agreed with the verdict.'

# CHAPTER 24

Despite his crumpled shirt, unshaven face and bloodshot eyes, the sales and marketing manager of Salt Castle Brewery looked a lot more human than when he'd staggered out of Gavin Thompson's front room that morning hunting for the nearest toilet to stick his head down. Nevertheless, despite the best efforts of the custody officer, the smell of stale alcohol and vomit lingered on, reaching into every corner of the interview room with its nasty fingers.

Tony placed a fresh cup of black coffee in front of him and took a seat next to Raven.

Across the table, Anthony's lawyer watched the development like a hawk. A small man, neatly dressed with a plain navy tie. This was no small-town budget lawyer. The Earnshaw family had money to spend, and weren't leaving anything to chance.

Raven kicked off the interview with a broad smile and an easy opening. 'How's your head, Anthony? Feeling better?'

*Police interview technique 101. Build rapport. Use casual conversation to encourage the suspect to open up.*

Anthony blew on his coffee and took a tentative sip. 'A little.'

'Good. Glad to hear that.'

The lawyer cleared his throat in annoyance. 'DCI Raven, I have advised my client not to respond to questions unless they are pertinent to the matter in hand.'

*Yeah, how well is that working?*

'You were lucky you bumped into Gavin last night. He took good care of you.'

The lawyer shot his client a stern warning and Anthony clammed up, sipping his coffee and saying nothing.

*So much for that tactic. Time to try a different approach.*

Raven put his elbows on the table and leaned in. 'All right, then. Time for some *pertinent* questions. Let's start with what happened twelve months ago, at the office party.'

The gambit took Anthony by surprise, throwing him off guard just as Raven had intended. 'What? You already asked me all about that yesterday.'

'And now I'm asking you again.'

But the lawyer was having none of it. 'DCI Raven, how is this relevant to the events that took place last night?'

Raven offered him a cryptic smile, then returned his attention to Anthony as if it was just the two of them in the room having a cosy chat. 'When we spoke yesterday, you told me that you and Marcus got on really well and trusted each other completely. But that wasn't true, was it?'

'I did get on well with him,' said Anthony.

'And trusted him?'

Silence.

Raven let it drag on, but Anthony refused to be drawn.

'Let me spell it out,' said Raven, 'just so there can be no doubt why this is relevant. On the night of the office party, you discovered that Marcus was having an affair with your wife. Correct?'

'No, I only found out yesterday.'

'There's no point lying, Anthony. Naomi told us herself that you discovered it a year ago. Can you confirm that?'

Anthony grunted.

'Please give a verbal response for the tape recorder.'

'Yes.'

'You discovered that they were sleeping together?'

'Yes.'

'How did that make you feel?'

The lawyer tilted his head. 'DCI Raven, how my client felt is not a relevant fact.'

Raven treated him to another of his smiles before returning to Anthony. 'If it was me, I'd have felt pretty gutted. Betrayed, confused, angry. Those would be normal reactions. Anyone would have felt the same.'

They were precisely the feelings that had hit Raven on learning that Lisa was sleeping with another man. It had taken him a good while to process them and leave them behind so that he could get on with his life.

Who was he kidding? The feelings of confusion and betrayal had never gone away.

'Did you feel betrayed, Anthony?'

Nothing.

'Confused?'

'No comment.'

'Angry? I would have been.'

'No comment.'

That solicitor was earning his money all right.

'Tony?' Raven waited for Tony to produce the first of his photographs. The DC slid a photo of Sam across the table. Sam – with the injuries sustained from the hit and run displayed in all their gory close-up detail.

Anthony and his lawyer took a moment to study the image. Anthony was the first to turn away, but it was his solicitor who spoke. 'DCI Raven, I question the relevance of this to the matter in hand.'

'It would have been entirely understandable if you'd decided to let off a little steam that night, Anthony. I'm not condoning violence, but people would understand if you'd had a bust-up with Marcus, perhaps even let your fists do the talking.' Raven dropped his gaze to the photo.

'And yet it was your younger brother, Sam, who ended up looking like this.'

'DCI Raven, once again, I would ask you to explain the relevance of this line of questioning.'

'Tony?'

On cue, Tony reached for his second photograph, laying it flat on the table for all to see.

The lawyer frowned at the green-and-white striped exhibit. 'An umbrella?'

'Do you recognise it?' Raven nudged the photo closer until it was almost under Anthony's nose.

'That umbrella belonged to Marcus.'

'That's right. But Marcus wasn't carrying it the night of the hit and run. Sam took it when he went outside to wait for the taxi. From behind, in the dark, he might have looked just like his older brother.'

Cogs began to turn in Anthony's brain, gears locking into position. 'No, I–'

But the lawyer was already one step ahead. 'DCI Raven, if you are suggesting that my client somehow mistook this man for his older brother and pushed him into the road, then–'

'Did you, Anthony? Because that's how this is beginning to look. You tried to kill Marcus when you first found out about the affair, then when you discovered yesterday that the affair was still going, you finished the job.'

Anthony shook his head vigorously. 'No. I would never have done that. I would never have tried to kill Marcus. He was my brother.'

'He slept with your wife.'

'I said no!' Anthony's fist came crashing down onto the table.

More silence ensued.

Raven was in no hurry to break it. He let it thicken until Anthony could stand it no longer.

'All right, listen. It's true that I found out about the affair that night. Naomi and I had a huge row about it. She promised me it would stop.'

'And you believed her?'

'Yes! Isn't that what married couples are supposed to do? Trust each other?' He looked imploringly at Raven. 'I thought it had stopped. But when I came home yesterday afternoon, I discovered that Marcus had been with Naomi while I was away. I knew it wasn't the first time. They'd been carrying on behind my back.'

Raven felt pity for the man whose trust had been so badly abused by his wife and older brother. Raven had imagined taking revenge on Lisa and Graham-the-accountant in all kinds of vindictive ways. The difference was, he had never actually pushed anyone under a moving vehicle or off a high walkway.

'Tell me where you went after I left your apartment yesterday.'

Anthony put his head in his hands. 'Oh God, I know how this looks. I went to the brewery and had it out with Marcus.'

'Witnesses say that you had a row with him outside the building.'

'Yes. I told him what a worthless, lying cheat he was. I threatened to tell Olivia. He didn't deny anything. How could he?'

'And then what?'

'And then I left. I went into town and started drinking.'

'And then what?'

'I just carried on. At some point I ran into Gavin and he took me back to his place. I couldn't go home and face Naomi. I just couldn't.'

Raven watched him for a minute, letting him feel sorry for himself.

'But before you met Gavin, and while you were still sober enough to think clearly, you returned to the brewery. Everyone had gone home except for Marcus. Maybe you waited for the others to leave, because you and he had unfinished business. Business that you first started a year earlier.'

'No, that's not true. I didn't see Marcus again after our argument in the car park.'

'You returned to the brewery,' repeated Raven, 'you went inside, pushed Marcus to his death, then wiped the CCTV clean to remove all evidence of what you'd done. Then you went back into town, a place where you don't normally go drinking, and arranged to "bump into" Gavin, so that he could be your alibi.'

'No, I swear, I never–'

'Only someone who was familiar with the brewery security could have wiped the camera recordings. Only someone at the party a year ago could have pushed Sam into the road. Only you had a motive to kill your brother.'

'DCI Raven,' interjected the lawyer, 'this is all speculation and wild fantasy. You have no evidence to suggest that my client attempted to kill anyone twelve months ago, or that he did so yesterday. There is no material evidence to place him at the brewery at the time of his brother's death, and nothing to indicate that he tampered with the CCTV.'

Raven knew that he had pushed that particular line as far as he could. Having made his accusations and got Anthony thoroughly rattled, he changed tack. 'In fact, this is not the first suspicious death connected to the brewery.'

Now Anthony looked confused. 'What do you mean?'

'I'm talking about Jeremy Green, the former finance director of Salt Castle Brewery.'

'But that was an accident,' protested Anthony. 'The coroner ruled accidental death. It was official.'

'Only because there was insufficient evidence to reach a conclusion of unlawful killing.'

'DCI Raven.' The solicitor's voice had reached a new level of sternness. 'I would suggest that the reason there was insufficient evidence to reach a conclusion of unlawful killing is because the death was accidental.'

Anthony nodded his agreement. 'The cliffs at Flamborough Head are bloody dangerous.'

'Not for an experienced walker like Jeremy. Let's

consider the facts, shall we? Crime-scene evidence proves that Marcus was pushed to his death at the brewery. An eyewitness account confirms that Sam was pushed into the path of a moving vehicle. Is it very far-fetched to imagine that Jeremy was pushed off the cliff?'

*Especially since only a complete idiot would go that close to the edge.*

But the lawyer was having none of Raven's imaginings. 'That is a completely unsubstantiated claim, DCI Raven. One that goes against the established facts!'

Again Raven ignored his protests, focussing on Anthony, who was looking more uncomfortable than ever now that Jeremy's demise had been brought into the mix.

*Interesting.*

'I understand that there was "bad blood" between you and Jeremy?'

'Who said that?'

'A reliable witness.'

Anthony blanched.

Raven cast a net out, hoping to catch a fish. 'It was over a financial matter.'

Anthony opened his mouth to speak, but his solicitor cut him off. 'That's quite enough. The death of Jeremy Green has been ruled as accidental, and has nothing to do with my client. It seems clear to me that you have no evidence to link my client to the murder of Marcus Earnshaw or the attempted murder of Sam Earnshaw and that you are simply fishing for information. I think we're done here.'

Raven eyed the lawyer's suit and tie and decided it was time to admit defeat, or at least a temporary stalemate. The lawyer was right. Much as Raven would have liked to pin all three incidents on Anthony, he didn't yet have enough evidence. There was no way the CPS would consider charging him.

But there was still time. He could hold Anthony for twenty-four hours without charge. Long enough for forensics to do their thing and hopefully place him at the scene of the crime. Long enough for more witnesses to be interviewed. Long enough for a lucky break.

'Let's adjourn for now,' he suggested, 'and try again later.'

The lawyer studied his watch, looking annoyed. Raven didn't know why – Saturday rates were double, surely? Perhaps the man had a dinner party to attend. Raven was glad he hadn't been invited to that merry gathering.

Once Anthony had been taken back to the cells and the lawyer had gone to do whatever lawyers did when they weren't being irritating, Raven spoke to Tony. 'We need hard evidence linking Anthony to Marcus's murder. 'Can you check out his alibi? What time did he arrive in the pub, and was he there all evening? Check the ANPR to see if we can pin down the movements of his car. And get onto the forensics team. Make sure they know that the clock's against us.'

'I'm on it, sir,' said Tony. 'What about you?'

'I'm going back to speak to Naomi. I want to find out more about what was going on between Anthony and Jeremy. If we're going to convince a jury that Anthony pushed him off a clifftop, we'll need to establish a crystal clear motive.'

# CHAPTER 25

When Raven emerged from the claustrophobic confines of the interview room, the stink of sweat, vomit and alcohol still tickling his nostrils, a constable was waiting for him in the corridor. 'Sir? There's a Mr and Mrs Earnshaw here to see you. They're asking to know what's going on with their son.'

'Okay, I'll come and deal with them now.'

Raven wondered which son was top of their list of concerns. The one who had just been murdered, or the one arrested for committing the crime. A nightmare scenario for any family.

He made his way immediately to the room where Greg and Denise were waiting. He was pleased to see that the constable had done his best to make them comfortable, moving them into a private space away from the Saturday chaos of the main desk, and fetching them tea and coffee, even if it was just the weak slop provided by the drinks machine in the corridor.

Greg rose to his feet as Raven entered, his chair scraping back as he pushed himself away from the table. 'Raven, what the hell's going on? I've been told you've arrested Anthony. Is that true?' His voice was just one level down from shouting.

Raven kept his own voice calm. 'I'm afraid it is.'

'But why?' Denise was red-eyed from crying, but the face she turned to Raven was hard and brittle. Her recent joy at seeing her youngest son recover from his coma had been cruelly snatched away, plunging her into an even blacker darkness. No mother should have to confront so much grief in so short a time. Raven wondered how much more she could take.

Greg looked angry enough to punch someone, and Raven knew that there was no way he could fob the grieving parents off with platitudes. They would have to be told the truth. However hard it might be to handle.

'Perhaps you'd like to take a seat,' he said to Greg, trying to bring a little peace to the situation. He would get nowhere if the confrontational atmosphere persisted. He sat down at the table himself, obliging Greg to do likewise. 'We arrested Anthony this morning. I've just finished questioning him.'

Greg's eyes hardened. 'And?'

'And we'll be holding him overnight while we continue to gather evidence.'

'You think he murdered Marcus?'

Raven hesitated, but knew that Greg and Denise would not be placated with anything less than full frankness. 'That's our current working theory.'

'But why?' wailed Denise. 'His own brother!'

'He would never do such a thing,' said Greg, each word more hostile than the last.

Raven regarded the grieving parents with compassion. It seemed they were giving him no choice. He would have to rub salt into their wound. 'I also spoke to Naomi this morning. She admitted to having an affair with Marcus behind Anthony's back.'

Fresh tears came to Denise's eyes. 'He wouldn't.'

'I'm afraid that he did, for over a year. Anthony has confirmed that he was aware of the relationship. He'd thought it was over, but yesterday he found out they were still seeing each other. That's why he went to the brewery and argued with Marcus.'

It was no consolation to Raven that he had guessed about the affair as soon as he encountered Marcus leaving the apartment in such a hurry just before his brother returned home. By tipping off Anthony to Marcus's visit, he may have unwittingly set in motion a train of events that ended with one brother dead and the other in the cells.

Greg averted his gaze, perhaps unable to look his wife in the face. However much Greg had known about the affair, the news had clearly come as a complete shock to her.

'I realise this is distressing to hear,' said Raven. 'On top of everything else. But I can assure you that we are investigating the matter using all available resources and following up a number of possible leads.'

Greg gave him a scornful look, clearly unimpressed. Denise seemed too upset to say anything.

*Following up a number of leads*. That was stretching the truth, given that they had only one suspect. Still, there were multiple avenues to the investigation, not least the attempted murder of Sam and the suspicious death of Jeremy Green at Flamborough Head.

'While you're here,' said Raven, 'I'd like to ask if you were aware of any disagreements that might have taken place between Anthony and the other board members. In particular, Jeremy Green.'

A frown crossed Greg's face. 'Jeremy? What kind of disagreement? I don't know of anything.'

'It may have been a business matter, or a personal one.' Raven looked to Denise, who shook her head.

The couple exchanged glances.

'You're not aware of anything?' pressed Raven. 'Anything at all?'

But neither Greg nor Denise had anything to give him.

The family was closing ranks.

★

By the time Jess had returned from the post-mortem it was far too late to embark on the three-hour trek that she and Scott had planned to take along the Cleveland Way as far as the old smuggler's haunt of Robin Hood's Bay. The gloom of evening was already closing in and Jess had no intention of stumbling along a rugged coastal path above steep cliffs in the dark.

She would leave that kind of reckless activity to Raven.

It was a pity, though, since it had been a bright sunny day. Still, a murder investigation wasn't something she or Scott could avoid, and however annoying it might be to miss a day's hike, it was nothing compared with the distress that had been visited on the Earnshaw family. After all they had been through with Sam's coma, for tragedy to strike again was dreadful.

She met up with Scott in one of the quieter pubs in town after he had finished at the crime scene.

'Hi! I bought you a beer. Salt Castle, of course.'

He sat down next to her. 'Of course. Can't get away from the place.' He took a sip, licking froth from his upper lip. 'Good beer, though.'

'Yeah.' Jess leaned forwards and took his hand in hers. 'How embarrassing was it when Raven came into the office and found us together looking at the CCTV?'

'Do you think he guessed we're a couple?'

'Oh yes. He guessed all right.'

Not that Jess and Scott had been doing anything inappropriate. They had simply moved to a new level of intimacy, sharing each other's personal space, touching each other without even thinking. Scott's defences were beginning to crumble, revealing the man beneath. She looked forward to getting to know him a lot better over the coming months. Which reminded her...

'What are you doing for Christmas?' she asked, keeping her voice casual. 'Any plans?'

'Not really. Why?'

'Just wondered if you'd like to come to stay with me at Rosedale Abbey?' Just dropping it into the conversation like it was no big deal. Like Jess's mum wasn't desperate to meet him. Like her dad wouldn't be on a state of high alert, checking him out as potential son-in-law material. Like the house wouldn't be full of legions of aunts, uncles, cousins and grandparents all firing questions at him.

Like there was no pressure at all.

His quick reply took her by surprise. 'Yeah, I would. Thanks.'

Duh. If she'd known he would agree so readily, she wouldn't have put off asking.

'But in return will you come somewhere with me?' he asked. 'Tomorrow.'

'Sure, where?'

Scott swallowed another mouthful of beer. 'I don't want to say. Can I just take you there?'

She hesitated. 'Well...'

'It's just that, if I tell you where we're going, you might think it's weird.'

'Scott, now you're making me worried.'

'It's perfectly safe, honest. Just a little strange. I want to tell you, but it's... personal. It'll be easier just to show you.'

Jess supped some beer herself, studying Scott's earnest face. She'd known when she took him on as a boyfriend that Scott wasn't quite like other guys. So it shouldn't keep surprising her when he behaved oddly. He had agreed to come to her home without making a fuss, so she felt obliged to return the favour. She would just have to trust him.

'Okay,' she said. 'Let's do it. We'll go there tomorrow.'

★

Anthony's parents may have been unwilling to say a bad word about their middle son, but Raven had a hunch he knew someone without such qualms. Naomi Earnshaw hadn't exactly displayed much affection towards her husband when he'd returned from his sales trip to Scotland, and she'd been terrified out of her wits upon learning of Marcus's death. Now, after a whole day alone to confront the idea that her husband had killed her lover, she might be persuaded to open up.

When Raven arrived at her apartment on the Esplanade, the chain was still on the door, but she was visibly calmer than when he'd seen her that morning, fearing that her husband might come to take revenge. 'Is Anthony still in custody?' she asked as soon as she let him inside.

'He is.'

'And has he confessed? Has he admitted killing Marcus?'

Raven could tell from the intensity in her voice that she had already made up her mind about her husband's guilt. 'Not yet. We don't have sufficient evidence to charge him, and we can only hold him for twenty-four hours without charge.'

Naomi's hand twisted over her mouth and her eyes grew wide. 'You mean he might be released?'

'That's why I need to speak to you. Can we sit down?'

She led him into the lounge where he took his usual seat on the cream sofa. Naomi sat opposite, her eyes like those of a startled deer, her hands tangling and untangling in her lap. 'What's going to happen next?'

Raven didn't feel ready to give her any more information just yet. Let her worry instead. He needed her own worst imagination to work at her conscience. 'We're still piecing together the events of last night. And earlier.'

'Earlier?'

'I'd like you to tell me all you know about Jeremy Green, the former finance director at the brewery.'

'Jeremy?' Naomi's eyes darted nervously to one side. It was dark outside and the windows that gave onto the sea were black, filled only with a reflection of the room itself. A ghostly version of Raven and Naomi sat on matching cream sofas against a framed backdrop of tasteful off-whites. She rose and went over to her pale twin, pulling the curtains closed.

'I've been told there was some kind of dispute between him and your husband,' prompted Raven.

Naomi returned to her seat, her fingers continuing to writhe like worms. 'I don't know anything about that. Anthony had known Jeremy all his life. He told me he was like an uncle to him. They got on really well.' She pulled her cardigan tight and folded her arms, shutting Raven out, just as she had shut out his mirror version.

'Naomi, if I'm going to make a case against Anthony, then I need to know all the facts. So far I have one confirmed murder and one attempted murder. So when I learn that Anthony was seen arguing with yet another of the directors of Salt Castle Brewery just before he died, I'm bound to investigate.'

She looked up, her face as pale as the walls of the room. 'But you can't imagine that Anthony had anything to do with Jeremy's death. That was an accident!'

'Was it?'

Her hands rose to her lips, trembling like butterflies. Fresh fear filled her eyes. 'Oh my God!'

Raven let her unease grow. Let her be frightened if it helped to loosen her tongue. If it brought him one inch closer to uncovering the mystery of Jeremy's death.

'Well.' Still hesitant. 'There is something you should know about.'

*No kidding.* But still she seemed unwilling to talk. Whatever secret she was hiding, it was a damn big one.

'Yes?'

Naomi bit her lower lip before finally taking the plunge. Her words came out breathlessly, as if speaking them softly might cost her less. 'Greg had always looked after the sales and marketing for the brewery. But he said he was getting too old to be travelling so much. He wanted one of his sons to take over, and since Marcus's expertise was in finance and Sam was too young, it was obviously the role that

Anthony was destined for. So, after working alongside Greg for a year, Anthony took over as sales director. He was really good at it too, bringing in loads of new customers. Business was booming.' She stopped, glancing at Raven before continuing. 'But then Jeremy discovered some... financial irregularities.'

'What sort of irregularities?'

'It was complicated. Basically, Anthony had started taking a little money on the side. He figured that he was doing all the work, running all over the country, doing negotiations, shaking hands, closing deals. He was bringing in so much extra custom, he deserved a bit of a bonus, especially since Marcus was taking such a big cut of the company profits.' She glanced around unconsciously at the lavish apartment, at the coordinated furnishings, at the modern crystal chandelier that hung overhead. It was no great mystery what Anthony's "bonus" money had been spent on. 'The gist of it was that when Anthony signed up a new customer, the first invoice he raised would be off the books, payable into a special bank account he'd set up. After that first invoice, everything was done properly, with invoices raised through the normal channel, receipts payable to the company. But that initial payment would always go to him. He didn't think Jeremy would notice.'

'Did none of the customers find this odd?'

She shrugged. 'Anthony had a plausible explanation for why it had to be done that way. He's good at convincing people, that's what makes him such a good salesman. And no one ever complained.'

'But Jeremy found out.'

'He wasn't as big a fool as Anthony had supposed.'

'What did Jeremy do?'

'He was pretty decent about it, actually. He told Anthony that if he repaid the money he would put everything straight with the accounts and Greg wouldn't have to know. It would just be between the two of them.'

'How much money are we talking about?'

Her fingers were on the move again, squirming around each other in denial, her gaze resolutely refusing to meet Raven's.

'How much, Naomi?'

'It was some tens of thousands. Maybe as much as fifty.'

Fifty thousand pounds. A lot of money to go walkabout. 'So, what happened? Did Anthony pay it back?'

She shook her head. 'It wasn't as simple as that. We'd put down a hefty deposit on this apartment. Anthony had bought himself a nice car for all his travelling. I'd bought some jewellery and clothes. We had the mortgage to pay, we had credit card debts... we couldn't just put together that kind of money.'

At some point during Naomi's confession, her story had stopped being about what Anthony had done, and had become about "we". Raven wondered if the scam had been her idea from the start. 'So what did you do?'

'Anthony was terrified that Jeremy would tell Greg and that he'd be fired from the company. He pleaded with Jeremy to let him pay off the debts slowly. But Jeremy said no, he couldn't allow that. We talked about selling the car, or even moving out of the apartment, but then...'

'What?'

She lifted her face to Raven's as she revealed the final piece of her sorry tale. 'Jeremy died. He fell off the cliff.'

'Didn't Marcus know anything about the missing money?'

Naomi gave a small shake of her head. 'We wondered if he would find out, but no. It seemed that Jeremy hadn't left any written notes or spoken to anyone else about it. So Marcus was none the wiser.' It seemed the eldest brother wasn't quite the hotshot financial whizz he claimed. A substantial fraud had taken place right under his nose. 'But Anthony would never have... he would never have killed...' Naomi's voice trailed off.

'Do you still believe that?' demanded Raven.

Her silence told him all he needed to know.

# CHAPTER 26

It was late by the time Raven returned to Quay Street. He could really have done with a quiet evening on his own, eating fish and chips out of a cardboard box and listening to loud music on his headphones. Gothic rock, his poison of choice: The Cure, The Sisters of Mercy, Joy Division. Immersed in a relentless drumbeat with banshee guitars wailing in his eardrums, he could lose himself in a feast of doom and gloom, spiced with a heavy dash of anguish and a side serving of angst. A consoling, cathartic pursuit, like sinking into a hot bath or curling up in your favourite armchair.

Back in the real world, the tangled, messy lives of the Earnshaws were dragging him down. On the surface they appeared to have everything – a thriving business, beautiful homes and spouses, a strong family bond. Yet they had to go and mess it up by stealing from each other and conducting illicit affairs. And now the eldest son was dead.

A real life tragedy, far less comforting than the imaginary version conjured by his song lyrics.

He slammed the door of his car behind him and trudged down the street towards his house. After dealing with the Earnshaw family, the last thing he needed right now was a confrontation with his own estranged wife but, as arranged that morning, Lisa was waiting for him on the pavement, next to the overflowing skip, piled high with rubble and rotting timbers, her blonde hair burnished gold by the streetlamp.

Well, there was no way he could put off the encounter now. Better to get it over with. Like a bitter pill, the divorce was something he would just have to swallow. Then he could move on with his life.

Alone.

Lisa looked less than pleased with the fact that he had kept her waiting. 'I was beginning to wonder if I'd got the right address,' she said, her words as ever loaded with implicit criticism of his own shortcomings. She gazed up at the old house that looked positively Dickensian in the yellow glow of the streetlight. 'Is this it?'

Raven grunted. If Lisa was unimpressed with the exterior of the building, she had a bigger shock awaiting her inside. 'Shall we go in?' He unlocked the door and pushed it open. 'Mind the hole in the floor.'

She stepped across the threshold and gasped. 'Good grief, Tom, this place is barely habitable. It's a wonder the council haven't condemned it.'

It was a fair comment, given the current state of the building work, or rather demolition work. Yet Raven felt compelled to defend his home. 'It'll be nice once it's finished. Haven't you always been keen on home improvement?'

Lisa edged cautiously across the plank of wood that spanned the entrance hall, tiptoeing into the living room, her coat gathered around her legs so that it wouldn't come into contact with the dusty walls.

'Wait here,' said Raven. 'Just give me a moment.'

He trudged laboriously up the stairs, noting the fresh round of destruction that Barry had unleashed. The builder's propensity for creating mess and disorder had spread to almost every room in the house. Skirting boards had been ripped off, floorboards pulled up, flaking plaster hacked from the walls. The bare bones of the house were being revealed day by day.

He changed his shirt and freshened up with a quick blast of deodorant. There was no time for a shower. In any case, he no longer had a bath. He would need to find a temporary solution to that – perhaps call in at the local swimming pool in the morning before work. He looked forward to the day, hopefully not too far off now, when he would be able to start each morning with a good hot shower and then select a shirt and tie from a built-in wardrobe. He didn't care much for luxuries, but he liked to keep up his appearance. Was it vanity? No, it was simply the way his mother had brought him up.

When he returned downstairs, he found Lisa inspecting the place where his kitchen had once been. 'I take it you weren't planning to cook dinner this evening, Tom?'

He returned her wry smile. 'Perhaps it would be better if we ate out. Under the circumstances.'

'You were never much of a chef anyway, were you?'

He didn't try to deny it.

Walking into town they passed the car park at the end of the street. Lisa cast a glance over Raven's car. 'You still have the Beamer, then? It must be almost as old as you.'

'It's not that old, thank you very much.' Her comments on the house may have been justified, but he wasn't prepared to accept any criticism of the BMW. 'It still goes perfectly well.'

'Just like you, eh, Tom?' She flicked her hair to one side, turning to study his face in profile. 'You're looking good, actually. Maybe it's the sea air.'

'The air's certainly fresher here than in London.'

Or perhaps it was simply being away from Lisa that had done the trick.

They strolled together to a quiet Italian restaurant near the town centre and were shown to a corner table complete with candles. The waiter had obviously mistaken them for a couple out for a romantic evening.

They perused the menu in silence. When the waiter came back to take their orders, Lisa chose a seafood tagliatelle and Raven asked for lasagne. He braced himself for a snide comment from her about his predictable choice, but she said nothing. Perhaps she was saving her snark for when she brought up the subject of the divorce. As she must inevitably do – perhaps after dessert.

There was no sense ruining good food, was there?

After the waiter had brought her a large glass of Sauvignon Blanc and a sparkling mineral water for him, she leaned forwards with her elbows on the table. 'So, here we are, Tom. You and me.'

'You and me.'

The warm light of the candles softened her clear blue eyes and a smile tugged playfully at her lips. 'We still make a good-looking couple, don't we?'

A grin crept across his face. 'I'd say so.'

He meant it. Lisa had always been a very attractive woman and still was with her blonde shoulder-length hair cut in a flattering style, her tastefully applied makeup, and her voguish fashion sense. When they'd first met he'd fallen for her immediately. And the early years of the marriage had been good. Having fun together. Making a home. Raising a daughter.

Growing apart.

Ultimately he knew he'd failed to live up to her expectations of a husband. His working hours were predictable only in the sense that they were long and variable; he showed little enthusiasm for her constantly-changing interior design whims; he insisted on driving his unsuitable car.

But his greatest failure had always been to put work before family. It was entirely his fault that she'd walked away from him and found another man.

'How's Graham?' Best to get the elephant in the room out of the way. Then perhaps they could start talking about what she was doing here in Scarborough, and what she wanted from him.

Lisa's smile faltered. 'We split up.'

Well, that wasn't exactly what he'd been expecting.

She raised her wine glass to her lips and took a nervous gulp, watching him intently, waiting for his reaction.

But what was he supposed to say? Sorry? Good riddance? Found someone else yet?

Her eyes sparkled with tears, but she wiped them away. 'Well, you could say *something*, Tom. I've just travelled several hundred miles to bring you my news. You could act like you cared one way or another.'

'I'm sorry.'

'That's decent of you to say so. But are you really? Or are you glad? In your shoes, I'd probably be feeling more than a little smug.'

'Well,' he admitted, 'maybe a little.' Yet in all honesty he had moved on from the wreckage of his marriage. The infidelity had started a year ago and he had known about it for months. Since then he'd moved to another town, built a new life for himself here in Yorkshire. What did it matter if Lisa's affair had come to an end? The damage was done.

'Graham broke up with me,' she continued, clearly feeling a need to explain. 'He said I was too *flighty*. He wanted someone more reliable. I told him he should have thought of that before starting an affair with a married woman.'

Raven did his best to keep his face straight. 'I hope you told him what a complete and utter shit he was.' Words he would gladly have delivered himself.

'I did. I called him far worse than that. But I know that everything was my fault really. I realise that now. I should never have treated you the way I did. I ruined everything. I'm sorry.'

'Thank you.' Raven sensed how much it must have cost her to admit that her year-long fling had been a mistake.

The waiter arrived with plates and bowls laden with food and went through an elaborate performance of dispensing black pepper from an oversized mill. When he was gone, Lisa reached across the table and grasped Raven's hand.

'I truly am sorry, Tom. If I could take it all back, I would. But I know I can't. I'm going to have to ask for your forgiveness and try and prove myself to you.'

'Wait, what are you saying, Lisa?' He gently freed himself from her grasp. 'What do you have to prove?'

'My contrition.'

'I don't understand.'

'I have to make it up to you. So that you'll take me back.'

He shook his head sadly. 'So this is why you came to Scarborough. To beg forgiveness. It's too late for that, Lisa.'

If she was offended by his rejection, she refused to show it. 'Don't say no, Tom. Not without giving it a chance. I want us to try again. Put the last year behind us. We could start with a family Christmas – you, me and Hannah.'

'Hannah?' Lisa must have known that she was playing her trump card. Raven had been longing to see more of his daughter ever since leaving London. He knew that of all his failures, not spending more time with Hannah when she was young was his greatest. 'I've already invited her to Scarborough for Christmas,' he said.

Lisa laughed, yet not spitefully. Her amusement at his foolishness seemed genuine. 'Oh, Tom, you can't possibly expect her to come and stay with you in that building site. How would you cook? Where would she sleep?'

Raven knew she was right. The prospect of his house being made habitable within the next few weeks was fanciful.

Lisa sensed his resolve crumbling. 'A friend recommended a really lovely hotel in the centre of York. I could travel up by train with Hannah. We could stay for a few days, visit the Christmas market, sing carols at the Minster, go on one of those open-top bus tours of the city. What do you say, Tom?'

The excitement was evident on her face, in her eyes, in

her voice. She was like the Lisa of old, the woman who had stolen his heart. She seemed sincere in her desire for reconciliation. And to spend Christmas with his wife and daughter... wouldn't that be a dream come true?

Yet Raven had been burned once. Could he risk a second time?

'I'll have to think about it, Lisa. Give me time to mull it over. I'll let you know when I see you again tomorrow evening.'

*

Tony pushed open the door of the pub and stepped inside. A front of warm air greeted him, making his glasses immediately steam up. A hazard of being short-sighted, especially for those who enjoyed a glass of beer on a cold winter's night. He waited until the fog had lifted enough for him to see again, then made his way over to the bar.

Saturday night and the place was heaving, with standing room only. But that was all for the better. Tony had come here to meet people, as many as possible. First, he could use a drink. He recognised the familiar Salt Castle design adorning two of the pumps and made his choice. 'A half of the IPA, please.'

He waited as amber liquid flowed into the glass, then paid and took his first sip. He licked his lips with satisfaction. Just the right balance of malty sweetness and bitter hops. Aromatic, refreshing and very flavoursome. One thing was for sure – that Gavin Thompson knew how to brew a good beer.

With his spare hand, Tony reached for the photo he'd brought along. Raven had asked him to pin down Anthony's movements the night before, and since the sales director claimed to have roamed around half the pubs in Scarborough, Tony anticipated a long night ahead of him. Still, there was some compensation to be had. He took another mouthful of beer and began his work. 'Excuse me, sir. North Yorkshire Police. Do you recall seeing this man yesterday evening? He may have been here or in one of the other pubs. Take a good look, there's no hurry.'

# CHAPTER 27

*S*unday morning, waking up. The day starts early when there's a small child in your world. Hannah rushes into the bedroom and tugs at Raven's arm. 'Daddy, wake up!' He rolls over and opens his eyes to look at her. She's all Lisa at this age – sparkling eyes, shining hair, a bewitching giggle. Raven's look will only emerge later, revealing itself less in surface features, more in a haunting undercurrent of sadness – a shadow behind the eyes, a hesitation in the laughter. Right now, she couldn't be happier. 'Daddy, it's time to get up, I want to go to the park!' Resistance is futile. 'Okay, okay.' Raven gives Lisa a prod and together they begin the morning ritual of shower, dressing, breakfast, under a constant barrage of questions and chatter from their little girl. They take her out for an early stroll around the park. It's surprisingly busy for this hour – full of dogwalkers, joggers and other families with small children pounding the twisting paths like crazy people. The trees stand like bare skeletons, but a rich carpet of yellow leaves rolls across the grass beneath them. Hannah swings between Lisa and Raven, one small hand in hers, one in his. 'I want to fly!' They lift her over a puddle, tiny pink boots skimming the muddy water. Lisa is wearing a long green raincoat, Raven is in his *customary black. 'Will it snow at Christmas?' asks Hannah. 'We'll have to see,' says Lisa. 'But it always snows at Christmas!' Hannah is at peak excitement about the coming festivities, old enough to know exactly what to expect, still young enough to be free of suspicion that the whole Santa Claus thing might be nothing more than an elaborate hoax, part of a broader conspiracy of elves, tooth fairies and pixies. 'Splash!' she yells as she stomps her booties in shallow pockets of rainwater, launching splatters of mud over Raven's trousers. His phone rings and he retrieves it from the depths of his jacket pocket. Lisa scowls. 'Do you have to, Tom? On a Sunday?' But he takes the call anyway. 'Something's come up,' he tells her. 'I'm going to have to go into work.' She turns away and a tiny fissure opens up in Raven's world, the beginnings of a crack that will one day widen into an almighty chasm big enough to swallow everything he loves...*

The phone was still ringing. Raven's hand sneaked out from under his duvet, fingers groping clumsily for it in the dark. 'Hello?'

'Sorry to disturb you on a Sunday morning, sir.'

'That's all right, Tony. What have you got for me?' Raven sat up and switched on the bedside light. It was eight o'clock, black outside, but the gulls already on the wing, shrieking loud enough to make sure everyone knew it.

'It's Anthony's alibi. It's shaky to say the least.'

'Tell me what you've found.'

'I did a tour of the pubs last night, like you asked, talking to landlords and regulars and showing Anthony's photo. I couldn't find anyone who was willing to state with certainty that they saw him last night. At least, not until he ended up in the pub with Gavin. Before that, there's no saying where he'd been.'

'So he could easily have gone back to the brewery and killed his brother. Thanks for letting me know, Tony.'

It was a step forward in building the case against Anthony, but he still didn't have enough to charge him with murder. He would need to apply for an extension to hold him for another twenty-four hours, and for that he would need the approval of the boss. Would Gillian appreciate a visit from him on a Sunday morning? Probably not, but there was no way to avoid it.

He dressed and headed out to his car, hands thrust deep into his pockets against the cold. Barely above freezing this morning, with an iron-clad sky threatening snow.

The old swimming pool next to Peasholm Park, where he had learned to swim, had been closed down, replaced by a shiny new sports village further out of town. He drove there and presented himself at the front desk, feeling starkly out of place in his black overcoat. The warm interior was all bright lights and colourful posters advertising swim classes, gym sessions and cardio workouts.

'Pool, gym or fitness studio?' enquired the keen, young thing at the desk, dressed in shorts and t-shirt.

Raven glanced awkwardly around the echoey cavern of the reception hall. 'Actually, I just want to use your shower facilities.'

The girl seemed dumbfounded by his request. 'I could offer you a swimming pass?'

'That'll do.'

'Pay as you go or membership?'

Raven pictured the current state of his bathroom. A hollowed-out space, bricks stripped bare of plaster. No heating, no floor, no hope. 'Membership, please.'

After showering and shaving he returned to his car and drove north. Detective Superintendent Gillian Ellis lived in the same part of town as Greg and Denise Earnshaw, though further inland, away from both sea and castle. The views here were of striped lawns, clipped hedges and tennis courts laid out in crisp rectangles, all orderly and neat. Gillian's detached house, with its Edwardian redbrick frontage, veranda and tall chimneys, was a far cry from Raven's own humble abode in the heart of the crowded old town. He rang the bell and waited.

She answered the door, a hint of annoyance crossing her brow when she saw who had come calling. 'Tom, what brings you all the way out here so early on a Sunday morning?'

'Sorry to intrude, ma'am, but I wonder if I might have a word regarding Anthony Earnshaw?'

She nodded her consent and led him through to a well-proportioned lounge where classical music was playing at high volume through ceiling speakers. To Raven's uneducated ears, the music sounded harsh and discordant. Undoubtedly modern, from a composer he would certainly never have heard of. Gillian turned the volume lower, leaving a lingering residue of atonal noise, just loud enough to set his teeth on edge.

Unlike Anthony and Oliva's apartment, there were no subtle off-whites in this room. The walls were stark white, all the better to display large canvases splashed in bold colours. As in all matters, Gillian's taste in interior design was strong and brash, not impeded by self-doubt.

She took up residence in a leather armchair next to a glass coffee table scattered with a selection of the more serious Sunday papers and invited him to take a seat opposite. No tea or coffee was on offer. She clearly didn't anticipate a long visit. 'So, what can I do for you, Tom?'

'I'd like to request an extension to hold Anthony Earnshaw in custody for another twenty-four hours.'

He could tell from her darkening expression that his plea had not been well received. 'And your reason for this extension?'

'He has a motive for killing his brother, Marcus, as well as pushing Sam into the path of the van that ran him over. He also has strong motive for murdering Jeremy Green, the former finance director of the brewery.'

Gillian's opening scowl deepened. 'I wasn't aware that you were investigating two murders.'

Raven laid out his case, outlining the financial fraud that Naomi had explained, how Jeremy had demanded that Anthony repay the money to the firm, how the timing of his death had been extremely convenient for Anthony.

'Dr Felicity Wainwright agrees that Jeremy Green may well have been murdered,' he concluded. 'But I need more time to continue investigating. So far, we have eyewitnesses who state that Anthony had a row with Marcus at the brewery just a few hours before Marcus's body was found. We've been unable to verify Anthony's alibi at the time of the murder, and we know that Marcus must have been killed by someone involved with the brewery, because they knew how to wipe the CCTV footage from the computer. What we don't yet have is firm evidence placing him at the scene.'

Cymbals crashed and a jagged staccato of notes spilled out from the concealed speakers. Gillian steepled her fingers pensively. 'I'm sorry, Tom, but this all seems rather far-fetched to me. The coroner ruled that Jeremy Green's death was accidental. I find nothing in the present inquiry to justify re-opening that case.'

The disappointment on his face must have been apparent because Gillian added, 'I admit I was initially sceptical about Sam being pushed under a vehicle. I now concede that you were right about that. But I can't accept your theory that Anthony is some kind of homicidal mastermind. Your theory is too elaborate. You need to stick to the facts. If you have no forensic evidence or an eyewitness account to place Anthony at the time and location of the crime, then you have no basis for continuing to hold him.'

'So my request to keep him in custody…'

'Is denied. Is that all for now?'

Raven stood to go. 'Yes, ma'am. I'll leave you to your Sunday relaxation.'

★

Raven returned from his visit to Gillian feeling frustrated. They were going to have to let Anthony go. He would call Tony and let him know. He wished he could have made a more convincing case for keeping him in custody. He knew he didn't have the evidence to support his theory, but he was convinced more than ever that Jeremy's death hadn't been an accident. Not after everything else that had gone on at the brewery. Two directors dead, one pushed under a van. Yet it looked as if Anthony had covered his tracks each time.

His phone rang, interrupting his thoughts.

When he saw that it was Hannah calling, his heart leapt.

'Hey, Dad, how's it going?'

'Good,' said Raven, automatically adopting his daughter's upbeat tone. No need to tell her that his house was a demolition site and his boss had just squashed all hope of solving his current case. Focus on the positive. 'How are things with you? How's uni?'

'Great. Really busy. Sorry I haven't been in touch more.'

'Don't worry about it. I expect you're too busy studying and having a good time.'

'Yeah, something like that. Listen, I heard from Mum. She says she's in Scarborough.'

'That's right. She surprised me with an unannounced visit.'

'So, what's going on? I hear she and Graham have broken up.'

'That's what she told me.' But what was going on exactly? That was a very good question. 'How would you feel about a family Christmas? The three of us together. Maybe in York.'

'I thought you wanted me to come and stay with you in Scarborough.'

Once again a vision of exposed brickwork, bare plaster, missing floorboards and a complete absence of bathroom facilities intruded into Raven's thoughts. It was like a still from a horror film, refusing to go away. 'My house may not be ready in time.'

'Okay, I'd like to. But if this is really about you and Mum getting back together, then that's up to the pair of you. Don't drag me into it.'

Raven sighed. He knew that Lisa's proposal for spending Christmas as a family was really just code for getting back together permanently. A trial reunion before a full reconciliation. But was that what he wanted?

If he was hoping for help from Hannah, it looked like she was wisely keeping out of it.

'Okay, darling. Let's all think about it. There's no hurry to decide. No rush at all.'

After all, there were still three weeks before Christmas.

# CHAPTER 28

It was destined to be a stilted affair, possibly one of the most awkward family gatherings ever. But Becca had little choice about whether to go along. She had to, for Sam's sake.

The gathering had been arranged to mark his return home after over a year in hospital and Becca had wondered if Denise would cancel or postpone the occasion in light of recent events. But if anything, Marcus's death had steeled her resolve to throw the best get-together possible. It seemed she was determined to celebrate the life of one son while mourning the loss of another.

'But I won't know what to say to anyone.' Becca had arrived early at the house before the other guests arrived, to take care of Sam, and was sitting with him in the lower half of the living room. He was ensconced in a big armchair while she perched on a stool.

He gave her a reassuring smile. 'Don't worry. You'll be fine. Just be yourself.' He reached out and held her hand tightly.

That was all very well for him to say. This was his home and his family, not Becca's. 'How did you sleep last night?'

'Like a log. It was good to be back in my own room. Hospitals are such noisy places.'

Becca smiled at him indulgently. Sam had slept for a whole year without stirring, no matter how much noise she or the doctors and nurses had made.

The house on Scalby Mills Road was enormous. Becca's grandparents lived not far away, but their house was much more modest. Loads of chairs had been set out for guests and Greg was busy laying out drinks coasters, adjusting chairs, moving between living room, hallway and dining room. He was wearing a dark suit and tie, as if for a funeral wake. Becca wondered if she was seriously underdressed in her loose trousers and polo neck top. 'How many people has your mum invited?' she whispered to Sam.

'Just family and close friends.'

She was on the verge of saying how big Sam's family was, but stopped herself just in time. *One son dead, another in police custody.* She would have to watch every word she said to avoid making some awful gaffe.

She withdrew her fingers from his, placing both hands on her lap. Normally she could relax completely in Sam's company but for some reason today she felt tongue-tied talking to him. She rose to her feet, feeling a need to move about and do something useful. 'I'll go and give your mum a hand in the kitchen.'

He smiled up at her. 'She'll appreciate that.'

She went through to the kitchen at the back of the house. Like all the rooms, it was huge – miles of granite worktop stretching out in every direction with a big island unit in the middle. Denise stood in front of the island, wearing a cook's apron over a dark, velvet dress, making Becca more convinced than ever that she ought to have worn something more formal. But Denise seemed not to notice her arrival. She was too busy keeping her mixed emotions in check by attending to mountains of food – sandwiches, mini quiches, sausage rolls, chicken drumsticks, samosas, salads and dips.

Becca lingered in the doorway, beginning to regret leaving Sam's side. She and Denise had exchanged some bitter words in the run-up to Sam's recovery. It had been Denise – and Greg too, with the encouragement of Dr Kirtlington – who had pushed for his life support to be switched off. Becca had begged repeatedly for her to change her mind, but she had been resolute.

They hadn't spoken of it since Sam had woken from his coma.

Denise glanced up from her work and Becca saw immediately that her eyes were red and puffy. She had covered her face in makeup to try and disguise the fact that she'd been crying, but her grief pushed through the layers of foundation and concealer to the surface.

Compassion tugged at Becca's heart and she knew that whatever had passed between them, Denise was Sam's mother, and Becca needed to find a way to put past quarrels behind them. 'Hi,' she said brightly, forcing a smile to her lips. 'What can I do to help?'

A sad smile animated Denise's face. 'Oh, that's so kind of you to help, Becca. Would you mind chopping those carrots and celery sticks?' She indicated a wooden chopping board piled high with scrubbed vegetables.

'No problem.' Becca picked up a long-bladed kitchen knife and set to work. The blade was sharp, slicing through the carrots and celery like butter.

Denise gazed around at the plates, dishes and bowls overflowing with food of all kinds. 'Do you think there'll be enough for everyone?'

Becca was sure there was enough to feed the five thousand. 'I'm sure there'll be plenty. It's only for family and friends isn't it?'

'Yes. People we've known for a long time. And one person we haven't seen for ages...' Denise trailed off, leaving Becca to wonder who she might be referring to.

'Anyone I know?' she enquired innocently. Despite the circumstances, she couldn't help switching into detective mode. Was it a hazard of the job, or had she always been so nosey?

Denise glanced out of the window, her gaze fixed on the distant grey of the sea. 'It's been such a long time. I do hope it was a good idea to invite him. But under the circumstances, I thought...'

'Yes?' said Becca, even more intrigued. She waited for Denise to supply some details, but before she could say more a bell chimed from the front of the house.

'Oh, there's the doorbell. I'd better get it.' Denise whipped off her apron and hurried out to the hallway. Becca had missed her chance to discover the identity of the mysterious guest, but with any luck she would find out soon enough.

Before long a series of voices raised in greeting and condolences floated through from the hallway. The party from hell had begun.

★

The A169 to the west of Scarborough cut a straight line through gentle fields of pasture. There was little to see of any interest, just lines of trees and the white dots of sheep against the green. The land sloped gently up as if it was climbing to meet the sky.

'Just keep going along this road. It's not far now.'

Jess had agreed to drive the Land Rover, with Scott giving directions. He was still acting all mysterious, refusing to explain where they were going. 'It's more fun if it's a surprise,' he told her.

'Are we going onto the moors?' she asked.

'Kind of. Okay, turn off the road just here. We'll stop in the car park.'

She pulled the Land Rover into what was little more than a layby by the side of the road. 'We're in the middle of nowhere.'

'Yeah.' He opened the door and stepped out. Jess jumped out and went to join him.

A sign marked the location as Saltergate Car Park,

although there was no sign of any village or houses nearby. They crossed the road, and after a short distance the ground fell away to reveal a large hollow. Jess peered over the edge.

A vast natural amphitheatre lay nestled in the moorland, stretching for a mile or more. In late summer or autumn it would be spectacular, a mass of purple heather. The flowers had all faded now, but the hollow made a patchwork of browns, greens and golds.

'It's called the Hole of Horcum,' Scott explained.

'It's beautiful. Is this what we came to see?'

'No, follow me.'

He led her back across the road and along a path heading east. 'They call this Old Wife's Way.' They followed the track for a little over a mile until it split in two. They took the left fork. 'Do you see it?'

There was no need for Jess to ask what "it" was. A squat conical hill rose before them, almost perfectly regular in shape.

'Its name is Blakey Topping,' said Scott. 'It's a sacred hill. Some people believe that hills like this inspired prehistoric burial mounds. The ground nearby is full of ancient features, cairns and standing stones.'

'Can we climb it?'

'Sure.'

It wasn't a difficult climb for Jess, but it was steep and slippery in places. When she reached the top, she was puffing and panting. But the view was well worth the effort. From here she could see for miles across the rough moorland. She sat down on the wet grass, her knees bunched up before her.

Scott squatted next to her. 'An old legend says that the giant, Wade, was having a row with his wife one day. He grabbed a great clod of earth and threw it at her. Fortunately his aim was poor and he missed, but the Hole of Horcum marks the place where he scooped up the earth, and Blakey Topping is where it landed.'

'And Old Wife's Way must be the path she followed to

run away.'

The moorland was full of myths and legends like that. Of witches, of faerie-folk but most of all, of Wade and his Old Wife, Bell.

'Do you see those stones?' Scott pointed out four weathered standing stones near the foot of the hill. 'Some people think they formed a stone circle. Others say they make up part of an alignment. Beyond them is an earth bank topped with more stones and beyond that lies the cairnfield and the barrows.'

'This place is special to you.'

'My Mum used to bring me here sometimes. We'd walk the way we just came and sit here on the hilltop. She'd tell me stories of giants and witches.'

Jess took his hand in hers. 'You really miss her, don't you?' Scott's mum had been murdered when he was only fourteen years old and he had been sent to live in a children's home.

'Yes. Today was her birthday. I always come here on this day, every year, to remember her. You see, this is where her ashes are scattered.'

A shiver ran down Jess's back. She glanced at the barren hillside, as if grey ash might suddenly start billowing all around. But of course there was nothing. The air was perfectly clear.

'You see,' said Scott, 'since I'm going to come and meet your family at Christmas, I wanted you to meet mine. Does that make sense?'

'I think so.' Jess realised that by bringing her here on this special day, he was letting her into his life, opening up, showing her everything that was important to him.

'My mum used to say that even though December marked the dying of the year, it was no reason to be sad. It was actually something to celebrate, because from now on, every month would be a little lighter. The ancient people who put these stones here used to gather at the solstice to welcome the sun back into their lives. And I come here because, although she's gone, I can still feel her' – he touched his hand to his chest – 'and even though she's dead, part of her lives on. I wanted to bring you here to show you to her. Because, now you've come into my life, it feels like the light will never leave me again.'

\*

Becca had nearly finished chopping the celery when the knife slipped across her finger. The blade was so sharp it sliced right through her skin. 'Damn!' She held her hand under the tap to wash it clean, then patted it dry with a paper towel.

Blood continued to well up where the knife had nicked her. She hunted around the kitchen for a box of plasters and found one in a drawer under the worktop. The cut wasn't deep and a single plaster was enough to stop the bleeding. Fortunately she hadn't got any blood over the food.

She put the chopping board and knife next to the sink then started carrying bowls of food through to the dining room where a long table had been set out with plates, glasses and cutlery.

'I'll give you a hand.' A young woman sporting a short, spiky haircut with purple streaks entered the room. If Becca had worried about being too casual, she needn't have bothered. The newcomer was even more dressed down than her, wearing a stripy top with denim dungarees. 'Gosh, look at all this food. Aunt Denise must be expecting half of Scarborough to turn up. I'm Ellie, by the way. Sam's cousin. I'm guessing you must be Becca, Sam's girlfriend?'

'That's right. Pleased to meet you.' Becca shook hands with her over chicken vol au vents.

'Sam should have introduced us sooner. But sometimes it takes a wedding or a funeral to bring people together.' Ellie's hands moved to cover her mouth in embarrassment. 'I shouldn't have said that. I mean, this isn't a funeral, is it? Although, actually, I don't really know what it is.'

Becca nodded, relieved she wasn't the only one who was finding the occasion hard to navigate. She had taken an immediate liking to Ellie, and together they carried plates of sandwiches and quiches through to the dining room. 'You're doing Sam's job at the brewery, aren't you?' asked Becca.

'I've been filling in for him. Initially I thought it would be just for a few weeks. But obviously I'm still there.'

'Do you think you'll stay on?'

'That depends on Sam.' Ellie moved closer to Becca and dropped her voice. 'What do you think? Is he planning to return to work? Does he want his old job back?'

'I honestly don't know. Sam's still got a long road ahead of him. The doctor says he's got to take things one step at a time.' Becca was aware she was slipping into the platitudes that Dr Kirtlington was so fond of. 'What about you, though? What do you want?'

Ellie's face lit up. 'I really love working at the brewery. I didn't think it would be so much fun, but I enjoy meeting clients and keeping them happy.'

'Then you should speak to Greg and tell him how you feel. Maybe there's room for both you and Sam at the brewery. Especially now that...' Becca tailed off, leaving the sentence unfinished.

*Especially now that Marcus is dead.*

This really was turning out to be a total minefield. Fortunately, Ellie seemed quite relaxed about it. 'You're right. I'll talk to Uncle Greg. Listen, what are you doing tomorrow? We should have lunch together. Just the two of us. Get to know each other.'

'Sure, why not? I'd like that.' It was a long time since Becca had done anything sociable with a friend and even though she and Ellie had only just met, she felt sure they had a lot in common.

They took the last of the food through to the dining room. More people had arrived now, including Marcus's widow, Olivia. Denise was fussing over her grandson, Freddie, who was sitting on Olivia's lap. Becca had

212

wondered if Olivia would show up today, so soon after her husband's death. But she could see that Denise and her daughter-in-law were taking comfort in their shared grief. Maybe that was the true purpose of this so-called party – to bring together those who had suffered so great a loss, and begin to make sense of it.

A man was standing in the doorway of the room, looking uncomfortable and out of place. Becca had never seen him before, but his similarity with Greg was striking.

'Have you met my Dad?' Ellie asked Becca. 'Let me introduce you. Dad, this is Becca, Sam's girlfriend.'

The man who looked so much like Greg they could have been twins turned in Becca's direction and held out a hand. 'Keith Earnshaw. Pleased to meet you.'

'Likewise,' said Becca. Perhaps this was the mysterious stranger Denise had mentioned. No one had ever spoken Keith's name all the time Becca had known Sam. She wondered what might have happened to drive a wedge between the two brothers.

Keith looked nervously over his shoulder. 'Is Greg around?'

'Here he comes now,' said Ellie.

Greg was stalking along the hallway, a beer bottle in one hand, a glass in the other. He stopped a couple of paces before Keith, his eyes blazing with anger. 'What are you doing here? On today of all days.'

Keith took a step back. 'I came because Denise invited me. But if you'd rather I left…'

'No, don't go, Keith!' Denise came forward, positioning herself between the two men. She turned to her husband. 'Greg, I asked Keith here today because we need all the family to come together. When something like this happens, you realise that life is too precious to waste on petty squabbles. Whatever's happened in the past, it's time for you two to put your differences aside. Please, for Marcus's sake.'

Greg's face was as dark as thunder, but after a moment the cloud seemed to pass over, ushering in a ray of sun. His voice cracked as he moved forward to grasp his brother. 'Keith.'

'Greg.' The two men wrapped arms clumsily around each other, standing in an awkward embrace in the middle of the room.

Ellie leaned in to whisper in Becca's ear. 'Bloody hell. I never thought I'd live to see that happen. They haven't spoken in years.'

'What caused the rift?' asked Becca, wondering just how much her new-found friend would be willing to divulge, but Ellie just shrugged.

When the two men had finished their emotional reunion and Keith had been furnished with a glass of beer, Ellie tapped him on the shoulder. 'Dad, Becca and I are having lunch tomorrow. Can you keep a table for us?'

'Sure,' said Keith.

'Dad runs a restaurant in town,' explained Ellie. 'Okay if we go there?'

'Sounds great,' said Becca.

The doorbell rang again. Denise had returned to the baby, and Greg had disappeared into the kitchen, so Becca went to answer it.

A middle-aged man and woman stood on the doorstep. 'Oh, hello there.' The woman bustled in through the open door and gave Becca a huge and unexpected hug. 'Let me guess. You must be Sam's girlfriend?'

'Becca, that's right.'

'Sam told me a lot about you. You know – before he had his accident. And I've heard how you stood by him the whole time he was in hospital. Not many girlfriends would do that, I can tell you.' The newcomer looked Becca up and down approvingly. 'Oh, I'm Sandra by the way, Greg's secretary from the brewery, and this is Gavin, our head brewer.'

The brewer, a tall, thickset man who looked to have bidden farewell to the last of his hair some years ago, inclined his shiny head but remained silent. Perhaps he was used to not being able to get a word in edgeways in

Sandra's company.

Becca wondered if they were a couple or if it was just a coincidence they had arrived together. 'Nice to meet you.'

'Come on,' said Sandra, seizing Gavin by the hand and dragging him over the threshold, 'don't just hang about outside. Let's go and find Greg and Denise.'

Becca stood aside to let them past. Sandra seemed to be the sort of person who would liven up any party, whether it was a celebration or a wake. Just as well, since no one seemed to know exactly what kind of event this was.

Becca returned to the dining room and put together two plates of food for herself and Sam. The party looked to be in full swing, with everyone drinking beer or wine, tucking into Denise's catering, and expressing a mixture of condolences and congratulations to Greg and Denise. Sandra was doing a round of the room, hugging and kissing everyone in her path.

Becca made her way into the living room where Sam was looking somewhat abandoned and handed him his food. 'It seems to be going well. There's quite a crowd.' Becca had left the front door on the latch so that new arrivals could find their way inside by themselves. Various friends and neighbours were dropping in, swelling the numbers considerably. So much for only close friends and family, it looked like half of Scarborough was here.

Sam pushed food around his plate with his fork. 'No sign of Anthony. You think they've charged him?'

'I don't know.' Becca had heard nothing more about Anthony's arrest and didn't know what was happening with him. Even if he'd been released from custody, would he have the courage to show up here after being accused of his brother's murder? The other person who was conspicuous by her absence was Naomi, Anthony's wife. It was hard to see how she could ever be welcomed back into the bosom of the family, having broken her own marriage as well as Marcus's and set in train a sequence of events that had ended with one son dead and the other arrested.

The doorbell rang again. One of the latest entrants must have locked the door behind them. 'I'll get it,' said Becca. She opened the front door and stifled a gasp.

Naomi Earnshaw, the scarlet woman herself, was standing on the doorstep as bold as brass, in a faux fur jacket over a short black dress. Her eyes flashed at Becca and she strode in through the open doorway, not bothering to say hello.

Becca followed her through into the dining room.

Naomi came to a halt in the centre of the room. One by one, conversations died away as eyes turned to stare in her direction. Becca wondered how many of the people there knew of the affair between Naomi and Marcus. Judging from the general reaction to her arrival, probably most of them. A rumour like that would spread like wildfire through such a gathering.

The silence stretched until it became painful, and then Naomi marched up to Denise, threw her arms around her mother-in-law and made an emotional declaration. 'I'm so sorry, Denise.'

Whether she was expressing sorrow over Marcus's death or apologising for the affair was not clear, but there was no denying the tears that ran down her cheeks.

Denise stood self-consciously, embracing her daughter-in-law with obvious reluctance. But then her own emotions seemed to overwhelm her and she burst into tears herself, hugging Naomi against her chest. The two women stood locked together for a few moments, and then stepped apart.

Becca observed Naomi's performance with admiration. Now that was the way to make a comeback against all odds.

The moment of awkwardness seemed to have passed, and the murmur of conversation resumed. Only Olivia's face remained icy, her eyes following her rival hawkishly wherever she went.

By four o'clock, people had started to disperse. Becca went around the room, clearing away plates and glasses.

As she was carrying them through to the kitchen, she heard raised voices coming from within and stopped.

'You've got a nerve, showing up here!' It was Olivia. Becca had never heard the normally gentle mother so angry. 'How dare you show your face in this house! Because of you, my husband is dead and Freddie is without a father. I hope you enjoy being the wife of a murderer!'

'Don't lay all the blame on me!' retorted Naomi. 'If you'd taken better care of your husband, he would never have turned to me. You just wanted a baby, you didn't want Marcus.'

'You bitch!'

'Anyway, don't tell me you didn't know the affair was going on. You knew Marcus was cheating on you when you saw us together the night of the party at the brewery, yet still you were content to play the passive wife and do nothing about it.'

Olivia looked like she'd been slapped. 'Marcus loved me. I thought your sordid affair would quickly fizzle out. I thought the baby would bring us closer together.'

'Well how did that work out?' Naomi glared at Olivia. When she spoke again, there was a catch in her voice. 'The truth is, in the end Marcus decided to come back to you. When I saw him on Friday, he told me the affair had to end.'

'You're lying!'

'It's true,' said Naomi. 'Even though I begged him to leave you, ultimately he chose you over me. So you'd won anyway. I was the one he jilted.'

Becca tiptoed away from the kitchen just as Naomi stormed out. She paused when she saw Becca to give some parting advice. 'Stay well clear of this family if you know what's good for you. They're bad news.' And with that she was gone.

Becca wondered if she ought to go and console Olivia, but decided it was best to keep her distance. Besides, she was busy processing what she'd just heard.

*I was the one he jilted.*

Olivia had been betrayed by her husband, but Naomi, the mistress, had also been spurned by her lover. Which of them had the greater motive for wanting Marcus dead?

*Hell hath no fury.*

Becca returned to the living room and found Sam where she had left him, still sitting in his chair. He looked rather forlorn and she realised she hadn't spent as much time with him as she ought to have done. She would make it up to him, but there was one thing she needed to do first. She took out her phone and started typing.

'What are you doing?' asked Sam.

'Just sending Raven a message.'

'Why?'

'Just something I overheard just now.'

'For God's sake, Becca, don't you ever stop?'

She looked at him in surprise. 'What do you mean?'

'You've hardly spoken to me all day. This was meant to be a private, family gathering. Not an opportunity for you to listen at keyholes and report back to your boss.'

Becca stopped typing, stunned by the resentment in his voice. Sam had never spoken to her like that before. 'I thought you wanted me to find out the truth,' she said defensively.

'That's what I thought too. But the truth's a blunt instrument isn't it? It doesn't care who it hurts. First Marcus ended up dead and then Anthony was arrested. Now you're spying on the rest of my family.'

'But–'

He turned his face away from her. 'Just go and tell your boss what you've found out. That's what you really came here for today isn't it?'

'Sam–'

'Just go!'

# CHAPTER 29

Raven had arranged to meet Lisa at her hotel after lunch. She had chosen a fine place to stay – a smart establishment above the south cliff – not cheap, but enjoying commanding views over the South Bay and spa. The hotel had a small terrace garden with chairs and tables but this was no weather for sitting outdoors. It was the kind of day to "blow the cobwebs off" as Raven's mother used to say. Clouds scudded across the big sky, gulls screeched and swooped on the gusting wind. Droves of white horses galloped across the curving bay before dashing onto the shore in a frenzy of foam.

The landscape was alive. It was impossible not to feel invigorated on a day like today.

Lisa was well muffled against the elements in a coat with a fur-trimmed hood. Raven turned up the collar of his overcoat. They set off walking towards the town.

'You get great views from up here.' Raven indicated the sweep of the bay with his arm. He pointed out the spa buildings down below, the harbour at the northern curve, the grey castle rising above the headland. 'See that church near the top of the hill? That's St Mary's. Anne Brontë is buried in the graveyard.' He thought Lisa might appreciate that little snippet of literary culture.

She took his arm and fell into step beside him. 'And when was the last time you read a book by Anne Brontë, Tom?' she teased.

'Never.' All the same, he felt a need to prove to her that there was more to this "*northern* seaside town" – as Lisa had once scathingly called it – than just windswept beaches and amusement arcades. They went as far as Birdcage Walk, stopping just before the footbridge that spanned the Valley Road. Ahead of them loomed the edifice of the Grand Hotel, Scarborough's most iconic landmark.

'My mother worked as a chambermaid in that hotel.' Raven had rarely spoken about his parents when they lived in London. Jean and Alan Raven had seemed like distant memories from another world. Now he was reminded of them constantly. A fishing boat setting out to sea, and he saw his father, strong arms ready to cast the nets. A glimpse of the Grand, and his mother was at his side, showing him the proper way to tuck in sheets and make a bed.

He pointed out the hotel's various architectural features for Lisa's benefit. 'See the towers at each corner? They represent the four seasons. The twelve floors represent the months of the year. There are fifty-two chimneys, one for each week. And originally there were three hundred and sixty-five bedrooms.'

'Shall we have a peek inside?' asked Lisa.

But even though it was half a lifetime since his mother had died, Raven feared the painful memories that the interior of the hotel might stir. 'No, let's go the other way.'

He led her along the winding footpath past the Victorian splendour of the spa and up through the Rose Garden and Italian Gardens that adorned the clifftops. The roses were nothing more than bare stems bending in the wind, yet even at this most austere time of year they held out the promise of better days to come.

Before long they were back outside Lisa's hotel. Elegant terraces on one side of the street, open sea on the other.

The safety of the harbour before them, rugged coastline behind. The wind, everywhere.

'I'm beginning to see why you like it so much here,' said Lisa. 'There's a kind of wild magic to the place.' She took his hand. 'Shall we go inside for a coffee?'

Her cheeks were red with cold and Raven couldn't feel his nose. He didn't decline her offer. They sat together in the warm lounge, drinking coffee and watching as colour slowly drained from the sky.

'You promised you'd let me know about Christmas,' said Lisa.

'I did.'

'And?'

After speaking to Hannah on the phone, he had to admit he'd warmed to the idea. If Lisa wanted a reunion and Hannah was okay with it, who was he to stand in the way? A family Christmas together. He was tempted, he couldn't deny it. And after that? Well, they could wait and see.

'I think we should give it a go.'

A smile broke out across Lisa's face, as radiant as the rising sun. 'Thank you, Tom.' She leaned across the table and kissed him on the lips. A soft, tender kiss that lingered, growing warm and hungry.

When she suggested they go upstairs to her room, he had no will to resist.

★

Anthony sat hunched in his thick winter coat in a deckchair by the open door of the family beach hut. When he'd been released that morning, he hadn't known where else to go. He couldn't go home and face his wife – not after the things he'd said to her, calling her a whore and a slut. And he couldn't go to his parents' house either. Would they think he had actually killed his own brother? Naomi would certainly think him capable of such a crime. So he had made his way to the North Bay and let himself into the old hut where he'd spent so many happy summers with his brothers.

The North Sands were deserted, save for the occasional dogwalker, hurrying to get out of the wind. Anthony remembered how the family used to come here during the summer, spending whole days down on the beach. Building enormous sandcastles, constructing moats and dams, hunting for starfish in the rock pools. The long row of brightly painted huts had enchanted him. The Earnshaws' hut was blue, its neighbours lime green and red. There were yellow and orange ones too. His parents had held on to the hut long after all three boys had grown up, maybe thinking that their grandchildren would enjoy coming here in their turn. The wooden hut was equipped with deckchairs, a kettle and a sink. There was even an inflatable mattress if he decided to spend the night here.

He stared out over the cold sea and thought about the chain of events that had led him to this point. He'd been foolish when he'd first joined the business, he could see that now. Embezzling money from the firm had been too easy. He'd wanted to give Naomi the best and had fallen into temptation. He'd thought he could get away with it, but Jeremy hadn't been the fool he'd taken him for. When Jeremy had threatened to tell Greg about the missing money if Anthony didn't pay it back, he'd felt trapped, desperate.

But he would never have killed to save himself.

He couldn't deny that the finance director's sudden death had come as a relief, letting him off the hook. The coroner had declared it to be accidental, but to Anthony it had seemed providential, as if some benevolent god was giving him a second chance. And he'd learnt his lesson. He'd never stolen a penny after that.

As for Marcus, he'd wished many a time that the same god would strike his older brother down. They'd always been rivals, growing up, and the affair with Naomi had sealed their antagonism. Marcus had broken a bond of trust that should have been unbreakable. But Anthony was no Cain. He would never kill his own brother.

Sam had always been his favourite. With Sam there was none of that rivalry that had marred his relationship with his older sibling. But he had let Sam down. He hadn't visited him in hospital as much as he should have done. He'd been too wrapped up in his own problems. And besides, he'd thought that Sam was as good as dead.

But Sam had woken up, against all the odds, and it was time for them to renew their bond of friendship.

As light turned to dusk, then disappeared completely, Anthony came to a decision. He would resign from the family business, give up the travelling, settle down somewhere new. If Naomi would come with him, they would move together, somewhere a long way from Scarborough and make a fresh start.

He shivered inside his coat. Coming to the beach hut had helped him get his head straight, think things through, but if he stayed here all night it would make him look like a fugitive on the run. He was innocent of the charges he'd been accused of and he needed to stand up and prove it.

The last of the dogwalkers had long gone home. The North Bay was deserted. He folded the deckchair, stacked it against the wall of the beach hut with the rest and fished in his pocket for the key.

It was cold enough for snow and his fingers were frozen. As he fumbled the key into the lock he heard footsteps behind him. One final lone dogwalker perhaps. He was about to turn around when he felt something cold and sharp against his back. The blade pressed softly into his flesh, almost painlessly, sliding easily between his ribs like ice.

He gasped for air, but no breath came. The knife withdrew, then thrust again, puncturing his second lung. Now it hurt. It hurt like the devil. Perhaps that benevolent god had returned, but this time for vengeance. Like Jeremy had said, a debt always had to be repaid.

He took another gulp, desperate for air, but still none came. There was only pain – a sharp burning in his chest.

He staggered, then fell, collapsing onto the sandy walkway by the hut. The key dropped from his fingers and lay on the ground, gleaming like gold as the world faded. The last thing he heard was the moaning of the wind. Or it might have been his final breath.

# CHAPTER 30

The call came through early and Raven left a sleeping Lisa in the comfortable king-size bed at the hotel to venture out to Scarborough's North Bay. They'd made love the previous afternoon, and again after dinner in the hotel, and it had been like the early days of their relationship – exciting and passionate. Lisa was a different person here in Scarborough – carefree, like the woman he'd fallen in love with all those years ago. Maybe she could be persuaded to leave London for good in favour of the rejuvenating benefits of a former spa town. They wouldn't be going for a walk today – not in the horizontal rain that was gusting in from the sea – but they had agreed to meet again that evening.

Right now Raven wished he could be back in the comfort of the hotel and not standing beside a dead body in front of a blue-painted beach hut while the wind whipped rain against his frozen face.

The area around the beach hut was sealed off with crime tape and Holly Chang and her team had shielded the body with a white tent. The polythene snapped and billowed in the wind and looked as if it might take flight at any moment. The CSI team had placed numbered evidence markers around the crime scene and were now examining the interior of the hut in minute detail.

The gruesome discovery had been made shortly after dawn by an early-morning jogger. DC Tony Bairstow had been the first detective on the scene and had been the one who had called Raven. Tony pulled back the flap of the tent so that Raven could peer inside.

'There'll need to be a formal identification,' said Tony, 'but it's definitely Anthony Earnshaw.' The body was lying on its side, the handle of a knife protruding from its back. 'That's a professional Sabatier kitchen knife. Judging from the size of the handle, I'd say the blade is probably around twenty centimetres long.'

'Plenty long enough to have punctured a lung,' said Raven. He kneeled down to examine the body more closely. 'There are at least two separate stab wounds.'

'His phone and wallet were still on him,' said Tony, 'and the keys to the hut were on the ground near his hand. Looks like he dropped them when he fell.'

'So we can rule out a mugging.' It looked like Raven's theory that Anthony was responsible for the Salt Castle murders would need to be revised. Whoever had killed Marcus and Jeremy and tried to kill Sam had probably also murdered the middle brother, even though the MO was different. 'There's been no attempt to make this look like an accident. Whoever is behind these murders is beginning to lose patience.'

DC Jess Barraclough's Land Rover drew to a halt a short distance beyond the sealed area and Jess emerged dressed in head-to-toe waterproofs. 'What have we got, sir?'

He let her take a look at the body before leading her and Tony to shelter behind a neighbouring beach hut for an impromptu team meeting.

'So now we're looking for someone who knew where to find Anthony, or guessed that he might be here. That same person killed Marcus at the brewery, wiping the CCTV.

They were also at the brewery the night Sam was pushed in front of the van, and they knew Jeremy too. We're looking at someone who works – or worked – for the brewery, or possibly a family member.'

'Do you still think that the attempt to kill Sam was a case of mistaken identity?' asked Tony. 'Or were all three brothers deliberately targeted?'

'I think that we can't rule out either possibility. Either way, we're no longer looking at a feud between the brothers, but something larger.'

'Perhaps someone with a grudge against the brewery?' suggested Jess. 'Or against the family?'

'Sir,' said Tony, 'I ran background checks on everyone who currently works at the brewery. Gavin Thompson, the head brewer, came up on a PNC search. Just over twenty years ago he was convicted of manslaughter after a punch-up in a local pub. He served a four-year sentence.'

Raven drew in a breath. 'Good work, Tony. I'll go and speak to him now. Can I ask you to stay and supervise things here?'

★

Despite the sour note that Becca and Sam had parted on the previous day, she was determined to keep her promise to call round and take him to his physiotherapy session. She had booked time off work especially. Besides, she wanted to be with him. She'd stayed by his side all the time he'd been in a coma. She wasn't going to abandon him now.

But when she rang the doorbell at the house on Scalby Mills Road, she was startled when a uniformed police officer answered it. Becca showed her warrant card and asked what the constable was doing at the house.

'I'm PC Sharon Jarvis, ma'am. Family Liaison Officer. I'm here to support the family during the murder investigation.'

Becca shook her head in confusion. 'But the FLO went

on Saturday. The family asked to be left alone to grieve in peace.'

PC Jarvis raised an eyebrow. 'You haven't heard, then, ma'am. A second murder has taken place. The middle brother, Anthony.'

'Oh my God.' Becca reached for the doorframe to steady herself. 'When did it happen?'

'Some time last night. The body was found this morning.' Sharon lowered her voice. 'The father has gone to the mortuary to ID the body. The mother is upstairs.'

'And Sam?'

'He's here. Do you want to see him?'

'He's the reason I came.'

Becca stepped over the threshold and went through to the living room where Sam was sitting, staring out of the picture window. The usual view over the headland and sea had turned to grey in the drizzly rain, but Sam didn't seem to notice. He turned as she entered and she saw that his face was stained with tears.

'Oh, Sam, I'm so sorry.' She went to him and they embraced.

'Becca.' His cross words of the day before appeared to be forgotten. 'I'm so glad you came.'

'Of course I came. I promised you I would.'

He seemed chastened. 'You know about Anthony?'

'I just heard. What have the police told you?'

'Nothing much. Just that he was found at the beach hut. You know, the one on the North Bay.'

'How did he die?'

'The police won't say.'

'That's normal,' Becca assured him. 'They'll want to get the post-mortem results before they make a statement.' But the FLO had been clear – she had called it murder. Becca's mind was racing. Two brothers dead, and an attempt made on Sam's life. Was someone engaged in a vendetta against the Earnshaw family? Was Sam in danger?

'So what are you going to do?' she asked him.

'Me? I'm going to my physio session at the hospital.'

'Are you sure? Don't you think it would be better to take a day off?'

A look of annoyance passed over his face. 'No. I was only discharged on the condition that I attend daily sessions. I don't want to give Dr Kirtlington an excuse to insist that I go back in as an in-patient. And besides, I want to get my mobility back. I hate being like this.' He gestured angrily at the walking stick propped against his chair and the wheelchair that was folded up to one side. 'I want to get better.'

'Well, if you're sure. I'll tell the FLO where we're going.'

Becca helped Sam into her car and folded the wheelchair into the back. It was a tight fit in the small boot, but she just managed it. She put the Jazz into gear and pulled away slowly, not wanting to give Sam a rough ride on the short trip to the hospital. She knew he wouldn't like what she was about to tell him.

'Sam, I think I'll stay at the hospital with you today. I don't want to let you out of my sight. And I'm going to ask Raven if we can station an officer outside your house.'

'What for?'

'Because you're at risk. Marcus and Anthony are dead, and someone tried to kill you. I think they'll come back and try again.'

He shook his head. 'That doesn't make sense. Who would want to kill me?'

Becca took the plunge. 'You have to face facts. Marcus and Anthony were most likely killed by someone who was at your house yesterday. A friend or a family member. Or someone who works at the brewery.'

'That's ridiculous. How can you even think that?'

'Because I'm looking at this objectively.' Becca kept her eyes on the road, but she could feel Sam's anger directed towards her.

'No, you're not. Everyone at the house yesterday was a close friend or family. I've known them for years. You've never liked my family and now you're accusing them of murder! How do you think that makes me feel?'

'I can't imagine how you must be feeling right now. But how else do you explain what's going on?' Becca turned the car into the hospital car park and began searching for a space.

She waited for him to reply. But he was looking straight ahead out of the window, his expression furious.

'Sam, both your brothers are dead. You could be next.'

She found a space in the far corner of the car park and squeezed the Jazz into the gap. He was still ignoring her, his arms folded across his chest. She retrieved the wheelchair from the back and went to help him into it.

'I can manage,' he snapped.

'Don't be silly.'

'I said I can do it!'

She watched him as he inched his way out of the car seat, every muscle in his arms tensing as he struggled to do it himself. A vein stood out on his forehead but he refused to let her help.

'Sam.'

Eventually he was in the chair. 'Don't come inside with me,' he told her. 'I can do it myself.' He gripped the wheels of the chair, his arms straining to turn them.

Becca stood to one side, swallowing her frustration at his behaviour, telling herself that his anger wasn't with her, it was because he'd just lost his two brothers. 'I'll come back later and pick you up,' she said.

'Don't bother. I'll give Dad a call. I can always depend on my family.' He set off across the tarmac, battered by the wind and rain, but determined not to accept her help.

# CHAPTER 31

The Salt Castle brewery had fully reopened in the wake of Marcus's death, and all the crime scene tape had gone. The concrete floor where Marcus's body had been found showed no traces of blood. Holly's cleaning tip had worked, or maybe the brewery workers knew a thing or two about hygiene themselves.

Raven found the head brewer adjusting the electronic control panel on one of the huge steel vats.

'Don't mind if I get on with this, do you?' said Gavin. 'Only we got a bit behind when we had to close the other day. Don't want this lot to spoil, otherwise that's a few thousand quid's worth of beer down the drain.'

'No, you carry on.' Raven hadn't yet explained what he was doing at the brewery, and Gavin gave no indication that he was aware of the latest murder. He seemed focussed on his task. Raven could sense the passion of the brewer for his work. Brewing beer was clearly more than just a job for him, it was a way of life.

Raven's hair was still wet from the rain. He pushed it back from his forehead, glad to be indoors, in the warm cocoon of the brewery. The thick resiny smell of hops filled his nose. Liquid bubbled and gurgled in the pipes like blood coursing through the arteries of some great beast. It was like standing inside a living creature, witnessing the creation of a strange new form of life. 'When did you last see Anthony Earnshaw?'

'Anthony? It was when I handed him over to you, on Saturday morning.'

'He didn't return to your flat after he was released on Sunday?'

'No. I didn't know he'd been released. Why d'you ask?' A note of caution had entered Gavin's voice.

'What did you do on Sunday?'

Gavin turned to face him, a frown deepening across his brow. 'I popped round to Greg and Denise's with Sandra – she's the secretary here. We wanted to pay our respects regarding Marcus. And of course to welcome Sam home.'

'Anthony wasn't there?'

'No. What's this about?'

'What about Sunday evening? Where were you?'

Gavin sighed at Raven's refusal to answer any of his questions. 'Sandra drove me home about four o'clock.'

'And then?'

'Beans on toast in front of the telly. I had an early night because I'd been up late the night before and knew there would be loads of work to catch up on today.' He gave a meaningful glance towards the upper gallery. 'Mind if I press on?'

'Go ahead.' Raven watched as Gavin climbed the metal staircase with ease, his long legs striding purposefully up the steps, grabbing the rails with his beefy arms. Raven followed at a more sedate pace, his leg as always holding him back. 'Tell me about Friday.'

Gavin threw a backward glance at him, clearly irritated by Raven's persistence. 'What about it?' He was becoming markedly less cooperative.

'What time did you leave work?'

'Late. I wanted to check everything was in order before the weekend.'

'Did you see Marcus before you went home?'

'He was in the office.'

'Anyone else with him?'

'No. And before you ask, he was alive and well when I left him.'

'One of my team has done a bit of digging into your background.'

Gavin's eyes narrowed. 'Aye? And what did they find, as if I didn't know?'

'That you were convicted of manslaughter.'

The brewer sighed, his shoulders slumping forward. 'I was wondering when you were going to bring that up. It seems that even after twenty years have passed I still have to pay the price for a moment's stupidity.'

'Tell me what happened,' said Raven, his voice not unkind.

Gavin leaned back against one of the steel cylinders. 'I was young and hot-headed. Got into a bit of a punch-up down the pub.' He held up his hands as if they were to blame. 'I'd had a few to drink, maybe more than a few. Some dickhead accused me of spilling his pint. He started pushing me about, threatening me. I should have walked away, but I was a fool. I threw him a punch, just the one. It wasn't even that hard. I wasn't trying to knock him out or anything. But he fell and struck the back of his head on the corner of a table. That was what killed him. I'm not proud of it, but I served my time. These days, I help out with the local boxing club, helping youngsters to channel their energy into something constructive. It teaches them discipline. Some of those boys have no one else in their life to show them how to behave. I like to think that I can help them avoid the kind of mistake I made.'

'You got a job here after you were released from prison?'

'Greg gave me my old job back. I've always been grateful to him for that. He was willing to give me a second chance when no one else would. I owe him a lot.'

Raven digested the information. 'You said that no one

else would give you a chance. Did that include Jeremy Green?'

Gavin's face was suddenly guarded. 'Does it matter what Jeremy thought?'

'Just answer the question.'

'Well, since you ask, the truth is that Jeremy didn't want me back. Greg had to persuade him. Even though the three of us went way back, Jeremy thought I was too much trouble.'

'And how did that make you feel? Knowing that one of your closest friends had lost confidence in you? That one of the company's directors didn't want you working here?'

'I kept my head down and got on with the job. Jeremy's path didn't cross mine very much. Look, why are you asking me all these questions? Has something happened to Anthony? Has he gone missing?'

'Not exactly.'

'Then what?'

'He's dead.'

The words flew out and hit Gavin like a slap. His face whitened. 'He's what?'

'You heard me.'

The brewer seemed to sink into himself. He shook his head in disbelief.

Raven regarded him, trying to measure whether his reaction was genuine or a calculated charade. He decided that he didn't know the brewer well enough to take a view on the matter. 'Don't go anywhere,' he cautioned. 'We'll need to speak to you again.'

*

Becca sat in the car, tears rolling down her cheeks in step with the raindrops trickling down the car's windscreen. She was still too stunned to drive. What had got into Sam? She knew this was a difficult time for him, but to just turn away from her like that! She had only been expressing concern for him.

She needed to find out what was going on with Anthony. She dialled Raven's number and was pleasantly surprised when he answered instead of letting it go to voicemail.

'Aren't you supposed to be taking some time off?' he said by way of greeting.

'I am. But I've just heard that Anthony has been murdered. What's going on?'

The line went quiet and she thought he wasn't going to tell her anything. That would be just like Raven. But then he seemed to think better of it. 'Anthony was found outside the family's beach hut first thing this morning. My guess is that he was killed late yesterday evening or last night. He was stabbed with a knife. Two puncture wounds to the back. It looked to me like they'd collapsed his lungs.'

'So there was no attempt to make it look accidental?'

'I think the killer has moved on from that stage. Whatever's driving them, it's becoming more urgent.'

Raven's statement confirmed Becca's worst fears. 'You think they'll kill again?'

'We have no way of knowing, but we can't rule it out.'

'Then I'd like some kind of protection for Sam.'

'I thought you were with him today.'

'I just dropped him at the hospital for his physio session.' It was too painful for Becca to admit that Sam had walked out on her.

'He'll be safe enough at the hospital, and he'll be safe at home with the family liaison officer to keep an eye on things.'

'What about when she leaves?'

'I'll arrange for uniform to put a car outside the house tonight.'

'Thank you.' It was just what Becca needed to hear. Whatever happened, Sam would be safe. 'What sort of knife was used to kill Anthony?'

'A Sabatier kitchen knife.'

A cold prickle ran down the back of her neck. 'I know someone who has a set of Sabatier knives.'

'Who?'

'Denise. Everyone was round at the family home yesterday. I helped chop the vegetables with one of those knives. Nearly sliced my finger off.'

'Could someone have taken one?'

'Sure. Anyone who was there. They were kept on the kitchen worktop.' It would have been a simple matter for one of the guests to go into the kitchen and remove a knife from the wooden block where they were stored. They might even have taken the knife Becca left on the draining board.

'You'll need to give me the names of all the guests.'

Becca told him all the names she knew. 'But there were also friends and neighbours popping in who I wasn't introduced to. You'll need to ask Denise for a definitive list.'

'I will,' said Raven, 'but did you say that Naomi was there? I thought she would have kept well away.'

'I was surprised too. But yes, Naomi turned up and made quite a grand entrance. She seems to have been accepted back into the family, although not everyone was so welcoming.'

'Olivia?'

'I overheard her and Naomi having a slanging match in the kitchen towards the end of the afternoon. Naomi accused Olivia of knowing about the affair the night of the hit and run. Olivia admitted it. Then Naomi said that on Friday, Marcus dumped her. One of them could have grabbed the knife on their way out and murdered Anthony. Olivia because she suspected him of killing her husband, or Naomi because she suspected him of killing her lover.'

The line went quiet again. 'What a tangled mess,' he said eventually. But he didn't tell her what his next steps would be. Typical Raven.

# CHAPTER 32

Raven was pleased when the door to Greg and Denise's house on Scalby Mills Road was opened by the family liaison officer. Becca had been right to alert him to the possibility that the killer may not yet have concluded their grisly business. Whatever the murderer's agenda, the Earnshaw family was at the heart of the matter, and the possibility remained that another attempt would be made on Sam's life, or that further members of the family would be targeted.

'DCI Raven.'

Raven had encountered PC Sharon Jarvis on a previous case and knew that the FLO was someone he could depend on. Short but broad-shouldered, she looked like she could handle anything that came her way. 'How's the family bearing up?'

'As you'd expect.' There was no need for Sharon to elaborate. Two sons dead. The parents must be devastated.

The house was silent. 'Are they at home?'

'Mr Earnshaw went to ID the body but he hasn't returned. Sam's at the hospital. Mrs Earnshaw is in the front room.'

'Do you think she's up to talking to me?'

'You can try. It might do her good.'

Sharon led him into the living room where Denise was sitting on a sofa staring vaguely into space. She seemed to have reached a state beyond grief, her features frozen, her face revealing no emotion. Her swanlike neck turned as Raven entered, but she gave no sign of recognition. A sad collection of sympathy cards consoling the family over Marcus's death crowded the mantlepiece in the spaces between the family photos. Another flurry of cards would soon be joining them.

A square of card seemed a poor consolation for a life, however heartfelt the sentiments it expressed.

Raven fixed a grim expression to his face. 'Mrs Earnshaw? I'm sorry for your loss. Would it be all right to ask you some questions?'

Her blank face studied his. After a moment she nodded dumbly.

'I wonder if you'd be able to help me by providing a list of all the guests who came to your house yesterday? There's no need for you to do it right now – perhaps you and Sharon could sit down after I've gone and go through the names. You might want to consult with your husband. It's important that you don't miss anyone off. Could you do that for me, Denise?'

She nodded.

'Right now, I wonder if you'd mind coming through to the kitchen with me?'

Sharon gave him a questioning look, but Denise nodded slowly. 'Yes. All right.' She rose unsteadily to her feet and Sharon stepped forwards to lend a hand. Raven followed them through to the back of the house.

The kitchen wasn't as sleek and modern as Marcus and Olivia's, but it was large and well equipped with top quality appliances – a Miele dishwasher, a filter coffee maker, a retro-styled food processor.

'Do you own any Sabatier knives?' asked Raven.

'Sabatier? Yes, why?'

'Could you check them for me please?'

Denise approached the granite worktop and pulled a wooden block towards her. Seven black handles protruded from the block, each one studded with stainless steel in the distinctive style that Raven had last seen on the knife sticking out of Anthony's back. She took her time examining them. 'One's missing.'

'Maybe it's in the dishwasher?'

Denise pulled open the dishwasher, sliding out a cutlery tray at the top. It was full of knives, forks and spoons, but there was no Sabatier knife.

'Could someone have put it in a drawer by mistake?' asked Sharon. 'You had a lot of people here yesterday.'

Denise slid some drawers open and started rifling through wooden spoons, spatulas, a whisk, a couple of vegetable peelers and assorted chopsticks. No knife.

'Could you describe the missing knife for me please?' said Raven.

Denise leaned against the kitchen worktop, her face pale. 'It's a chef's knife. About this big.' She held her hands about eight inches apart. 'I use it for chopping vegetables. Carrots, parsnips, butternut squash.'

'It's sharp then?'

'Very.' There would need to be further tests, but it looked as if they'd identified the murder weapon. Denise's lower lip trembled. 'Was the knife used to kill Anthony?'

There was no point in Raven denying it. Denise had drawn the obvious conclusion for herself. 'I'm very sorry, Mrs Earnshaw.'

Denise closed her eyes, steadying herself against the kitchen cupboards.

'I think it's best if we all go and sit down,' said Sharon, giving Raven a reproachful look.

They returned to the living room and took seats near the window. 'Did you see anyone take a knife from the kitchen yesterday?' asked Raven.

'Only Becca. She helped me prepare the food. But

anyone could have taken it. I was busy with my grandson and the other guests.' A look of horror slowly spread across Denise's face as realisation dawned. 'The man who murdered my sons was in this house yesterday!'

'Man or woman. We can't rule anyone out at this stage.'

Her hands curled into fists in her lap and she fixed Raven with a beseeching look. 'Chief Inspector, why is someone destroying my family?'

'I'm sorry, I don't yet know. But perhaps you could tell me more about the early days of the business, when it was just your husband, Jeremy and Gavin. I'd like to hear more about that.'

She nodded and relaxed, her hands uncurling. 'It was always Greg's ambition to build his own business. He didn't really mind what kind. Jeremy didn't mind either as long as there was a profit to be made. He had a keen financial mind. The brewery was Gavin's idea. I'm not sure there was any rationale to it, other than Gavin liked beer.'

'So it was Gavin's passion project?'

'In a way. But all three brought their own passions to the business. It would never have got off the ground without Greg pushing it so hard. Once he had a goal there was no stopping him.'

Denise looked as if she was raking up long-distant memories, staring directly into the past. Raven was happy to let her talk.

'I expect you already know about Gavin. He made a silly mistake and got into trouble. When Gavin got sent down, it looked as if the business would fail. What's a brewery without its brewer? But Greg worked hard and found a replacement brewer. He made a success of it.'

'And then when Gavin was released from prison, Greg brought him back?'

She smiled. 'That's Greg for you. He's loyal to a fault. Friends and family always come first.'

'Were you ever involved in the business?'

'I helped out with admin in the beginning, but when

Marcus came along, I stepped aside. Sandra had already proved herself to be more than capable.'

'Tell me more about Jeremy. When I was last here you told me that his wife died young?'

Denise sighed. 'Breast cancer. It was terribly sad. I think the brewery became like a substitute family for him.' She looked wistful. 'Those early days were hard on all of us. A struggling business, Jeremy's bereavement, Gavin in prison. And Greg away such a lot, always travelling. But the brewery thrived despite it all. Greg poured his heart into the company. It's why it matters so much to him. And why he's always been so determined to pass it on to the next generation. You can't imagine how hard the loss of Marcus and Anthony has hit him.'

'Do you think that Sam will want to carry on the business? Perhaps with Ellie's help? Have you spoken to him about it?'

'I know that Ellie's very keen to stay on. She enjoys the work. I'm not so sure about Sam. After everything he's been through, he might decide to go in a different direction.'

'Did Greg's brother never want to have anything to do with the brewery?'

'Keith? He and Greg haven't always got on.'

'Do you know why?'

'Greg's never opened up to me about Keith. They were close when I first got to know him, and for the first few years of the business. Then something happened, I don't know what.'

Raven waited to see if she had any more to add, but it seemed that her recollections had come to an end. He stood up. 'Thank you very much, Mrs Earnshaw. I'll leave you in Sharon's care now.'

★

Keith's restaurant enjoyed a good location in the heart of the town. It occupied the ground floor of a four-storey

Victorian terrace on York Place and described itself as a bistro.

Becca was greatly looking forward to her lunch with Ellie. After her argument with Sam, she needed some cheering up, and Ellie seemed like a lot of fun. Ellie was already waiting outside the bistro when Becca arrived, slightly out of breath, having hurried from the nearby multi-storey where she had struggled to park even her modest car in the narrow spaces half-blocked by pillars. Raven wouldn't have stood a chance in his BMW. She wondered what he was doing right now and whether he had followed up her tip-off about the knife. The thought that Anthony had been stabbed with the same knife that had sliced her finger was chilling. It confirmed her theory that someone at the party was responsible for the killings. She shuddered at the notion that she had so recently rubbed shoulders with the person who had pushed Sam under the van and then murdered his two brothers.

If only you could tell a murderer by their face or the way they spoke. *Some outward sign of evil.* But Becca had been a detective long enough to know that a killer generally walked among their peers unseen.

She greeted Ellie with a kiss on each cheek. 'Sorry I'm late. Parking nightmare.'

Ellie gave her a beaming smile in return. 'No worries, let's go inside.'

Keith welcomed them into his restaurant. Once again Becca was struck by his close resemblance to his brother. Even his voice was the same. He took their coats and ushered them to a table just inside the big bay window at the front of the restaurant. The circular table was set for two and adorned by a narrow glass vase holding a red carnation. It looked like he'd reserved the best spot in the house for them. 'What would you ladies like to drink?'

Normally Becca never drank while driving, but after the morning she'd had, she was sorely tempted by a glass of wine. 'Well… I shouldn't really but…'

'It's your day off, isn't it?' prompted Ellie. 'Go on, let

your hair down.'

'Oh all right,' said Becca. 'Just the one.' It wasn't like she had anywhere to go afterwards. Sam had made it perfectly clear he didn't want to see her.

Ellie ordered two glasses of house white and Keith went away, leaving them to peruse the menu.

The bistro offered a surprisingly wide choice of dishes, a mix of traditional British meals, French classics and Spanish tapas starters.

'Dad's a fantastic chef,' enthused Ellie. 'Don't look at the prices. He always lets me dine on the house.'

'That's very generous.' Even so, Becca didn't like to take advantage. She chose a simple poached salmon with salad and fries. Even that seemed extravagant compared with the usual lunchtime sandwich she ate while working. Ellie went for the more expensive *Moules à la Crème*.

'Now tell me what's upset you,' said Ellie after Keith had taken their orders. 'I can see from your eyes that you've been crying.'

Becca hadn't realised she was so transparent. Normally she didn't get emotional, but the argument with Sam had left her disoriented. 'It's Sam. We had a row.'

'It happens to everyone,' said Ellie sympathetically, taking a sip of her wine. 'If you want to talk about it, I'm happy to listen. But if it's private, then I won't pry.'

Becca wasn't sure if she did want to talk about it. She didn't usually share such personal details with strangers. But Ellie seemed like a good listener and Sam had always been close to his cousin. Maybe she'd be able to help Becca understand his frame of mind and how to handle him.

'You've heard about Anthony?'

Ellie nodded. 'Shocking isn't it?'

'Two brothers dead.'

'You think Sam might be in danger?' Ellie had gone immediately to Becca's main concern.

'I do. But Sam won't hear of it. He thinks I'm making a fuss.'

Ellie regarded her thoughtfully. 'I don't think you're

making a fuss at all. Someone already tried to kill Sam once. What's to stop them trying again?'

'Exactly. But he won't hear of it. I don't know what to say to him.'

'Do the police have any ideas about who's behind it all?'

Becca hesitated, on the brink of telling Ellie about the knife. She stopped herself just in time, police training kicking in. 'I think it must be someone very close to the family, probably connected to the business.'

Ellie arched her pale brow. 'Wow, that's shocking. But it does narrow the field of suspects, doesn't it?'

*Especially now that two family members are dead.*

Who did that leave? Becca looked across the table at the young woman sitting opposite. She had only met Ellie the day before, yet here she was having lunch with her, sharing confidences. Had Ellie known that she was a police detective? She surely must have. Had she invited Becca here so that she could find out where the investigation was going?

Ellie had joined the company after Sam's injuries had unexpectedly created a vacancy. Now two more of the company directors had been eliminated. Greg had always made clear his intention to pass the business on to the next generation, but if Sam died, who did that leave? Ellie was the closest blood relative. Would she inherit the lot?

Keith arrived, a dish in each hand. He placed the food in front of Becca and Ellie. '*Eh, voilà*. Your orders, ladies.'

Ellie beamed up at her father. 'Thanks, Dad.'

He returned her smile warmly. 'No problem. You know I'd do anything for my daughter.'

# CHAPTER 33

Back at the station, Raven gathered Jess and Tony together for a debrief. He'd just come out of a meeting with Detective Superintendent Gillian Ellis where she'd told him in no uncertain terms to get a grip on the situation before anyone else was killed. She didn't need to add, 'Or before I take you off the case.' Raven could feel the precarious nature of his position only too keenly.

On the whiteboard under the heading "victims" he wrote four names: Jeremy, Marcus, Anthony and Sam.

'For the purpose of this exercise,' he said, 'I want us to work on the assumption that Jeremy's death was no accident. It's too much of a coincidence that three directors from the same company should end up dead within the space of two years, not forgetting the attack on Sam, which he barely survived. We should also bear in mind that this is a family business and that three of the victims are brothers. It's clear that we're dealing with someone closely connected to the family.'

He fixed a photograph of the knife that had been recovered from Anthony's body to the board. 'We're also working on the assumption that the murder weapon was taken from the kitchen of the Earnshaw family home during the gathering that was held on Sunday to mark Sam's return from hospital and Marcus's death. Only close friends and family were invited to that event.'

He pinned up the list of guests that Sharon Jarvis had sent him after consulting with Denise. A total of some thirty names. 'One of these people killed Anthony Earnshaw.'

He wrote the word "suspects" on the board and underlined it. 'Who wants to go first?'

When no one spoke, Raven delved in with his own thoughts. 'One of the problems with this case is that we can't be certain whether Sam was an intended victim or if he was mistaken for Marcus. The night of the hit and run it was dark, the weather poor, the streetlighting offering limited visibility and Sam was carrying Marcus's umbrella. The attempt on his life could easily have been a case of mistaken identity.

'Marcus had a clear motive for wanting Jeremy out of the way, so that he could take over as finance director. And when we learned that Sam had seen Marcus and Naomi together at the party, we speculated that Marcus may have tried to silence him so that the affair would remain a secret. But when Marcus died, it appeared that he had been the intended victim all along. The person with the strongest motive then became Anthony. Anthony had an even stronger motive for killing Jeremy, because Jeremy had found out that he was embezzling money from the business. We also know that Anthony learned about his wife's affair the night of Sam's hit and run, and that he confronted Marcus on the day of his murder. According to Gavin Thompson, Anthony kept repeating, "He's a dead man!" But now Anthony is dead too.'

Tony raised a hand. 'Sir, is it possible that we're looking at more than one murderer? Perhaps Marcus pushed Sam under the van, or it might have been Anthony, thinking he was pushing Marcus. Then Anthony killed

Marcus. Jeremy's death may simply have been an accident.'

'Then who killed Anthony?'

'Well, I don't know.'

'How many killers can one family contain?' said Raven. 'They're not the Borgias.'

*Or were they?* He parked that thought in the dark recesses of his mind. 'Let's run through the possible suspects. What are our thoughts on Gavin Thompson, head brewer?'

'He seems like a good bloke,' said Tony. 'Straightforward. Takes pride in his work. He gave Anthony a bed for the night when he needed it.'

'Gavin admitted to me,' said Raven, 'that Jeremy opposed taking him back into the company after he was released from prison. Gavin certainly had reason to bear a grudge. Perhaps he was settling an old score. He was also the last known person to see Marcus before he died.'

'And he does have a conviction for manslaughter,' Jess pointed out, 'so we know he's capable of taking things too far.'

'That was one moment of anger,' said Tony. 'These murders are all characterised by careful planning.'

'What would he have to gain by killing Marcus and Anthony?' asked Raven.

'Well, Gavin's a traditionalist,' said Tony. 'He longs for the old ways. Marcus and Anthony wanted to sell out to a big brewery. That's against everything Gavin believes in.'

'Good,' said Raven. 'Let's move on to the wives of the murdered brothers. Starting with Naomi. We know that Jeremy found out that Anthony was embezzling money from the company. Jeremy threatened to tell Greg what was going on if Anthony didn't repay the stolen money. That gave Anthony a clear motive for killing Jeremy, but the same is true for Naomi. She enjoyed the lifestyle that the extra money bought.'

Raven was gratified to see Tony and Jess nodding in agreement.

'Then we come to the night of the party. Sam caught her with Marcus, and we can't rule out the possibility that she tried to silence him. More recently, Marcus refused to leave Olivia for her. She could have killed him in a fit of jealous rage. And she might have killed Anthony because their relationship had irretrievably broken down. If he divorced her, she'd lose half her money.' He paused. 'What about Olivia? Any thoughts?'

Jess put up a tentative hand. 'If we're thinking outside the box, then a lot of her motives are the same as Naomi's.'

'Go on,' said Raven.

'Well, she might have killed Jeremy so that Marcus could take over as finance director. It's possible that she pushed Sam in a case of mistaken identity after she found her husband with Naomi. And she might have killed Marcus because of the affair.' She faltered. 'But I can't think of any reason why she would want to kill Anthony. He hadn't done anything to hurt her.'

'Maybe we need to look at the extended family,' said Tony. 'What about the cousin who took over Sam's job?'

'Ellie,' said Raven. 'I was just coming to her. Greg is always talking about how important it is to build a business that can be handed down to the next generation. But what happens if all the heirs to the business are eliminated? With the brothers out of the way, presumably Ellie would inherit the lot. And then there's Greg's brother, Keith. We know that he and Greg have been feuding for years. Is he behind all this on behalf of his daughter? If he is, could Greg and Denise be his next targets?'

They stared at the list of names.

'That's a lot of suspects,' said Jess.

And time was running out. 'Damn,' said Raven. 'We're still missing something crucial.'

*

Becca and Ellie were the last of the lunchtime diners still in the restaurant. Despite Becca's earlier misgivings about

Ellie, her new friend had offered sound advice about Sam – *just be there for him, he'll come to you when he's ready* – and had deftly moved the conversation on to more upbeat topics. Music, food, local events. It seemed that she and Becca shared many interests and held similar opinions on a range of topics.

Becca soon began to loosen up again. The food was excellent, the wine relaxing and the company stimulating. The notion that Ellie could be the murderer quickly faded. It was a relief for Becca to unwind after all the stress she'd suffered this past year. She was only just beginning to realise the toll that Sam's coma had taken on her. He had lost a year of his life, but so had she.

It was time to move on and make a fresh start.

It was only when Keith turned the Open/Closed sign around on the door that she realised how much time had passed.

Ellie looked at her watch. 'Oh no, is that the time? I'm going to have to shoot off. I've got a call with one of our clients. We should do this again sometime.'

'I'd like that,' said Becca.

Keith came over to the table. 'I was hoping to join you ladies for a coffee before you go.'

'Sorry, Dad, I've got to get back to the brewery.' Ellie looked at Becca. 'But you can stay, can't you?'

Becca looked up at the man who reminded her so much of Greg. Strong brow, thick dark hair, thin lips. It was funny how Sam looked so different to his father, with his fine blond hair and easy smile. He took more after his mother.

Becca wasn't sure what she and Keith would have to talk about, but it seemed churlish to turn down his offer after she'd enjoyed his hospitality. Besides, it wasn't as if she was needed elsewhere. Sam had told her not to collect him from the hospital, and she didn't have to go to work.

'All right, then,' she said. 'Why not? But perhaps I could have some tea instead?'

A smile creased Keith's mouth. 'Of course.'

Ellie embraced the two of them and then left. From the window Becca watched her purple hair disappearing round the corner. It felt good to have made a new friend. She'd lost touch with too many while spending time at Sam's hospital bed, willing him to wake up.

Keith brought two cups to the table and sat down in the chair that Ellie had vacated.

'Lunch was delicious,' said Becca. 'Thank you.'

'Oh, you're welcome.' Keith seemed hardly to register the compliment, but gazed out of the window distractedly. There was clearly something he wanted to talk about. When he turned to face her, she could read the concern in his eyes. 'I saw you with Sam yesterday. Is everything all right between you two?'

'It's fine.'

'You don't sound too sure.'

Becca wondered what Keith had seen or heard. While she'd been happy to unburden herself to Ellie, she was less comfortable discussing her personal life with a man she barely knew. Even if he had just treated her to a free lunch.

Keith's eyes didn't leave her. 'Sam's a good boy. He's lucky to have you. And Greg should be proud of him. I would be, if he were my son.'

Becca shrugged. She was beginning to wish she'd refused Keith's offer of a drink. But she could hardly walk out of the restaurant now.

'Do you love him?' he asked.

The shock of the question startled her into replying. 'Yes.'

She wiped away fresh tears with the back of her hand, angry at herself for revealing so much to a man who was little more than a stranger. What business did he have poking his nose into her private affairs?

Keith nodded, as if her answer had somehow given him permission to continue. 'Love's a powerful emotion, isn't it? It can catch you unawares, make you do almost anything. But the love a parent feels for their child is the strongest of all. It's an unbreakable bond.' He leaned forwards, resting his forearms on the table. 'I've always done my best for Ellie. I've tried to give her everything she needs.'

This wasn't at all the kind of conversation Becca had been expecting. She had no idea where Keith was going with this, but he seemed to be expecting some kind of response. 'I'm sure you have, Keith. Ellie seems very happy.'

'It's not easy for a father to bring up a girl alone. Ellie's mum suffered a breakdown after the birth. A kind of depression, you'd call it. I tried to help her, but she never recovered. For years I wondered if it was my fault, but now I think it was just the way she was. She left us when Ellie was still a baby. She just walked out one day. I never heard from her again.'

'I'm sorry to hear that.' Becca took a sip of her tea, sensing that Keith was only just building up to what he had to say.

He drummed his fingers on the table, conflicting emotions playing over his face. Then he stood up and went over to the door and locked it. He returned to his seat as if nothing had happened. 'I should have brought this to an end sooner.'

Alarm bells were going off in Becca's head. What was going on? Why had Keith locked the door? 'Brought what to an end, Keith?'

He didn't answer her question. 'Ellie tells me you're a police detective, is that right?'

'Yes.'

'The man in charge of the investigation, Raven, is he any good?'

'He's the best we've got.' She'd meant it to be an endorsement, but it sounded lame to her own ears.

Keith pursed his lips. It wasn't what he'd wanted to hear. 'When Ellie's mum went away I was left alone to look after a baby girl. I could have used some support from my family. But the only family I had was Greg, and he was too focussed on building his business. He had no time for anything else. He neglected those closest to him. I reached out to him, but he turned me away.'

Keith was avoiding Becca's eye. Perhaps it was easier for him to speak that way, to tell her what he had to say. His coffee was untouched, growing slowly cooler.

'I could see what was coming, like a train crash in slow motion. Inevitable.'

Becca's thoughts were racing. Was Keith trying to tell her something about his own daughter? Ellie seemed perfectly normal, but surface appearances could be deceptive. A young girl growing up without a mother, her father busy running a restaurant, Keith's own brother refusing to help… could something very wrong have happened to that girl?

'Keith,' said Becca, 'if you're trying to tell me something about Ellie…'

He shook his head, dark eyes flashing. 'This is not about my daughter!'

His voice became quieter, more normal again as he picked up where he'd left off. 'I tried to warn Greg, but you know how he is. Obstinate. Stubborn. Good qualities for building a business, not so good for being a husband.'

He cast Becca a sideways glance to gauge if she was catching on to his drift. She thought she knew where he might be heading, but wanted to hear it from his own lips.

'I tried to tell him. *Greg, you have to spend more time with Denise.* But he was having none of it. It was no surprise when she turned to Jeremy for comfort. Jeremy had lost his wife to cancer. Denise was as good as widowed with Greg away for days, weeks at a time, acting like he cared more about that damn brewery than he did about his own wife. I told him. I said it would happen. But he refused to listen.'

The truth was beginning to sink in. Becca listened, held rapt by Keith's story.

'When Marcus was born, I could see Jeremy's face in that baby. How could Greg not have seen it too? I held my tongue, and the same with Anthony. But when Sam was born I had to say something.' A sadness entered Keith's eyes. 'Greg didn't speak a word to me again for more than twenty years.'

'Marcus, Anthony and Sam were Jeremy's sons?' But Becca already knew the answer to her question. It had been staring her in the face all along. Greg's dark hair; Sam's so light in colour. Greg's broad build; Sam's slim frame. Even their faces were different. Now she knew it, she wondered how she could ever have been fooled.

Keith resumed his tale. 'When Jeremy died, I paid no attention. It was an accident, everyone said so. Then Sam was run over by that van.' He shook his head, angry with himself. 'Nobody suspected anything. It was made to look like an accident. I couldn't have known, not then. But when Marcus was killed... I should have spoken up. I should have put an end to it then. But who would have believed me?' He turned the full weight of his gaze on Becca. 'Now Anthony is dead too. The time for silence is over. Who will be next? Sam? Denise? Greg's taken leave of his senses. He's always had a vain streak. All this talk of passing something on to the next generation... it's really all about him. He imagines he's like some Roman emperor building something that will last for centuries. He may be my own brother, but he's out of his mind.'

'Keith,' said Becca, 'I have to call this in.'

He nodded. 'I'm glad you believe me.'

'I do.' Her phone was already in her hands and she dialled Raven's number. As soon as she heard his voice, she told him. 'I know who the killer is.'

# CHAPTER 34

When his father wheeled him out of the hospital and helped him into the back seat of the car, Sam was surprised to find his mother sitting in the front. Sunken in a black coat, her face ashen, she looked like a mourner at a Victorian funeral. She stared straight ahead, clutching her handbag on her lap. Well, she had lost two sons, she was entitled to grieve.

His dad, by contrast was all smiles and jollity. 'Don't forget to do your seatbelt up, Sam. We don't want anything to happen to you on the way home!'

Sam buckled up, feeling like he was five years old. He really needed to get fit again and reclaim his mobility and independence. The physio sessions were helping, but they were hard work and he knew that it would take time before he could walk properly, drive a car, and do all the things he had once taken for granted.

While his dad pushed the wheelchair round to the rear of the car and folded it into the boot, Sam leaned forwards and rested his hand on his mother's shoulder.

'All right, Mum?'

Slowly, she turned her head to face him and he saw

something more than grief in her eyes.

It was fear. The sight was enough to chill his blood. 'What's the matter, Mum?'

She laid a cold hand on his and opened her mouth to say something. But before she had a chance to speak, the driver's door opened and his dad jumped into the car. He slammed the door closed, started the engine and said in a loud, jovial voice, 'All aboard!'

His mother withdrew her hand as if it had been burned.

*All aboard!* Now Sam really did feel like a little kid in the back of the car. It was what Dad used to say when they were about to set off on a family holiday. Being the youngest, Sam had always sat squashed in the middle of the back seat between Marcus and Anthony. The piggy in the middle as they squabbled and fought. He'd hated that. How he missed his brothers now.

His dad revved the engine, reversed out of the parking slot way too fast with barely a glance in the rear view mirror, and sped to the exit. There he drew to an abrupt halt, tapping his fingers impatiently on the steering wheel as he waited behind a short queue of cars for the barrier to rise. 'Won't be long!' he said cheerfully.

What on earth had got into him? Was this his way of dealing with the recent tragedies? Reverting to a time when they'd all been one, big, happy family? But there was no big family anymore, only empty seats where Sam's brothers should have been. He could understand his mother's mute grief and pain, but not his father's forced bonhomie. When they got home they needed to sit down and have a proper talk. It was long overdue.

Sam was bitterly sorry now that he'd pushed Becca away. What had he been thinking? There were times when he was so confused, he didn't know who to trust anymore. Dr Kirtlington at the hospital, his own parents – they had wanted to turn off his life support and leave him to die. He could barely stand to think of that. But he knew he could rely on Becca. After all she'd done for him, sitting at his bedside, hour after hour, day after day, month after month.

She could have been out enjoying herself, making a new life without him, but she'd stuck by him even when she'd thought he would die.

He should never have doubted her. Becca had good instincts – that's what made her such a good detective. If she had suspicions about who was behind the murders, then he ought to have listened to her and taken her concerns seriously. Somebody close to the family, she'd said. Somebody at the house the previous day. Somebody who worked at the brewery.

He caught his dad's eyes staring back at him in the rear view mirror. Eyes he thought he knew so well. Eyes that he'd always thought he could depend on. There was a glint in those eyes now of – what? Suddenly it felt as if they were the eyes of a stranger.

The eyes of a madman.

★

As soon as Raven finished on the phone to Becca, he made a call to PC Sharon Jarvis. The family liaison officer picked up almost immediately. 'Sir?'

'Where are you?'

'At the hospital.'

'Are you with the family?'

She missed a beat before replying and Raven knew instantly that something was wrong. 'They've given me the slip, sir. Greg asked me to go and fetch some coffee. When I got back, he'd gone. He's taken Sam with him.'

'Shit.'

'Should I make my way back to the house?'

'No,' said Raven. 'Greg Earnshaw is dangerous. There's a high probability that his intention is to kill Sam and possibly also Denise.'

When he came off the phone, Tony and Jess were staring at him wide-eyed. 'Greg is the killer,' he explained. 'He's not the father of Denise's children – Jeremy Green was. He's just abducted Sam and Denise from the hospital.

There's an immediate threat to life and we need to get to his house right away. I'll take my car. Tony, authorise backup, then join me there.'

★

The line of cars waiting at the exit barrier finally shifted and it was their turn to leave the hospital grounds. But instead of turning left and heading north up the Scalby Road, Greg swung the steering wheel to the right and pulled out into the main road, narrowly missing a bus that tooted its horn loudly at them.

'Dad!'

They were going south instead of towards home.

'Where are we –' began Sam.

But his father cut him off. 'Since it's just the three of us now, I thought we'd go for a little spin!' Still that holiday-mode cheer that was really starting to grate.

His mum said nothing, appearing frozen in her seat. From the back, Sam felt helpless. Like a child. He decided to play along and engage his father in conversation.

'Where to, Dad?'

'You'll see when we get there. A surprise!'

'Don't you think it's getting a bit late for a day trip? It'll be dark soon. I'm exhausted after the physio. Can't we just go home instead? Do this another day?'

'Don't be such a wuss!' His dad's teasing tone was the same one he'd used to coax Sam and his brothers into the sea as little boys when the water was freezing – as it often was in Scarborough. 'You'll enjoy it when you get there.'

*Dad's finally lost it.*

Sam was done playing games. 'Turn around, Dad!' he commanded. 'I've had enough of this nonsense and so has Mum.'

Those stranger's eyes glared angrily at him in the mirror.

His father stamped his foot down and jumped a red light. Tyres screeched. Horns blared. The car accelerated away, leaving chaos in its wake.

*Okay, that didn't work.* His father was intent on doing whatever he had in mind. *A surprise.* Sam had no idea where they were going, but resolved to sit tight and see where they ended up. He started paying attention to the route they were taking.

*

As soon as Becca had alerted Raven to her suspicions, she sent a text to Sam. There was no easy way to tell him that the man he thought was his father was actually a homicidal maniac, so she confined her message to the bare essentials, keeping her words simple and trying to avoid over-dramatising the situation. She didn't want him to panic.

*I think Greg is behind everything. Stay at the hospital. I'm coming to fetch you.*

She left the restaurant and hurried back to her car. The town was in a post-lunch slumber, a quiet period when people were still at work and the shops were fairly empty. Becca set off walking before breaking into a run. She had just made it back to her car when her phone pinged with Sam's reply.

*In the car with Mum and Dad. Leaving Scarborough, heading south in direction of Cayton Bay.*

Shit!

Greg ought to have been driving back to the family home. If he was leaving town, then he must already be one step ahead of the police. What was he planning? Becca didn't dare think about it. One thing she knew – he had to be stopped before he could harm Sam.

Frantically, she called Raven. He was in the car by the sound of it. 'Sam just texted me,' she told him. 'Greg's on the A165, heading south out of Scarborough. Sam and Denise are with him in the car.'

Raven swore loudly. 'I know where he's going.'

'Where?'

'Flamborough Head.'

'Are you sure?'

'It's where he claimed his first victim, Jeremy Green. Now he's going back there.'

There was no need for Raven to spell out Greg's plan. He had already murdered Jeremy, Marcus and Anthony and had attempted to kill Sam. Now he was going to finish what he'd started.

'We've got to stop him.' Becca ended the call and tossed her phone into the pocket of the car door. For once she wished she had Raven's BMW instead of the little Honda with its 1.3 litre engine.

She started the car and snapped the gearstick into first, pushing her right foot down and letting the clutch bite hard. Tyres squealed and the car leapt forwards. She swung it round the tight corner of the multi-storey and down the first ramp, giving the steering wheel a sharp yank to negotiate the one-eighty turn at the bottom. She bumped the car down the second ramp, cutting across another vehicle that was attempting to move off. At the exit she fed her ticket into the machine and was out of the car park just as soon as the barrier rose. Keeping in a low gear until the engine screeched in protest she shot onto the main road, darting through the traffic lights just as they were turning red.

The Jazz had never seen such action before.

∗

They left the built-up area and moved onto open road. Signs marking the village of Osgodby and the Cayton Bay holiday park flashed past Sam's window. But his dad ignored the turnings for both and kept on the main road, heading in the direction of Filey. He barely slowed as he passed the turnoffs, ignoring the speed limits and the signs welcoming careful drivers. The sea made a grey smudge on Sam's left; on his right, holiday homes looked drab and neglected in the off season.

He tapped out a message to Becca.

*Gone past Cayton Bay, heading for Filey.*

'What are you doing?' roared Greg from the front of the car.

'Nothing,' said Sam, tucking the phone into his jeans pocket.

'I saw you using your phone. Were you messaging someone?'

'No.'

'Give it to me!'

'What? No way.'

'Hand it over now!'

'No, Dad.' The phone was Sam's lifeline to Becca. No way was he giving it up.

But to his surprise, his mum turned to him. 'Do what your father says, Sam.'

Sam shook his head. 'I'm not a kid. You can't order me about!'

The eyes of the madman blazed at him from the rear view mirror. 'If you don't give me that phone I'll run this car off the road and kill us all!'

As if to prove his point, his dad jerked the steering wheel, sending the car careering across the white centre dashes of the road and into the path of an oncoming lorry. The driver of the vehicle hooted his horn.

His mum's eyes were wide with fear. 'He'll do it, Sam. Give him the phone.'

'Whatever.' Sam handed the phone over and his Dad snatched it from his fingers, returning the car to the left hand lane as the lorry thundered past, missing them by seconds. He lowered the driver's side window and tossed the phone through the gap.

'Hey!' yelled Sam. 'That's my phone!'

'Just sit there and be quiet!' bellowed his dad. 'If everyone in this family did what I told them' – he shot an angry glare at his wife – 'we wouldn't be in this situation now.'

The light was beginning to fade and his dad switched the headlights to full beam, ignoring warning flashes from oncoming drivers blinded by the glare. A roundabout approached and he shot straight across it without slowing down, not even thinking about giving way to other vehicles. Fortunately the road was clear.

A sign came into view, marking the Filey turnoff, but he kept going, heading now in the direction of Bridlington.

A cold feeling began to creep up the back of Sam's neck, hairs standing on end. Suddenly he knew their destination. There were still seven miles to go but at this speed they'd be there in ten minutes or less.

He wished he had his phone to tell Becca. But maybe she'd already guessed where they were going.

*Flamborough.*

His father was taking them to Flamborough Head.

★

Raven pulled up outside the Earnshaw family home on Scalby Mills Road, confirming what Becca had just told him. The windows were dark. There was no car on the driveway. Greg had given him the slip.

Damn! Raven hit the steering wheel with the palm of his hand, furious with himself. Why hadn't he seen it? He'd jumped to the obvious conclusion, wasting vital minutes driving to the wrong side of town. Greg had fooled him just like he'd fooled everyone else – first the coroner investigating Jeremy's death, then the original police inquiry into Sam's hit and run, and now him too.

He'd let Sam down, putting his life in danger. Now he needed to get all the way to Flamborough before something terrible happened.

He called Tony to let him know what was happening.

'Backup's on its way, sir,' said the detective. 'Should be with you any minute.'

'Never mind that, Tony. Greg's on the A165, heading south. I believe he's planning to go to Flamborough Head.'

Tony wasn't fazed by the change of plan. 'I'll get another car dispatched immediately.'

'All right.' Raven jammed the car back into gear and swung it around in the middle of the road. The nearest police presence to Flamborough was the station at Bridlington, but it was just a small team with a handful of officers. Raven wasn't going to depend on local bobbies to get the job done. By the time they reached the clifftop it might all be too late.

If Sam or Denise died, he would never forgive himself.

'What about you, sir?' asked Tony.

'I'm driving straight to Flamborough.'

How quickly could he get there? It was a good forty minutes from Scarborough if you drove sensibly and stuck to the speed limit. He'd do it in half the time.

*

The car park at Flamborough Head was dark and deserted when the car screeched to a standstill, braking so hard that Sam was thrown forwards against his seatbelt. His father killed the engine, letting a deep silence close in around them. The only sound now was the moaning of the wind and the hissing of the waves as they broke against the cliffs below. The only light came from the lighthouse far above, its bright narrow beam reaching out across the blackening sea beyond.

Four white flashes every fifteen seconds. A beacon for ships at sea, warning of rocky coasts, and guiding sailors to the safety of harbour. Sam longed to send a similar message to Becca, but without his phone he was helpless. He could only pray that the police were on their way.

At least the mad drive here was over. It was a wonder they hadn't all been killed on the road.

'Here we are! Everyone out!' His dad flung open his door and climbed out. A gust of wind reached into the car, bringing cold, damp air inside. The boot of the car opened and Sam heard the wheelchair being dragged out.

Thoughts raced through his mind. Could he wrestle the keys from his father's hand and drive his mother away to safety? But no, his arms and legs were wasted. He doubted he could even get into the driver's seat in time. He struggled to walk, and hadn't driven a car for more than a year. And after a day of hard physio, he was already exhausted. There was no way he could make a getaway even if he somehow managed to get hold of the keys.

His mum started to open her door.

'No!' said Sam, laying a hand on her shoulder. It was imperative that they stay in the safety of the car. Becca's message had warned him that his father was the killer. Sam didn't understand why, but his behaviour in the car had confirmed it. His dad appeared to have lost his mind. There was no way he had brought them to this desolate spot tonight to admire the view. 'Don't get out of the car, Mum.'

But it was too late. She appeared not to hear him. He watched helplessly as she stepped out into the black night.

Sam's door opened too.

'You too, boy,' ordered Greg over the roar of the wind. 'Stop skulking in there.'

Sam knew he had no choice. With a deep sense of foreboding, he clambered out of the car, hauling himself through the gap. A gust of wind almost threw him off balance, but he steadied himself against the doorframe of the car, standing upright on shaky legs. 'What are we doing here, Dad?'

His voice, still weak from the long months of disuse, was barely audible above the howling wind. The darkness was absolute, broken every few seconds by a blinding beam of light. A brilliant white flash that bathed the clifftop in a ghostly glow. His mum was standing with her back to him.

'Sit down.' His dad put a hand on his shoulder and forced him into the chair.

'Where are we going?'

'We're taking a little walk.'

The wheelchair began bumping along a rough grass track. Sam gripped the arms, afraid of being thrown from his seat. His dad said nothing more, but the roaring and crashing of the waves grew steadily louder.

★

The M6 chewed up the miles between Scarborough and Flamborough Head and spat them out. Raven didn't even glance at his speedometer, aware only of the deep-throated howl of the five-litre engine, the firm grip of the wheel under his hands, the way the car obeyed his every command. A beast unleashed and fully under his control. Twenty minutes flat, and he was there.

And yet he wasn't the first to arrive at the scene. Another car was pulling in as he arrived at the foot of the lighthouse. Brake lights painted a red glow in the darkness. The car door flew open.

*Becca. Of course.*

He should have known she wouldn't hang around while Sam's life was in danger.

He stopped the BMW next to hers and jumped out.

She was already peering in through the darkened windows of Greg's car, shining her phone into the abandoned vehicle. 'There's no one here!'

Raven put his hand on the bonnet. The engine was still hot, clicking faintly as it cooled. They couldn't have gone far. 'I know where they are,' he told her. 'Quick. Follow me.'

# CHAPTER 35

The wheelchair pitched and jerked across the rough ground. One wheel plunged into a hole made by rabbits or some other creature and the chair tipped to the side, almost throwing Sam from his seat. He clung on tightly, his knuckles white as his dad grunted and strained to shift the stuck wheel. Eventually it came free and the journey resumed, bumping and bouncing wildly into the darkness.

It was a moonless night, thick grey clouds concealing the sky, the sea as black as oil yet glittering like diamonds every time a blinding beam swung across its shifting surface.

His mum stumbled along beside them. More than once she cried out as her foot caught in some unseen dip or hollow, but she ploughed on regardless, desperate to keep up. His father's ragged breathing came from behind as he forced the wheelchair across the untamed headland. The sea roared to Sam's left and increasingly from straight ahead.

They were drawing closer to the edge of the clifftops.

'For goodness' sake, Dad, just stop!' shouted Sam.

His father pushed on implacably. 'Almost there, now!'

The sea was getting louder and there could be absolutely no doubt where they were heading. Sam had a vision of them marching right to the edge of the cliff and over, chair and all.

He wasn't going to allow that to happen.

He grabbed the brake handle and yanked it as hard as he could. The wheels came to a juddering halt. He felt himself thrown forwards, tumbling out of his seat like a ragdoll. He landed with a thump on the cold, wet ground and slithered along the grass, striving to put as much distance as he could between himself and his father.

'That was a bloody stupid thing to do,' Greg shouted.

Sam struggled to find his footing, but his legs were too unsteady, the ground too rugged, the grass too wet. He scrabbled helplessly, his hands pulling up clods of mud, tears welling in his eyes. He was too weak to stand, too frail to fight.

His father appeared over him, panting hard, breath pluming in the freezing air like some monster. 'Get back in that chair!'

'Dad,' begged Sam. 'Please!'

But strong arms reached down and seized him by the shoulders, dragging him along the muddy path, hauling him up by his arms, lifting him back into the chair.

Sam slumped in the seat in exhaustion, tears smarting his eyes, sobbing at his own helplessness. 'Why are you doing this?' he demanded.

'Tell him, Greg!' His mother's disembodied voice seemed to come from out of nowhere. In her black coat she was all but invisible against the night sky. 'Tell him the truth. All of it.'

Sam waited, fearful of what he might be about to learn, yet knowing that he needed to hear it.

His father leaned heavily against the back of the chair, panting breathlessly. When he spoke, his voice was surprisingly gentle. 'I was a good father to you, wasn't I, Sam?'

'You were, Dad.' The words rang true enough. Sam remembered the good times, plenty of them. Family holidays, days on the beach, riding high on his father's shoulders. 'You've always been a great father.'

His dad seemed pleased by his answer. 'Do you remember coming here when you were young? We walked along the clifftops, just you and me, looking at the drinking dinosaur, eating ice creams in the café.'

'I remember it, Dad. We had a great time.'

'Jeremy never brought you here, did he?'

'Jeremy?' Sam looked from one parent to another. His father's face contorted with rage, his mother's blushed deep with shame.

And suddenly it all made sense. The little kindnesses that Jeremy had shown over the years. The well-chosen Christmas and birthday presents; the keen interest in how he was getting on at school; taking the time to show him the ropes when he started working for the business.

His mum was crying now. Loud, wrenching sobs that tore at Sam's heart. 'I'm so sorry, Sam. I've been wanting to tell you for a long time.'

'Liar!' Greg spat the word at her. 'Don't believe a word she says, Sam.'

'I never meant it to happen,' she continued, undaunted, 'but in the early days of the business, your father' – she glanced at Greg then turned back to Sam – 'was never around. I was so lonely. Jeremy's wife died and he was lonely too. Jeremy and I – we understood each other. We were a comfort to one another.'

'You were his whore!' Greg bellowed. 'I trusted you. When my own brother tried to tell me what was happening, I turned him away. You betrayed me!'

She flinched at his voice, but stood her ground. 'How did you find out?'

Greg smiled. A nasty twitch of the mouth that made him look even more deranged. 'It was two and a half years ago. I had some genetic tests done at the hospital, remember? To see if I was at risk of developing cancer or

Alzheimer's like my father. I wasn't. But the test threw up something more interesting. I have a rare chromosomal abnormality that makes me infertile. I couldn't have fathered our children.'

Sam let it all sink in. Two and a half years ago. A chance discovery that had set in train a terrible course of events. Jeremy's death, his own attempted murder, the killing of his two brothers. Cold, calculated murders, designed at first to look like accidents. The sick actions of a twisted mind.

Denise nodded. 'Is this about revenge, Greg? If it is, then let Sam go. He's innocent. I'll pay for my mistake, but please let him go.'

Greg sneered at her. 'Killing Jeremy was my revenge. Now it's about putting things right. The way they should have been. I don't want my lifetime's work falling into the hands of one of your bastards!'

The word stung Sam like a slap to the face. *Bastard.* Is that what he was?

Greg advanced on Denise. 'You're no better than a common whore!'

'And you're a murderer!' she screamed.

The accusation rent the air like a knife.

Sam was frozen to the spot – everything he'd known and trusted had crumbled away like a sandcastle crushed under a gigantic wave.

Greg reached out and struck his wife across the cheek.

'Mum!' cried Sam. He tried to stand but his father shoved him roughly back into place.

'Stop snivelling!' he shouted. He placed both hands on the back of the wheelchair and pushed.

'Dad?'

But the wheels were already turning. The brake was off, the grass was sloping. From behind, Sam heard his mother scream.

Greg pushed harder and the wheelchair picked up speed.

'Dad, stop!'

But the only response was Greg's heavy breathing as he pushed the chair towards the cliff edge. Faster and faster they went, as the slope of the headland steepened, the roar of the sea growing ever louder.

Sam could feel the sting of salt spray against his cheeks, could see the vast expanse of the sea opening up before him. They were almost at the very edge. 'Dad!' he screamed.

'Don't call me that!' shouted Greg. 'I'm not your father!'

★

'Over there!' shouted Becca. 'Come on!'

She had moved ahead of Raven, his old leg injury slowing him down. The headland was a death-trap in the dark, a minefield of unseen hollows and troughs waiting to snag unwary feet. The grass was wet and slippery, the rough path uncut. Raven swung his torch, aware of the sheer drop just yards to his left. He could hear the unrelenting boom and crash of the waves as they threw themselves against the chalk cliffs below.

And somewhere in the darkness a homicidal maniac was going about his work.

Raven grunted with the effort of keeping up with his younger colleague. He could just pick out the line of the clifftops in the distance. They were halfway there already, nearing the spot where Jeremy had met his untimely death. Behind them the lighthouse stabbed a beam into the darkness, picking out three figures.

'Approach with caution,' he called to Becca. 'We don't want to spook him.'

A woman's scream cut the night like a knife.

*Denise.*

'It's too late for that,' said Becca. She broke into a run.

Cursing his leg, Raven quickened his pace.

★

Sam was too weak to put up a struggle, and Greg was strong. Powerfully built, like a bull. Sam had always wanted to grow up like that, to be as broad and muscular as his dad, brushing all obstacles from his path. But he had taken after his father – his true father – growing into Jeremy's likeness. Taller than Greg, and slender. Fair haired, fine featured.

He was no match for his adversary, especially with his limbs in such a wasted state.

Tears came to his eyes as he hurtled towards the cliff edge, washing away the salt of the sea. All he could feel now was cold, fear and helplessness. He had woken from perpetual sleep into a living nightmare. It would have been better if he'd never regained consciousness.

And then he thought of Becca. Where was she now? What was she doing? He hoped she would find a way to go on without him. He knew that she could. She was stronger than him. Braver.

Suddenly he knew that he didn't want to die. Not here like this. With the last of his strength he hurled himself sideways, capsizing the wheelchair and rolling on the ground. He flailed his arms, struggling to stop, but momentum took him right to the edge before he could bring himself to a halt.

Below him the waves crashed, throwing up foam, heaving up rocks and dragging them back. A relentless assault against the fragile land.

The wheelchair clattered right over the edge, plunging down the precipice and dropping into oblivion.

Sam began to claw himself back up the slope.

But his freedom was short-lived. Rough hands gripped him by the throat, squeezing the air from his lungs. He tried to resist, but his energy was spent. Greg grabbed him by the arms, turned him around and dragged him back to the cliff edge.

Sam had bought himself seconds, but his efforts had come to nothing. He was still going to die, although now at least he knew he had done his utmost to save himself.

Out of the corner of his eye, he saw his mother appear on the clifftop. She was drawing something out of her handbag. He heard the jangle of keys. And then she was raising her arm and stabbing Greg in the neck.

The hands that had dragged Sam right to the very edge of the precipice released him. Greg cried out and turned to face his wife.

She continued her attack, stabbing him in the face, in the eye, in the throat. A mother protecting her young. Greg roared in pain, a primal howl, and threw up his hands to defend himself. For a moment he was blind, staggering and defenceless.

Before Sam realised what was going to happen, Denise rushed at Greg with both arms outstretched and pushed him over the edge of the cliff.

*

'Sam!' Becca sprinted the last hundred yards, only slowing as she approached the dangerous clifftop. 'Are you all right?'

He was lying on the ground, his chest heaving, his face a mask of anguish. She knelt and put an arm around him. 'Where's Greg?'

'Somewhere he can't hurt anyone else,' said Denise, emerging from the blackness like a phantom. Her voice was strangely calm.

Greg was nowhere to be seen. But the roar of the hungry sea told its own tale.

Raven arrived, lumbering across the landscape, another black phantom in the night. 'Are you hurt, Mrs Earnshaw?'

'No,' said Denise. 'But I want to make a confession.'

'No, Mum.' Sam turned away from the cliff, sitting up with Becca's help. 'It was an accident. Greg was trying to push me off the cliff. He slipped and fell.'

Denise shook her head. 'No, Sam. He didn't.' She turned to Raven. 'I killed my husband. I pushed him over the cliff.'

'You don't have to do this, Mum,' wailed Sam. 'Nobody saw what happened.'

But Denise was unwavering in her desire to come clean. 'No more lies, Sam. I can't live with any more.'

Raven nodded reluctantly. 'We'll discuss this back at the station.' He led her away to his car.

Becca was left alone with Sam. He was shivering and she wrapped her coat around him.

'I'm so sorry,' he whispered. 'I should have listened to you. You were right all along.'

'I wish I hadn't been,' said Becca, cradling his head in her arms. 'I really wish I hadn't.'

# CHAPTER 36

When Raven turned up at Lisa's hotel the next morning, the smell of grilled bacon and fresh coffee greeted him in the entrance lobby. He followed his nose through to the dining room, but Lisa wasn't one of the guests taking breakfast there. Raven made his way upstairs and knocked on her door.

'Come in!'

She opened it with a smile and drew him into the room, throwing her arms around his neck and giving him a kiss on the lips. She smelled of hotel soap and shampoo. 'I missed you last night.'

'I got caught up in something.'

Raven's mind flashed back to the scene at Flamborough Head. He'd arrived too late to prevent another death but at least Sam had been saved, although understandably shaken by his ordeal. As for Denise, she remained in custody. Raven had been given no choice other than to arrest her, although he would be recommending a charge of involuntary manslaughter by reason of loss of control. A good lawyer might get her off, arguing self-defence. A jury would go for that, or at least

Raven hoped they would. There was no doubt whatsoever that Greg had intended to kill Sam, and quite probably Denise too.

'Never mind,' said Lisa. 'You're here now.'

Her suitcase lay open on the bed and she folded a dress into it. Her brief stay in Yorkshire was coming to an end.

She hadn't asked him anything about his work here in Scarborough. To her, being a police detective was just a job. A job that had often kept him away from her, a job that had ultimately pushed them apart.

But he'd been given a second chance, an opportunity to put things right. Happiness was finally within his grasp. A fresh start together with his wife and daughter. All he had to do was reach out and take it.

Lisa continued to pack. 'I'll book the hotel in York when I get home. I'll speak to Hannah and arrange some dates. You can leave all the details to me.'

She stopped when she noticed the expression on his face. 'What?'

The realisation had come to him as he stood on the windswept cliff looking at the wreckage of a family destroyed by betrayal. If he took the life Lisa was offering him, there would always be a voice inside, nagging away, reminding him of her unfaithfulness. Greg Earnshaw had ignored that same whispering voice for years, and in the end it had driven him to madness.

Raven knew that it wasn't just work that had pushed him and Lisa apart. It wasn't even her affair. The cracks had been there from the beginning. Miscommunications, misunderstandings, breaks in the bonds that should have held them together. Almost invisible at first, just scattered instances when the wrong thing had been said, or no word spoken when one was required. Decades of unexpressed thoughts, weighing on the marriage with ever-increasing force, slowly forcing the gaps wider until it became easier to say nothing at all.

'I'm sorry, Lisa. It's over. Our relationship, our marriage, everything.'

It had taken him twenty-five years to realise he didn't love her. But scarcely the length of a single heartbeat to tell her.

'What! Just like that?' Lisa looked incredulous. 'Don't you believe in second chances, Tom?'

He shrugged. Maybe he didn't. Some things were broken and could never be fixed. To pretend otherwise just made things worse.

He had to refuse her. Not to be cruel, but to be kind.

What more was there to say? He turned and walked out of the room, and out of her life forever.

★

Raven walked down to the harbour and out along the eastern pier. The tide was low, leaving a thick layer of mud in the basin. A rich environment for shellfish, worms and shore crabs, and good winter feeding for birds.

He stopped at the end of the pier to rest his leg. It was still aching from the previous day's exertions but it wasn't something he chose to dwell on. Low-level pain was a nagging constant in his life. You could think of it as a penance if you were that way inclined, which Raven was.

He gazed out across the bay, the coastline curving south and east. Forty miles away, less as the crow flew, the lighthouse at Flamborough Head was just visible. Despite everything that had happened, Raven found the sight a comfort. No matter how rough the seas, that light would always be there, a beacon of safety in the storm.

It was starting to spot with rain, dark clouds rolling in across the bay. Soon there would be a downpour. It was time.

He thrust a hand into his coat pocket and pulled out a small, metal object.

His wedding ring.

A simple, gold band, but imbued with so much significance.

He remembered that day at Kensington and Chelsea

Register Office. A sunny Saturday in May. Lisa in a cream, silk dress, he in a plain dark suit adorned with a single buttonhole. His best man had been a serving officer from the army. He had no family, and few friends. The guests had almost all been Lisa's. They had looked into each other's eyes and promised to love and cherish each other, forsaking all others, till death did them part.

In a way, death had parted them.

It was Raven's job as a homicide detective with the Met that had kept him away from the family home. Too many times, he hadn't been there when Lisa had needed him.

But ultimately she had broken her promise to him. And because of that he could never completely trust her again. He wasn't prepared to spend the rest of his life in a relationship like that, whether it was here in Scarborough, back in London, or anywhere else.

He dropped the ring into the harbour where it sank into the mud. Maybe an enterprising sandpiper or a greedy gull would find a use for it. It was no good to him anymore.

He knew that he was making a habit of this. Throwing the relics of his past into the sea. Peeling away the outer layers, leaving nothing but raw skin. Stripping back to the core.

But now he'd revealed the bottommost layer. There was nothing left to remove.

'It's over,' he said to the gulls.

# EPILOGUE

*Three weeks later*

'More Christmas pudding anyone?' Sue Shawcross looked hopefully around the dining table. 'Sam? Can I tempt you with a little more?'

'Maybe later,' said Sam. 'That was delicious, thank you.' Sam had made remarkable progress in the last three weeks and Becca was very proud of him. He no longer needed a wheelchair and was steadily regaining strength, building muscle by lifting weights.

Sue beamed at him. Under the table, Becca reached for his hand. They were, of necessity, having a scaled down Christmas. Just Becca and Sam, Sue and David, Becca's grandparents, and Liam.

'Such a shame Raven couldn't join us,' said Becca's grandmother.

Becca looked away in embarrassment. 'I expect he had other plans.'

For some reason, Sue had hatched the idea of inviting Becca's boss to join them for Christmas dinner. 'I hate to think of him all alone at Christmas,' she'd said. Becca didn't have the heart to tell her mum that inviting Raven was the worst idea ever and there was no way it was happening. There was a reason Raven was spending Christmas alone. Becca imagined his dark, brooding presence at the dinner table and was glad she hadn't asked him.

'I could manage a piece of Christmas cake,' said Liam. 'With a slice of Wensleydale.'

Cheese and Christmas cake – a long-held Yorkshire tradition. It was a combination that should never have worked, yet somehow it did.

Sue smiled at him indulgently. 'Of course. I'll go and fetch you a plate.' She returned with a generous helping of cake and cheese.

After even Liam had admitted that he was "totally stuffed", he persuaded everyone to play a game of Monopoly. Even as a young child he'd had a taste for wheeling and dealing on the property board and now he did it for real, building a small empire in Scarborough's burgeoning holiday rental market. As he negotiated deals with other players until he owned half the board and had hotels on all the best London streets, Becca reflected that some people were cut out for business and others weren't. She certainly wasn't one of them. Sam didn't do too badly at the game, holding onto the Strand, Fleet Street and Trafalgar Square for as long as possible, but in the end even he had to sell out to Liam's demands for rent on Mayfair and Park Lane.

'Too bad, mate,' said Liam, shaking Sam's hand once he'd swiped all the cards and was sitting on a huge pile of toy money. 'Win some, lose some, that's what I always say.' He turned to Sue. 'That game's given me a bit of an appetite. Any chance of a turkey sandwich?'

Becca and Sam retreated to the sanctuary of the lounge.

'Your brother's got a keen eye for a deal,' said Sam.

'You mean he's a shark.'

'Perhaps business is in his blood.'

'Maybe.' Her own parents did a good job of running the B&B, but she hadn't inherited their business acumen. Sam looked like he had something on his mind. 'What is it?' she asked.

'Business isn't really in my blood.' She knew he was referring to the fact that Greg wasn't his real father. 'But it's certainly in Ellie's. She's done amazingly well, keeping the brewery going these past few weeks. Now she's going to take over permanently, with Keith's help.'

'I'm sure she'll make a good job of it,' said Becca.

'Gavin knows what he's doing when it comes to brewing beer,' continued Sam, 'and Sandra is happy to stay on and take over more of the account management.'

'And what about you?' asked Becca. 'Have you decided what you're going to do?'

Sam nodded. 'That's what I wanted to talk to you about. Ellie doesn't need me and I'd just be a distraction, a reminder of all the bad things that have happened. I have other plans.' He reached out and clasped her hand.

Becca felt a frisson of anticipation. For so long all the decisions had been down to her. Sam had been unable to express an opinion. But now he'd clearly made up his mind about something. She nodded at him to continue.

'The thing is,' said Sam, 'I can't go on living in Scarborough. I have to get away from here and make a fresh start.'

'Okay.' Becca wondered what he had in mind. A job in York or Leeds, perhaps, or maybe Newcastle. It would be tricky, but they would still be able to see each other at weekends. They would find a way to make it work.

His hand gripped hers tighter. 'You know I've always wanted to travel. Remember how we talked about it before the accident?'

Becca remembered. They had tossed around the idea of taking a month off work and having an adventure. South America, Asia... she'd never really thought it would happen. But if that's what Sam needed to get over recent events, then she was sure she could find a way. She had a few weeks of annual leave due to her.

Sam gave her a tentative smile. 'So I thought we might go to Thailand and then explore Malaysia and Indonesia and make our way down to Australia. There are great opportunities in Oz, Becca. We'd have no problem getting jobs there.'

'Wait! What are you saying?' Becca pulled her hand free. 'You want to go to Australia? To live?'

He nodded eagerly. 'It would be a fresh start for both of us. It's just what we need. I can't stay here. I have to get away.'

Becca was lost for words. She'd had no idea that Sam was planning something so drastic. She thought of everything she'd been through in the past year – sitting by his bedside in the hospital, clinging to hope when everyone else thought the situation was hopeless. She couldn't have done it without her own family. Sam's family had been destroyed, but she still had her parents and grandparents, and her brother too, even though he could be infuriating at times. She couldn't abandon them and go and live on the other side of the world. And then there was her job as a detective. Working for Raven wasn't just any job. And Raven wasn't just any detective.

She tried to imagine a future for herself alongside Sam, living and working so far from home, but couldn't. Instead she saw herself working for Raven, her family close at hand.

The revelation came as a shock, but she knew it was true.

'Tell me what you're thinking,' said Sam.

'I think,' said Becca, 'that Australia would do you the world of good. It's just what you need.'

'But?'

'But I'm not coming with you. I belong in Scarborough. This is my home.'

*

The microwave pinged and Raven retrieved the Thai green chicken curry in its plastic container. He peeled back the film covering and spooned the steaming curry onto a plate of hot rice. It wasn't exactly what you'd call a traditional Christmas dinner, but it was what he'd fancied when browsing the ready-meals at Marks & Spencer. It was surprising what you could do with limited cooking facilities if you put your mind to it and it made a change from fish and chips and takeaway pizza.

He carried his meal over to the table – a plastic one that he'd picked up in a sale from a local garden centre. Winter was a great time for finding bargains on outdoor furniture, and there was no point buying anything decent until his house was finished. There was still no proper heating in the house, just a portable electric heater, so he wore his thick black coat to eat. He sat down, opened his laptop and logged in to Skype. After a few moments, Hannah materialised on the screen, looking even more grown up than he'd remembered her.

'Hey, Dad, Merry Christmas.' She held up a glass of wine.

'Merry Christmas to you too, sweetheart. Are you having a nice day?'

'Great thanks. Eaten too much turkey, but that's how it goes.'

'How's your mum?'

Hannah laughed. 'Asleep on the sofa. But don't tell her I told you. She's had rather a lot to drink.'

'I won't.' He had finally filed for a divorce and Lisa had raised no objection. It's what they ought to have done years ago. Looking back, Raven saw now that they should never have got married in the first place. They'd been far too young, not yet certain of what they wanted from life, or where life was taking them.

He'd been running when he'd found her. Running from his time in Bosnia, running from his home town, from his father's violence, and from his biggest regret of all – inadvertently causing his mother's death.

He'd been running half his life. It was time to stop.

'How's the house coming along?' asked Hannah.

He was tempted to say that it was almost finished, but the time for pretending was over. He angled the laptop around the room to take in the tins of paint, the bare walls and floor, Barry's ladder propped against one wall.

Hannah raised a hand to her mouth. 'Oh my God. How can you live like that?'

'It's not so bad. And it won't be like this for much longer.'

The truth was, the house was still weeks, maybe months away from completion. The morning after finishing the murder investigation, instead of fleeing the house at the crack of dawn, Raven had waited in for the arrival of Barry and his assistant. They'd had a frank exchange of views.

'What have you done?' demanded Raven, gesturing at the ruin his home had become. 'I can't live here anymore. You've ripped the guts out of my house.'

'Nah, don't be like that, squire.' Barry had looked around, seeming pleased by what he saw. 'We've just stripped out the rot. I know it looks a bit... what's the word?'

Raven knew some choice words. 'It looks like a fucking disaster, Barry.'

'Yeah, mate, I know. But trust me, the messy work is done. This is as bad as it gets. Next we start putting it back together. When we're finished you won't recognise it. We're gonna make this place amazing. What do you say, Reggie?'

The young lad looked up at Raven, his face giving nothing away. He shrugged his shoulders, his skinny arms reaching out in an unfathomable gesture.

'See?' said Barry. 'Reggie thinks so too.'

To be fair, since then Barry had begun to make real progress. Walls stripped bare were now covered in a smooth pink layer of fresh plaster. Rotten floorboards and skirting had been replaced with good timber. In the kitchen, gleaming copper pipework emerged from the floor, ready to connect to brand new appliances. New life was appearing where all had been laid waste. The old house wasn't derelict – it was receiving a deep detox.

Raven found himself repeating one of Barry's favourite sayings to Hannah. All about making omelettes and breaking eggs. Somehow it had sounded more convincing when the builder said it.

They chatted about university for a bit, then bade their farewells, both promising to stay in touch more frequently.

Raven's curry had grown cold as they talked, so he returned it to the microwave for a quick blast. Then he put on some music and tucked in to his meal. It had been a rotten year, dismal in every way. But as with his house, he had finally cut out the rot. The coming twelve months could surely only be better.

★

The view from the top was breathtaking. Jess gazed out across the valley floor, a patchwork quilt of fields, each one a different shape and hue. Greens, browns, yellows, purples. They were never quite the same on any two occasions, changing constantly with the seasons. The wind was bleak, the air bitingly cold, but fresh and utterly invigorating.

She looped her arm through Scott's. 'That wasn't too bad, was it?'

He grinned in reply. 'Not bad at all. Your folk are nice. And your mum's a great cook. I wish I had a family like that.'

She was impressed at how well he'd withstood the onslaught of uncles, cousins, sisters-in-law, maiden aunts and nieces he'd been subjected to over the Christmas holiday. Four whole days of celebration – not to mention the minute scrutiny from family and friends – and he was still standing. If he could endure that, he could survive anything.

At least they'd been able to get out onto the moors during the short hours of daylight. Snow had fallen on Christmas Day, lending a fantastical quality to the proceedings, and the temperature had hardly risen above freezing the whole time, but they'd wrapped up warm and gone out each day regardless. On Boxing day they'd hiked up the steep slope of Ingleby Incline – four hours there and four hours back and had looked out across the moors, feeling they were on top of the world. Now they were taking a shorter walk, up Chimney Bank, just outside the village. The narrow road followed a hill pass leading to Hutton-le-Hole and was famous for being the steepest road in England. A gradient of 1 in 3 at its most precipitous. Jess's heart was pounding by the time they reached the summit, and she was glad to pause for a breather.

She couldn't imagine ever leaving this landscape behind. Scarborough might have its attractions – not least the ever-changing sea and the coastal paths that overlooked it – but her heart was in Rosedale Abbey and always would be.

Dusk was falling as they returned to the village and headed indoors to enjoy the warmth and noise of the Coach House Inn. One last drink before facing the family again. It was a traditional pub and restaurant, built from solid Yorkshire stone to keep the elements at bay. With a darts board and a pool table it doubled as the beating heart of the small community. A blazing log burner greeted them as they entered, together with a warm hubbub of conversation.

'What would you like to drink?' asked Scott.

'Anything,' said Jess, 'as long as it's not Salt Castle beer.'

He set off in the direction of the bar and she went in search of a table. Taking a seat close to the fire, she shrugged off her parka and removed her hat, letting her hair tumble free and enjoying the feel of warmth against her skin.

She allowed herself a small sigh of relief. There had been no need for her to worry. Coming to Rosedale for Christmas had been the best idea ever. Scott had really opened up and relaxed, and their relationship finally seemed to be on a firm footing. They were going to be all right. She could tell.

★

Scott stood at the bar, waiting his turn to be served. He felt at home here, in the heart of the North York Moors, in this small, friendly village. Being surrounded by family was a novel experience for him. Growing up, it was always just him and his mum. In recent years, him alone. He'd come to associate Christmas with loss and loneliness. Now, with Jess at his side, he was discovering that it could be a time of happiness and celebration.

His phone vibrated with an incoming message. He took it out of his pocket and checked the screen.

*I have news about your mum. We need to talk.*

Scott didn't hesitate in typing back a reply. He'd been waiting for a day like this for a long time. *Tell me when and where. I'll be there.*

# DEEP INTO THAT DARKNESS
# (TOM RAVEN #4)

**A cold case to solve. New truths to uncover.
A killer to catch.**

When the body of one of his own colleagues is found in Scarborough harbour, DCI Tom Raven throws himself into finding out what led to the young man's death.

The killing shows similarities to the unsolved murder of the victim's own mother. Might his off-the-books investigation into her case have got him into deep water? Or could his death be related to the attacks on women that are taking place at night? The dead man left a trail of cryptic clues to his final movements that might lead Raven to the truth.

Drawn into Scarborough's shady night life in his quest to find the killer, Raven faces temptations of his own.

Set on the North Yorkshire coast, the Tom Raven series is perfect for fans of LJ Ross, JD Kirk, Simon McCleave, and British crime fiction.

# THANK YOU FOR READING

We hope you enjoyed this book. If you did, then we would be very grateful if you would please take a moment to leave a review online. Thank you.

# THE TOM RAVEN SERIES

The Landscape of Death (Tom Raven #1)
Beneath Cold Earth (Tom Raven #2)
The Dying of the Year (Tom Raven #3)
Deep into that Darkness (Tom Raven #4)

# THE BRIDGET HART SERIES

Aspire to Die (Bridget Hart #1)
Killing by Numbers (Bridget Hart #2)
Do No Evil (Bridget Hart #3)
In Love and Murder (Bridget Hart #4)
A Darkly Shining Star (Bridget Hart #5)
Preface to Murder (Bridget Hart #6)
Toll for the Dead (Bridget Hart #7)

# PSYCHOLOGICAL THRILLERS

The Red Room

# ABOUT THE AUTHOR

M S Morris is the pseudonym for the writing partnership of Margarita and Steve Morris. They both studied at Oxford University, where they first met in 1990. Together they write psychological thrillers and crime novels. They are married and live in Oxfordshire.

Find out more at msmorrisbooks.com where you can join our mailing list.

Manufactured by Amazon.ca
Acheson, AB

10762532R00171